Mind Lies

HARLOW STONE

MIND LIES

HARLOW STONE
SPIRITED HEROINES AND THE HEROES WHO LOVE THEM

The Ugly Roses Trilogy
Reading Order:

Frayed Rope
Concealed Affliction
Blinded by Fate

Standalone Novels:

Mind Lies

HARLOW STONE

COPYRIGHT

Mind Lies

Written by Harlow Stone

All rights reserved.

Registered Copyright through the Canadian Intellectual Property Office. No part of this book may be reproduced, scanned, or distributed in any printed or electronic form without permission from the author. Please do not participate in or encourage piracy of copyrighted materials in violation of the author's rights. Purchase only authorized editions.

This is a work of fiction. Names, characters, places and incidents are either the product of the author's imagination or are used fictitiously, and any resemblance to actual persons, living or dead, business establishments, events or locales is entirely coincidental.

Trademarks:

This book identifies product names and services known to be trademarks, registered trademarks, or service marks of their respective holders. The author acknowledges the trademarked status in this work of fiction. The publication and use of these trademarks is not authorized, associated with, or sponsored by the trademark owners.

© 2016 Harlow Stone

ISBN: 978-0-9940376-7-1

Edited by Gregory Murphy at Gregory J. Editing

Cover Images purchased from Adobe Stock

Cover design by Harlow Stone

MIND LIES

FOREWORD

When Jerri wakes up from a twenty-two day coma post car accident- her memory is gone.

Well... most of it.

She doesn't remember the friends she wakes up to, her home or the business she owns. The only thing she remembers is *him*.

Locklin.

Her pretty and reckless.

The passion between the two in her dreams is far too powerful to be a cruel joke of her amnesia filled mind. Portia — Jerri's best friend of ten years— has no idea who the man is; leaving the doctors to think thirty two year old Jerri's lost her fucking marbles a few decades too early.

But Jerri doesn't give up.

"Sing to me, Jerri girl."

Determined to find the motorcycle riding Irishman who begs her to sing in her dreams, she does just that.

Sings.

One woman, and one heartbreaking YouTube video, Jerri finds out exactly why Locklin never comes. She finds out why sometimes memories of the past are best left exactly where they came from.

The past.

#LOVELOCKLIN

DEDICATION

To everyone who thinks they can't.
Trust me, you can.

PROLOGUE

"This is the last time," I tell them.

Tears fall freely down my cheeks, but my voice is steady.

Clear.

Definitely not strong, though.

No.

Because I'm breaking.

What they see on the outside: The beautiful dress, shiny hair. Shoulders squared and perfect posture where I stand poised like a woman who has her shit together on the small stage....

It's a lie.

A ruse.

A wolf in sheep's clothing.

A gift, the packaging far prettier than what's to be unwrapped.

I feel like a fraud, but I don't tell them that. I feel like I'm dying. All these cracks that have continuously hurt my heart are ready to crumble.

Ready for it all to fall apart.

I'm ready to fall apart.

They don't know what it's like to stand up here, calling out to the love of your life, crying to him for months, begging him to find me. To hold me and shelter me and put me back together.

But he never comes.

He never crushes me in his strong arms and tells me that I'm not crazy . . . and that he's here. He never shows up to tell me he loves me, needs me, will never let me go.

He never comes.

He never shows up.

The crowd begins to boo. Not because they don't want to hear me, but because they don't want me to give up the fight. They don't want me to let go.

I'm not a quitter, but sometimes you need to know when to stop, when to toss in the towel. Because no matter how many times you cry your heart out in front of strangers, the end result is always going to be the same. Always going to end the same.

MIND LIES

With me.

Crying my heart out.

Alone.

Not with the man I'm supposed to share my life with.

I take a deep breath, reciting pretty much the same thing every time I sing to him. The only difference is that this time the crowd is much larger. This time, it's not Portia aiming a web cam at me while I search for my soulmate.

The one nobody knows.

The one the doctors tell me could very well be a product of my overactive imagination due to my amnesia-filled brain.

Lies.

But I know in my heart he's real.

I know he's out there.

Because I can *feel* him.

Giving a light smile, the same one that never reaches my eyes, I tell them again, "This is the last time. I don't think I'll be able to speak after I do this, so I'm going say what I need to now. And I hope you'll listen."

I watch them all, those who I can see clearly, as they settle into their front row seats with their eyes trained on the stage. I wait for the hushes and murmurs to die down, all eyes on me, before I continue. "I can't thank you all enough. What started out as an idea and a YouTube video riding on nothing but *hope*—you all clicked *view* or *share* and turned it into something viral overnight."

Applause and cheers echo throughout the theater. I absorb the sound's positivity, the vibrations filling me before adjusting the mic to continue. "If it weren't for people like you, and my best friend's support, we wouldn't be here; and if we weren't here, he might not hear me call for him."

I pause to swallow past the lump in my throat. "That video-gone-viral gave me hope." My voice breaks on the word "hope," but I power through. "It gave me hope that the man in my memories would come back to me. It gave me hope that after so many of you shared that video—I wouldn't be without him. Millions of people have watched that video, and I was sure that he'd be one of them."

I blink, letting tears roll freely before giving my audience another empty, watery smile. "But he's not here," I softly say.

Shaking my head, I sigh. "I can't keep doing this. Singing to the man I remember, the last song we sang together. I *can't*. Not because I'm giving up, but because it hurts too bad."

MIND LIES

Wiping my cheeks, I lift my head, prepared to give them my signature line: "Maybe I imagined him. Maybe my amnesia is fierce and playing cruel tricks on me. Or maybe, just maybe,"—I pause waiting for them to say it with me—"I've lost my fucking marbles."

My hollow laugh joins more boisterous ones. I watch as a few tissues are drawn from purses, people discreetly wiping their eyes. They've followed this love story as I have lived it. They've watched me cry my heart out for the man I used to know.

The man in my memories.

The one who never comes.

"So this is it, ladies and gents. This is the last time. Not because I don't love him. Not because I don't think of him often, but because it just hurts too damn bad."

Squaring my shoulders, I face my cheering squad with little determination and a lot less hope. "So, to the man with dark hair and beautiful, bright blue eyes whom I remember, . . ." I pause, letting that term hang loosely because I'm a woman with amnesia who remembers nothing aside from him. After they chuckle, I finish, "who goes by the name of *Locklin*. This is from me, to desperately missing you."

The lights in the theater dim, the spotlight above remaining lit while I sing to the man I love.

Whether or not my mind lies, I give it all I have—my heart, my soul, my love—and sing to the man from my memories, begging him to come to me.

One.

Last.

Time.

CHAPTER ONE

Not knowing who you are is probably the most terrifying thing you could ever experience in your lifetime.

Of course, losing a child, a loved one, or finding out you're dying would be equally or more painful. But I'm not there yet. Or, at least, I don't think I am.

I know nothing.

I don't know my name. I don't know my hair color, or if I have any family.

I don't know how old I am or where I came from, and I don't know who the woman holding my hand is. I can hear her, though.

A man called her Portia.

And she called me her best friend.

The sister she never had.

So why can't I remember her? Why do I know nothing of this room, or the people in it?

Why can I only remember *him*?
More importantly, why isn't *he* here?

The man from my dreams never comes when I'm awake, which makes me want to stay asleep more often because it's the only time my heart feels full.

I want answers to the million questions I have; but if he's not here, who will give them to me? Or more importantly, why hasn't Portia mentioned him?

The only person I remember.

A beautiful man named Locklin.

* * *

"How long?" a groggy female voice asks.

I still don't recognize it, but I know she is Portia and it sounds as though she's in pain.

Not physical.

No.

It's the kind that tears you apart inside and shatters your soul.

Emotional pain.

"As you were told over the phone, it's been ten days since she was brought in," an emotionless voice replies.

A quick bang follows before Portia continues. "I damn well know how long she's been in here! I want to know when she'll wake up!" She ends on a sob.

The man sighs. "The force of impact caused a great deal of trauma to her brain. Not to mention the blood loss and fractures. We have no choice but to keep Ms. Sloane in a coma until the swelling on her brain has reduced."

Sniffles can be heard before her small voice asks, "Back to my original question, Doctor. How long?"

"Could be a few days, could be a few weeks. Everyone heals differently."

The woman cries, the sound soothed by a caring masculine voice "She'll pull through, Portia."

I feel terrible for the couple. No doubt this news is heartbreaking, and I wish I could take away her pain. Wish I could wake up, give some answers, and ease minds.

"I should also inform you that it's not clear what to expect when she wakes," the doctor says. "When we pull Ms. Sloane out of the coma, you need to be prepared."

"For what exactly?" A male voice asks.

"Anything," the Doctor says. "She may have little voice. The damage to her neck and vocal cords is not something we can predict the outcome of. We also have to be prepared that although she seems strong, and has fought this far, we don't know what kind of memory she will have, if any at all. These circumstances aren't easy to predict. And unfortunately we'll know nothing until she wakes up."

"But she will wake up?" Portia asks.

"There is always a small chance that sometimes people don't pull out of these things; however, I feel strongly that she'll pull through. She's a healthy woman. Her MRI shows that she's healing well. And following each scan, her brain activity increases."

"That's good news, Portia." I can hear the smile in the man's voice and the subsequent happy sob, followed by, "I'll take it."

The Doctor, whose voice is not nearly as interesting to listen to, cuts off my eavesdropping. "Talk to her. Talk about things present and past. It always seems to help."

He's incredibly stoic and clearly needs some help in the bedside manner department, but I'm happy that they have good news. And when I wake up, I plan to tell them so.

The voices begin to drift off, and I welcome the sleep that starts to pull me under.

Strangely, it's the only time I feel lucid.

It's the only time I get to see *him*.

CHAPTER TWO

"Eggs?" he asks. Most likely the thirtieth question of the day, and I can't help but smile at his handsome face before I answer. Full, dark hair flips out a little at the base of his neck. His beautiful bone structure is covered in two days' worth of stubble, which makes you uncertain whether you would call him pretty or reckless.

The only thing I call him is mine. Because at this moment, that's exactly what he is.

Mine.

I smile as I answer his question: "Smothered in hollandaise sauce."

He chuckles. "Benny then."

"Always," I tell him as he reaches out and brushes my hair away from my eyes. I'm sure my hair's a mess after the many hours spent rolling in this bed last night. But I don't care. The way he looks at me is nothing if not precious. His features are relaxed, save for the small tip of his full lips. His eyes are soft and filled with so much adoration it makes me certain my bedhead is the last thing on his mind.

It's the last on mine too.

To say my hair isn't important would be an understatement. It's just that he is so much more important that everything else falls to the wayside. I wish I could hold onto this moment forever, hold onto the way he's looking at me, hold onto his warm body as he holds onto mine, hold onto the feeling . . . and never let go.

A tender hand moves down the side of my face, over my neck, and down my back. I sigh as he rubs my lower back before resting on my hips. "Open your eyes, Jerri girl."

I shudder. From his voice, his touch, and the energy that hums between us. I absorb the sensation, having never felt anything like it, hoping—praying—that I never have to let it go. His lips touch each of my eyelids. And when they leave, the second I open them, he pulls my leg up over his hip and enters me with one swift thrust.

"Eyes on me, Lass. Keep them open," he rasps. I do exactly as he says, continuing to hold on, taking everything he gives me and still wanting more.

Gently rolling me onto my back, he settles himself between my legs, his strong arms creating a cage I never wish to be released from.

"Stay," I tell him.

Or ask?

I don't know because I can't figure out why he would leave.

MIND LIES

Why he might want to leave when I, lying here, would never want to be anywhere else.

Be with anyone else.

I try to focus on his eyes, hoping they can tell me the answer I desperately seek. But, unlike last time and all the other times when I focus too hard on them, his face starts to blur.

Features unable to be discerned.

Striking eyes, too dark to see clearly.

I don't get his answer.

Because then I wake up.

* * *

"Alright, woman, now that everyone's gone, we're going to dive into Jerri and Portia's box of shit that's never said aloud, but I'll never let you forget," Portia says.

The first day I heard her, she was all distraught and somber. These past few days, she's been nothing but fierce. She's a fighter this one, and I've come to realize she likes to talk to me.

Her best friend.

Whose name is *Jerri*.

I don't know why I can hear but can't wake up, but I love the stories she tells me. Even though I strain to keep my mind awake, I try to consume everything she chooses to share.

"First in the box of shit would be home waxing kits. We didn't know each other then, but we each have our horror stories," she snorts. "It's no doubt the reason your asshole is still a virgin, and I saved for years just to get laser hair removal. Moral of the story: if you forget a lot when you wake up, always remember home waxing is a big fat no!"

I laugh but there's no sound.

She sighs. "Second in the box is the time I thought it would be cool to try out a D/s relationship, not you and I together, and it was long before those books came out. Any who, in case you don't remember, I'll remind you now: do not let a man spank your ass unless he knows what he's doing. I lived off Ben and Jerry for a week and didn't leave your couch for days. Oh, and we called in sick to work due to a death in the family so you could stay home and look after me," she pauses to take a breath. "I know, I know. We shouldn't have pulled the *death* card. But seriously, there was no other way we could get away with both of us being off work at the same time. I was young, stupid, and thought that because I was twenty-two I had all the answers in the world."

She squeezes my hand and I try to squeeze back, but it remains limp. "We'll fast forward to one of the biggest mistakes of your life: Tom Black. You never saw him coming, but we'll agree to disagree when it comes to men with good looks and hair. 'Cause seriously, when it comes to something that's all shiny and pretty on the outside, it's probably rotten leftovers on the inside. Either way, *you* learned your lesson, *I* may or may not have broken a finger, and *you* look so much better without him. If I saw you in another pantsuit, I was seriously going to kick your ass, strip you down to your knickers, and burn that stuffy sucker."

It's quiet for a few moments, and I take the time to try and place the memories. Running through all the images she gave me, I try to picture things as she says them. But I come up blank. Other than my own interpretation of how she described them to me, nothing sounds familiar.

"That's the bulk of our most embarrassing times and life lessons. The big ones anyway. Visiting hours are almost over, and if you've heard me when I speak to you, you'll know that I like to say what's important before I go. So, I love you, Jerri Sloane. I've loved you since we met in night school. I've loved you for the past ten years."

Ten years.

"I need you to wake up so we can meet for coffee on Thursday. Arabica isn't the same without you. Actually, that's an understatement; it's just too fucking quiet," she laughs, stifling a sob. "Most of all, I need you to pick up the phone because it really sucks you haven't been picking up lately. I burnt the damn beef when I tried to make Cooper dinner last week, and I knew you'd help or tell me how to fix it, or you'd just show up with a bottle of wine and takeout because you know I can't cook for shit when Cooper's around. Anyway, come back to me babe. I miss you so much. Please wake up."

I try. Lord do I try.

I can hear, I can smell, but I can't move. I didn't think about it before, but the not moving bothers me more than not waking up. I try to stretch my neck but it won't budge either.

Why can't I move?

What if I'm paralyzed?

I will my legs to move. In my mind, I'm kicking them.

I'm pulling with my hands, but they don't catch anything.

I feel like I'm suffocating. The loss of pressure on my hand, and its sudden drop in temperature, is the only indication I might have feeling in that particular body part. Portia has let go.

Don't leave, Portia!

"What's happening, Jerri?" Portia's shrill voice echo's in the room, overpowering the incessant beeping. Like an alarm clock on steroids, the beeping won't stop, just gets faster.

MIND LIES

Louder.

Beep, beep, beep, beep.

I feel sweat coating my forehead. I think my eyes are moving, but I can't see anything.

Jesus Christ, I'm blind.

Fuck, somebody help.

"Somebody help me!" I scream.

But it's useless because there's no sound.

I struggle but there's no movement.

CHAPTER THREE

"What's happening?" Portia asks, breaking through the fog.

"Ma'am, just stand back for a few minutes," a woman says. I think she's a nurse; I've felt her cold hands poking at me before.

Felt, Jerri.

You're not paralyzed. You can feel.

The Doctor announces himself as he comes in. I feel a sharp pain in my foot, followed by blinding lights that send jolts of pain through my head. I hear the machine again, beeping quick and loud, begging for attention.

"Ms. Sloane is waking up. It might not happen immediately, but she's trying. O'Brian, let's get another MRI scheduled, and make sure she's not in any pain."

Too late Doc.

My eyes are throbbing, my head too. I feel awful, my body a painful deadweight.

Portia's hand closes over mine. I recognize the feel of her rings and the jingle of bracelets that follows her movement. "Wake up, Jer. I'm right here, honey. And if you wake up, I promise I'll clean the shop for like a week,"

She's been promising to clean this *shop* every time she's in here. I don't know what the shop is, but I assume cleaning it is not on her list of favorite things to do.

I roll my eyes around in my head. They feel cold and sticky.

Unused.

The nurse pokes something in my arm again, which doesn't bother me as much as the pain radiating through the rest of my body. None the less, I flinch.

"Did you see that?" Portia exclaims.

"Keep talking to her," the nurse says.

"Wait! Where are you going? What do I do?"

"There's nothing any of us can do until she wakes up. So when she does, you just press the button on the bed and I'll come back." Her footsteps echo as they leave the room.

"And how long does that take?" Portia shouts.

"Could be five minutes. Could still be five days," she shouts back.

"Dammit! Shit!" Portia huffs in frustration. She's clearly not getting the answer she was hoping for. I keep rolling my eyes, putting energy into opening them. Portia's hand stays in mine, but I hear her sit down. Her voice now level with my head. "C'mon, Jer, and prove that stick-up-her-ass nurse wrong. If you can hear me, I know you're trying. Five days my ass. Wake up, woman. We have a shop to run and shit to do."

I don't know where it comes from, but a small laugh bubbles from my throat. It hurts. It's a dry laugh that could be confused with coughing. But all the same, it's there.

"Holy shit," Portia whispers.

I squeeze my eyelids, dryness keeping them stuck together. I feel a hand on my face, wetness on my arm. "Wake up, Jerri. C'mon, babe, you can do it."

I squeeze again, rolling my eyes at the same time until the first sliver of light comes through.

It's too bright.

It hurts.

I open my mouth. It too is drier than the Mohave, but I push my lips together, trying to whisper the word.

"Bah" whispers past my lips.

"I'm listening, Jer."

"Bhri," I try again, hoping for moisture. Taking pity on my plight, Portia lets go of my hand. I panic for a minute before a cool wet cloth is pushed against my lips. I try to get as much water from it as I can. I don't get enough to swallow because my tongue and mouth absorb it all.

"Brighd" barely leaves my lips.

She stutters it all back to me. "Bah, Bri, Brighd. Bride!" she shouts before giving a watery laugh. "You better not have eloped on me."

I do my best to shake my head. It's small and it, too, hurts but she manages to catch the negative. Squeezing my hand, she says it all again to herself: "bright."

Lightly, I squeeze her hand back.

I give her a small tip from my lips, and I'm quickly rewarded with more darkness. I don't know if a light was on or if the blinds were open, letting through the daylight. Either way, my eyes are grateful.

"Okay, babe. Open those eyes for me," she coaches. I lift them lightly, afraid to feel the pain from before, but determined to wake up.

The first sliver of pale light comes through. It's nowhere near as bright as before. It's blurry, but I'm thankful that whatever happened to me didn't take my sight. "That's it, Jer. You got this."

My eyes roll, trying to clear through the fog, to make sense of the shapes in front of me. One of them is round, and I blink a few times, bringing it into focus. Pale skin and pink-rimmed eyes framed by messy blonde hair. She's pretty, Portia, with an edge that matches the fierceness of her tone over the last few days.

Or weeks.

I don't know the time.

Her lips part, and tears run down her cheeks before a smile breaks out on her face. "Hey, pretty lady. I've been waiting a long damn time for you to wake up."

I blink a few times, wishing I could place this woman who I've only just laid my eyes on. She seems so happy. I don't want to say something to hurt her feelings, but I have no idea who she is aside from the woman who speaks at my bedside. My best friend named Portia who I do not recognize.

Not one bit.

Thinking it over for a moment, I whisper my first important question. "How long?"

I heard her ask the same thing, and I know she'll answer me truthfully. She sobs with her smile still stuck in place. "Twenty-two of the longest days of my life."

I close my eyes, trying to piece it together but finding nothing.

Instead, I ask for water.

MIND LIES

"I just paged the nurse. If she's half as fast as she was before, she should be here by tomorrow at two." Portia chuckles but is proven wrong when a nurse comes into the room.

"I take that back; maybe she wants to meet the woman who is the talk of the hospital," she says with an obvious eye roll.

"Welcome to the land of the living, Ms. Sloane."

I nod slightly in her direction. But, checking the machines at my bedside, she pays no attention. "If you're in a lot of pain, you let me know. Doc should be here any minute. He'll give you a once over and see what kind of shape you're in."

"Water?" I ask her.

Of course she shakes her head. "Nothing to drink yet, Ms. Sloane. You'll need to have everything checked out before Doctor Havan can permit food or drink."

I feel as if I'm dying or have died and come back to life. I just want some water. Of course I don't say any of that because my mouth is too dry to speak. My throat too sore. My neck on fire.

I don't dare ask for the pain meds yet because I know they will put me to sleep, and I need to know what is wrong with me, what my injuries are.

How old I am.

Where I'm from.

Where *he* is.

"Ms. Sloane!" a man exclaims brightly before coming to my bedside. He's tall, stiff, and his smile doesn't quite reach his tired eyes.

"Hi," I murmur lightly.

Leaning forward, he flashes a god-awful light in my eyes a few times. "Speaking will be difficult, Ms. Sloane. But I'm happy all the same that you can speak. There was a fair bit of damage done to your neck in the accident. You've also suffered trauma to your brain. Now, this may seem soon, but it's important to get a few tests out of the way so we can determine the extent of your injuries and the remainder of your recovery."

I simply nod and wait for him to continue. He pokes in places and moves limbs. He looks down my throat and checks under sutures. Aside from making me walk, he does just about everything, leaving the most painful for last. "What can you remember about the accident, Ms. Sloane?"

I shake my head lightly and whisper, "Nothing." It causes me to cough, and I look to the nurse and Portia and mouth, *"water."*

"Small sip for now. Let's see how you handle it," the Doc says. The first sip is like heaven, rain after a long drought. I cough. All too soon, the straw is pulled away. "That's enough for now."

MIND LIES

Doctor Havan adjusts himself on the chair beside my bed before continuing. "You remember nothing about what happened in the accident. What about what happened before the accident?"

I squint and shake my head again.

"Okay, let's try something different. What is the last thing you remember?" Concerned eyes meet mine across the room. I think back, remembering only one thing.

One man.

* * *

"If you could travel anywhere in the world, right now, where would you go?" I ask him. We're laying on the bed, facing each other. His elbow is bent and his head is propped on his hand. The black Celtic tattoos on his arm are a stark contrast to the white linen sheets. The moonlight cutting through the blinds dances over the shadows of his skin.

He's beautiful.

My own version of pretty and reckless.

A smile takes over his handsome face. I have no doubt his answer will be truthful, as all of them have been. I absorb his features, noticing he looks older than in my last dream.

My last memory of us: we were getting to know each other.

"If you're still in my bed, I don't want to go anywhere," he confidently says, making me smile. "But, if I had to choose and you wanted to come with me, we'd go to Ireland."

Smile still on my face, I tell him, "Good choice. Do I get to ask why?"

He leans closer, pressing his lips to my bare shoulder. "Because, it's still home. We may have some bad memories, and I may not travel there often anymore. But when I do, it still feels like home."

I take a moment to absorb his words, how he speaks of a place that's clearly important to him. Perhaps important to both of us if his reference to bad memories is anything to go by.

But it matters.

Matters and means something to him.
I press my lips to his jaw and then his chest where another tattoo meets his collarbone. Wrapping his hand around the back of my neck, he places another kiss on the top of my head. I curl into his warm body, our naked flesh coming together to ward off the chill in the room.

"Stay," I whisper.

MIND LIES

He replies the same way he always does: "You know I can't."

CHAPTER FOUR

"Ms. Sloane?" the Doctor asks again, shaking me out of my memories as I look at Portia. I have no doubt she knows me, but I'd hate to tell her that I can't say the same.

Why can't I remember her? Why do I only know her name?

"Do you know who this is?" Dr. Havan asks while motioning toward where she stands. I feel a light sheen of tears coat my eyes. I close them before whispering, "No." My voice is so faint I'm surprised anyone heard me, but the loud, choking sob confirms Portia did.

The whimper that follows is painful and gutting. It pierces my heart in a way that shouldn't for someone I don't know. Like a coward, I keep my eyes closed. Perhaps if I can't see it, it's not really there.

Out of sight, out of mind.

Hear no evil, see no evil.

Only this isn't evil. This sounds as if someone's heart has been ripped from their chest. As much as my body hurts, my heart hurts more to know that I have been the one to inflict that kind of pain.

MIND LIES

To be the one who caused it.

The Doctor starts speaking again, but I can't hear him over Portia's cries. I've upset her. Talking at my bedside, she's been wonderful to me, and I feel as though I had just told her someone died. But perhaps that's true?

Someone has died—to her, anyway.

That someone is me, and I'm saddened by the fact *she* may very well be dead to me too.

I've listened to Portia talk about the woman she believes me to be, the *me* who I don't remember. She's told me stories, so many stories and memories and things that we've shared together. A lifetime of happiness and regret, sadness and fulfillment.

But that's all it is right now.

A story.

A blank canvas.

My mind is that blank canvas.

A huge, empty white canvas that allows anyone and everyone to paint on it. And for the days that Portia has been here, she's added color to it, color with vibrant tales of our life together and shadows of our past mistakes.

There's a large, empty spot in the middle of my canvas—a portion that cannot be painted over or erased—

where *he* is. I feel as if it's an outline, like the beginnings of a tattoo before you have it colored in. But no matter how deep I dig, I can't access more than the outline. And I ask myself why he's not here, filling in the gaps for me.

Where did he go?

Why isn't he with me, not to tell stories, but to re-live the memories?

Some of the best I've ever had.

Or so I can remember.

I know I can feel it, feel *him*.

I know that he's out there. And if he knew where I was and what happened to me, I know that he would be here. He would never leave me alone with these people who I don't remember.

Giving my eyes one last squeeze for good measure, I accept the inevitable, the fate that will surely leave people disappointed. I open my eyes and look across the room to Portia, the woman who has shared so much and has been with me at my bedside—the beautiful woman who has done nothing but care for me.

Her eyes are somber, the tears running down her face falling off her cheeks, the weight of them too heavy for her face to hold onto. A man holds her close to his chest. He's handsome, with dark hair and brown eyes, and clearly thinks the world of her. I may not remember anything, but from the way he embraces her, I'm no fool to think otherwise.

Gaining eye contact, I softly tell her, "I am so, so very sorry."

The poor woman's knees buckle, sending her toward the floor, but the strong man's arms catch her.

Never letting her fall.

Holding her close, he brushes the hair from her tear-streaked cheeks before placing a kiss on her forehead. He whispers something against her skin, something I cannot hear but am immediately jealous of. I'm not jealous because of what they have together; I'm jealous because my own man is not doing the same for me.

Feeling the coolness of my own tears trickle down my temple, I move my hand toward my face. I cry out half-way, pain jolting through my arm like a stab wound to the bone.

"Don't, Jer!" Portia exclaims as she rushes to my bedside. Grabbing a tissue off the side table, ignoring her own as they continuously fall, she wipes my tears. "It's okay," she sobs. "We'll figure it out, babe. Don't worry about it."

I can tell from the agony on her face that it's not something to let go. She's worrying about it, but she's more concerned with putting on a brave face for me.

"It's not okay," I tell her. "You're hurt."

She squints her eyes at me. "No, babe. You're hurt. Don't worry about me," she replies before fluffing the pillow behind my head to busy herself with something monotonous and un-important. "We'll get you fixed up in no time. You're alive. What's a little memory loss?" she jokes.

I place my hand on her arm, giving it a little squeeze, stilling her movements so she'll look at me again. "It's everything. To you, it's everything. I'm sorry I don't remember."

Leaning her head onto her arm, she lets out a soft cry. "You're everything, babe. You're my best friend."

I watch her lips quiver before the man comes and puts his arm around her, offering a safe haven from the shitstorm around her. The shitstorm I've created. "I'm Cooper, Portia's husband," he says.

I give a small smile. "The one she burns dinners for, I'm told."

He gives a small one back. "The one and only."

He doesn't say it with any sort of contempt, or displeasure. He says it with pride because he's clearly happy to be standing next to this woman. The brave and strong one who has kept me company, filling the role of best friend. The one he'd happily accept burnt dinners from.

MIND LIES

Portia pulls her head out of his chest. "You heard me?"

I smile at her and nod. "I did."

She smiles. "I'm glad. Maybe once we get you home, things will start to come back." She shifts nervously before asking. "Is there anything you remember? Anything at all?"

Grateful she's given me the chance to bring it up, I say, "Yes, but I don't know his name. Who am I seeing? Or am I married? I can see him; I have memories of him." I finish on a smile.

Cooper and Portia share a look before she sits down in the chair beside my bed. "Jer, you've been single for years. Unless you're thinking of someone you used to be with, I'm not sure who you're talking about."

I avoid eye contact for a moment, wondering if I'm crazy when she asks, "What did he look like?"

I smile, a little less hopeful this time, and tell her, "Dark hair. Sort of longer in the back. A Celtic tattoo—actually a lot of tattoos, but you can't see them unless his shirt is off."

She's shaking her head. "That's not a description of the last guy you dated, Hun. But it could have been someone from before I met you."

"How long have we known each other?"

Her face goes soft. "Ten years."

I shake my head at her. "This guy was no teenager, Portia. And I know in my heart that I *know him.* I remember eating with him, being on a bike with him, being—" I pause, glancing at the room of people before lowering my voice, "being in bed with him. I remember it all. There has to be somebody?"

She squints, deep in thought. "You could have met someone new when you left for Salem last month."

"Sorry, where?" I interrupt.

She shakes her head. "It's okay. I guess we have a lot to go over. We live just outside of Boston, Massachusetts. We run a shop together. Mostly furniture. Every so often, you'll take off for a day or ten to scout out new merchandise for the shop." She pauses. I nod for her to continue. "So last month you left on one of your jaunts. You said you were heading north. Small towns around Salem and whatnot. We didn't talk for a few days. And then when I tried, you were missing."

Squeezing Cooper's hand to gather strength, she continues. "After a lot of phone calls, we finally found you in Brockton, which is south of Boston, not north. You'd been brought to the hospital here after a car accident in a small, nearby town. They figured you must have swerved to avoid hitting something because it was the middle of the night, and nobody else was on the road."

Leaning back on the pillow, I run everything she told me through my head. I said I was going one place, but I ended up in another. I live near Boston and run a furniture shop.

MIND LIES

"You said I could have met the guy I remember when I left?"

"Could have. You left on the third of April; the car accident happened on the seventh. I didn't find you until the eighteenth." She cries, "I'm so frigging sorry, Hun."

Shaking my head, I reply, "I don't get it. What do you have to be sorry for?" Cooper answers for her: "We were on our honeymoon, Jer. Normally you guys talk all the time, but we agreed no contact unless there was an emergency. When we got home and found out the shop hadn't been open since we left, we knew something was wrong. That's when we started calling the cops and then hospitals."

I'm not upset with Portia. I understand, after what Cooper had told me, that it's not her fault. It doesn't sound as if it's anyone's fault. Some shitty circumstances and a lack of communication may be at play, but this is definitely not anyone's fault. I reach out to take Portia's hand. "I'm not angry with anyone. The only thing I'm angry about is that I don't remember much of anything. I just want to get out of here."

My hand in hers, she squeezes back. "You just need to rest for a while. Once your scans come back, we'll figure out when we can take you home. Okay?"

I nod, not sure if I'm more worried about where home is or the fact that I feel completely alone. Portia's phone rings. It breaks the moment. She says that it's Cory. "One of our employees," she tells me. "He's been keeping the shop going since we've been here. I'm going to go give him an update."

I watch as she leaves the room. Cooper takes the seat at my bedside. He glances around the room—half uncomfortable, half curious—before asking me about the man I remember.

"Can you tell me what else you remember about the man? Perhaps I can help."

I nod. "You seem stronger than she is at the moment. I don't know if she'd tell me anything, but you need to let me know if there's something she left out. You look quite curious."

He gives me a small smile. "Neither your attitude nor your forwardness have changed, Jerri." I smile back. "Wish I could say I'm glad, but I don't know who, or what, I am right now."

He nods in acceptance. "There's a lifetime she left out then. And I'm sure over the next days or weeks she'll have a lot to fill you in on. But for the time being, I think it's most important that you focus on getting better. Let the rest fall into place."

Cooper shifts uncomfortably in his chair, avoiding eye contact when I scowl in his direction.

"That's not what I asked," I begin. "I don't know you, but obviously I did at some point. I truly hope I'll remember. But I feel like you're leaving something out, that same something that I feel like she's not telling me. Am I dying or something?"

His heads snaps up. "Jesus no, Jer. It's not like that."

"Then tell me what it's like if you don't think she will."

Scrubbing his hands down his face, he takes a quick glance over his shoulder before looking back at me. "The guy you're remembering," he says. I nod. "Maybe he is real. I don't know, Jer. But it seems like every time you take off to look for furniture, you come home a different person. Sometimes you're happy. Sometimes you're pissed off. If you're pissed, you say it's about the lack of good merchandise to be found. But I've been around you for a long time, and I think it's something more than that."

I mull over his words. "And Portia? What does she think?"

"She brought it up a few times. If she gets pissed enough because you're not telling her something, you take her with you on the next trip."

"And am I to assume correctly that when she comes with me nothing is amiss? No strange men or new friends I introduce her to?"

He nods. "You'd assume right."

CHAPTER FIVE

Cooper and Portia went home for the evening, leaving me to a restless night.

The next morning was not welcome.

I have more questions than answers. No matter how hard I push to remember the answers, the only thing I receive is a pounding headache in my forgetful brain.

"That's incredibly normal for this type of trauma," the Doctor assured me. Not the same man who was originally in my room when I woke up, but the Doctor who specializes in head trauma and memory loss. Nice woman. Late forties, I would guess. She's dressed casually in black slacks, a pale-purple blouse, and chunky jewelry.

"Do people in my position ever remember?" I had asked her.

She gave me a kind smile. Not a sympathetic one I would have hated, but one that said, *I'm here to answer your questions, and there is no such thing as a stupid question.*

"I truly hope you do regain your memory, Jerri. And it is absolutely possible. Why don't I explain some cases to you? I can tell you that memory loss is different for everyone. It very much is. But I don't think that's the answer that you're looking for."

I shake my head. "No, it's not."

Crossing her legs, she moves forward. "I'll give you some past examples: One of my patient's brain had swollen so badly that a portion of the skull needed to be removed in order to compensate for the amount of swelling. He'd been in a coma for months and had broken half the bones in his body. And when he opened his eyes to see his wife of two years, he had no idea who she was."

"That's terrible."

Nodding, she confirms, "It is. But as soon as that man saw his brother, his parents, and his best friend, he knew who all of them were—just not his wife."

I squint at the familiar pull. "I think I've heard a similar story to that. It sounds familiar."

She smiles, and I can't help but smile back. "You're right," she says. "There is a movie about something similar, but we're talking a true story, in this case. And in this story, the reason the man didn't remember his wife was because she was the one he was trying to forget in the first place."

I wave her on to continue.

"He found her cheating on him. So he went on a bender and crashed his car," she said.

I nod as it comes together. "So he didn't remember her because he didn't want to. Whether he knew it or not."

"Exactly."

"So, because I remember nothing, really, are you saying maybe I don't want to remember at all?" I ask. That would be awful, and after meeting Portia and Cooper, two incredibly kind people, I can't see that being the case.

"No, that's not what I'm saying. Let's go with story number two. Patient was in a work accident. She was a quiet gal who kept to herself. But when she woke up, she knew nothing—not even her name. She didn't remember a movie, like you may have just remembered. She didn't have visions or memories of a man, like you do. She had absolutely nothing.

"Turned out, her life was more traumatic than her head injury. She'd been abused her entire life in ways neither of us want to imagine. There were no signs of permanent damage to her brain, and although we still discover new things about the brain and memory loss every day, I don't think there was anything physically wrong with her. I think her brain was just filled with so much horror that it wouldn't let her remember, more or less." She pauses to take a breath. "I could be wrong; we all mistreat and misdiagnose. But I've been doing this for twenty years, and sometimes I think there's a reason the brain keeps us from remembering."

"Do you think that's what my brain could be doing? Blocking me from remembering something?"

MIND LIES

Folding her notebook, she shrugs. "I don't know, Jerri. It sounds like the past ten years of your life haven't been too bad. You have great friends and a sound business. And you're an attractive thirty-two-year-old single woman. The only thing we don't know is what happened in your first twenty-two years. Portia said you didn't talk about them much. I could be wrong, off my rocker, out in left field. But maybe, just maybe, there's something in there that's keeping a wall up. I also think it's too soon for us to make assumptions."

She could be right, and I'm no expert. So I'm not about to argue with her. "What should I do?"

Throwing her Kate Spade bag over her shoulder, she says, "I'd see what you can find out at home. Live in it. Try to make yourself comfortable in the space, and look through whatever you can get your hands on. Your home is what you made it. Start there and see if you can find any clues, something that will spark a memory. Maybe it will come. Maybe it won't. You have my card. Call me and we'll go over things again when you get settled."

"Thanks, Doc."

"No problem, Jerri."

* * *

"Jerri?" the barista shouts from the end of the counter. Locklin squeezes my hip before getting our order as I claim the love seat by the window. It's a beautiful spring day outside. The sun is shining, trees are in bloom, and the man I am absolutely infatuated with is spending the day with me.

Bliss.

"Here, babe." I eagerly accept my latte and settle in so I can enjoy the view. Not the scenery, not the cafe, but the view beside me. His face is shadowed, giving me little to remember him by. But that's how dreams go, right? They give you so much and yet nothing at all.

I see his hair, its usual raven color showing burnt-copper highlights in the sun. I see his jaw. Strong, masculine, with full lips.

I see his build. Broad shoulders, muscular thighs. Hands resting on them that show signs of use. Small calluses and a few scrapes.

Working hands.

His smell. It's clean and woodsy with notes of leather and spice.

It smells like home.

"Penny for your thoughts?" he asks.

I quirk a brow. "Just a penny?"

MIND LIES

Moving his hand from his thigh to my arm, he traces it lightly with his fingers all the way up until it rests on the back of my neck. Pulling me forward until his lips are touching mine, he tells me, "A monetary value cannot be placed on a woman like yourself. Because you, Lass, are priceless."

I whisper back against his lips, "Smooth talker."

He grins before pressing his lips firmly to mine. Reaching out with the hand not holding my morning brew, I grab hold of his leather jacket to keep him close. If we weren't in a public place, I would already be in his lap, and his tongue would have invaded my mouth—perhaps other parts of me as well.

Breaking the kiss, reluctantly, we settle in to a comfortable silence for a while. He rarely takes his eyes off of me. But when I turn to stare back, his face is blank, blurry, as if a fog keeps me from seeing exactly who he is.

"How's the shop doing?" he asks.

Twining my fingers through his, I tell him, "I'm sure you already know the answer to that, but I'll humor you by saying it's doing well."

He casually runs his thumb over the palm of my hand, back and forth, back and forth. It's hypnotic, and I close my eyes to absorb the feel of him beside me; if I can't see his face, I'll take the most of his presence and inhale as much of his scent as I can.

He is truly a beautiful man, both inside and out. Sometimes I think he's just lost his way. Or maybe he's stubbornly set in his own way. Locklin is a mystery that you can't help but want to decode. But regardless of how little time we get to spend together, I do my best to enjoy and savor the moments we have.

Like this one in the cafe.

I shift on the sofa, cringing lightly at the soreness between my legs. He smirks at me in a way that says, "You will still be feeling me for days, Jerri girl."

One thing: Locklin is not is a selfish lover. He consumes you, owns you, and makes you crave every bit of contact he gifts you. I watch his hands. Strong fingers that are capable of such wonderfully depraved things caress my own.

"Have you thought anymore about what I asked you?" I ask.

His thumb stops its movement.

"You know I can't," he firmly replies.

Frustrated and disappointed, I tell him, "You won't. You can, but you won't."

Giving my hand a squeeze, he then pulls me up off the love seat and tosses our empty java cups in the trash on his way out of the café. "I'm not the man you think I am."

MIND LIES

I shake my head at him. In defeat? In disappointment? I don't know. "And apparently I'm not the priceless woman you make me out to be."

Slamming his hand against a nearby news stand, he shouts, "Dammit, you know I can't change anything now. I care for you, Lass, deeply. You know I do. But this changes nothing. It can't."

Passing me my helmet, he mounts his motorcycle. After I've fastened it, I reluctantly take his hand to get on behind him. The engine revs and rumbles beneath us as he maneuvers the streets on our way out of town. I rest my cheek on his back, tighten my hands around his waist, and pray that my desperate whisper is taken with the wind.

"Stay."

The wind took nothing, because he answer's back. "I can't."

CHAPTER SIX

"We already know she can wipe her own ass, Doc. That's not what we're asking."

I laugh. It's been a long three days, but they've been made shorter by Portia's antics. How she makes me laugh, I don't know. But I am incredibly grateful to have had someone like her by my side. She's arguing with the doctor, in my defense of course, to get me the hell out of here and into the comfort of my own home, since I'm able to wipe my own ass.

Embarrassment—albeit very little—aside, she has a point. I've done some walking, and the swelling in my brain is pretty much non-existent. Other than my useless left arm, everything is functional. Agonizing, but functional.

There is more blue on my body than skin tone. The seat belt bruising. My bruised, swollen legs from their impact with the dash. Cuts, scrapes, and stitches mark around the blue. Small cuts all over my arms from glass. The stitches in the side of my head from its impact with the window. Lacerations to my neck from a tree branch. Thankfully, it didn't hit a main artery.

But I'm alive.
Apparently, I wrote off my SUV.

MIND LIES

"What we worry about in these situations is basically an overload in the sensory department. You're still in the fragile faze, Ms. Sloane. And although I can't necessarily keep you any longer, I hope that if you experience any of the symptoms I mentioned that you will get yourself to a hospital immediately."

Portia gives him what looks like a scout's honor symbol. "I'll be on top of it, Doc. You can count on me."

His thin-lipped smile says otherwise as he mumbles about getting paperwork on his way out the door.

"He's such a dink."

I sputter, "A dink. Really? I may not remember anything, but for some reason I think you would use more colorful language than that."

She puts her hands up in defense. "Hey, I'm all about the colorful. And on the plus side, since you don't remember, I'll get back to using all my colorful language while I'm around you. Just not in front of Cooper. We have a bet going. He doesn't think I can tone down my sassy swear words before he knocks me up."

"What's the bet?"

"I have a weak stomach. If I can go a month without swearing, he has to change shitty diapers for the first month after the baby's born."

"Will he not have to work?" I ask.

"Pfft. Oh he'll work alright, but he'll do it from home. Cooper runs his own software company, so he can pretty much work from anywhere and change shitty diapers while he does it."

I nod. "And what happens when he's not around?"

She smirks. "You're my neighbor. You live above the shop, which would take about a five second walk for you to come help me with the little spawn."

"And before you object, you already offered!" she hurriedly throws in.

"I'm guessing I enjoyed the idea of you having a child?"

She shrugs. "Of course you did. You'll be Aunt Jerri. We're family, and although it sounds depressing that I'm your only family, we've had a good run. No complaints from me. And as far as I'm concerned, you haven't had any either."

That's something else I learned. I met Portia in my early twenties when we were both taking the same night class at a local community college. Apparently I had no family. I bounced from foster home to foster home because my family died when I was young. At least that's what I told her, but she hinted that I left out a lot. Just as well. It's not something I liked to talk about.

She said she'd asked me about the foster families, and although I had a few kind words about them, I never really said much more than that. I asked if it bothered her, and she told me that, in a way, it did, but if I didn't want to talk about it, she wasn't going to push. We continued being friends in our business class and met a few times to study over a coffee. And as they say, the rest was history.

We've been running *Eclectic Isle* for close to six years now, and it's practically a landmark in the area. Business is great, and she says I have an eye for all things unique.

A nurse bustles into the room with a wheelchair and tells me that when I'm ready, I can sign forms at the desk and pick up prescriptions. I want to avoid the wheelchair and walk out on my own. But after dressing in the thin cotton pants and button-up shirt Portia brought me, I've about maxed out my energy for the day.

The nurse helps me get settled in the wheelchair before pushing me to the release desk. As I sign the release forms, Portia assures me that all the financial stuff has been taken care of, courtesy of Cooper's credit card. Insisting that I could have paid the bill myself, I argue with her as we leave the desk and head to the elevator. In truth, I don't know if I would have had the money.

"Do I not have money? Is that why Cooper has already paid?" I ask.

Portia shakes her head and replies, "You've got money, babe. But I have no idea where your purse is. I have to call the police station and ask if they have found it in your car. I cancelled the company Visa, since that's what you usually shop with. Your debit card is with the same bank, so I told them to cancel that too. We'll pick up a new one this week."

"Do we not have health insurance?"

"No, Jer. I'm covered with Cooper. You've rarely ever had a cold and probably wouldn't go to the hospital unless you were dying. If you did, you'd pay cash."

Figuring that's enough—and deciding that when I go to the bank, I'll look into my financial situation—we head out of the hospital. Cooper is waiting in the drop-off point with an SUV.

"Ready to get the hell out of here?" he asks.

I smile, thankful. "You have no idea."

* * *

I take in the sights and smells.

The street is busy but quaint.

The building is clean and not too tall or overwhelming.

Cooper guides the vehicle into a parking spot in front of a cozy, modern-looking shop with large display windows. The sign above it reads, *Iclectic Isle* in a weathered font, and I press closer to the window to take in as much as I can without actually moving from the vehicle.

MIND LIES

"This is it babe. We'll tour later after we get you settled in," Portia says.

It's beautiful. It looks light and airy but warm and cozy at the same time, like some place you would wander into to find treasures and lose yourself for an hour or two.

"It's lovely."

She spins in her seat. "It's your pride and joy, Jer. You spend more time in that shop than you do sleeping."

I give her a small smile, happy that I have so much passion for something. At the same time, I feel sad because I wonder what else I'd do with my life if the majority of it is spent behind those windows. It sounds like a hobby and a passion, but it also sounds empty and alone.

Much like I feel at the moment.

Empty.

Blank canvas.

Cooper continues and points across the street. "We live there, Jerri. On the top floor."

I look at the historic building. The third floor is the top floor, and from what I've learned from Portia, they live on the entire floor; Cooper owns the building. Apparently, software development is a lucrative career.

Turning down an alley, we come to a stop at the rear of the building. There's a large garage door, which they tell me is for deliveries, and a small overhang over a set of steps that leads to a door. Cooper pulls up so my door is closest and parks the vehicle.

"Home sweet home, Jer." Portia tells me.

By the time I unbuckle my seat belt, Cooper is at my door to help me out. It's slow moving, but eventually we manage to get my feet on the ground. Once that is accomplished, he guides me to where Portia is, holding open the door. I step into the landing and eye the large staircase ahead with misery.

"I'm gonna carry you up, Jer," Cooper tells me.

I deflate in thanks, my legs already throbbing from the short trip from the hospital. Portia bounds ahead of us up the stairs as Cooper carefully lifts me. My broken arm is positioned away from him to avoid having it pushed against his chest as we ascend to my home.

The first thing I notice are the exposed beams along the fifteen-foot ceilings. The outer walls are made up of exposed brick and various colorful paintings on canvases that are much fuller than my own. A mismatch of furniture and large-screen television is pulled together by an abstract rug to make up the living space. To the right, a long island with blood-red stools sits in the middle of the kitchen, and adjacent sits an espresso-colored, heavy-wood table complete with high, leather-padded, ladder back chairs. The set looks like something from the Viking era .

MIND LIES

There's a set of patio doors off the kitchen that opens to a rooftop outdoor area, which I plan to explore later. Cooper sets me down between the living area and kitchen. Portia guides my good arm through hers. "This is it: the other half of your happy space. Anything look familiar?"

My eyes roam over the furniture, the art, and the stack of mail on the island.

"It's beautiful, but unfortunately no."

She nods, resolute in her words. "It's okay. It'll come. Let's get you cozy."

She walks us toward a door that slides on a track. It's heavy and is made of old wood and metals. It's industrial-looking but warm. It suits the space. On the other side is a bedroom, my bedroom. A low king-size bed sits against the only exposed brick wall in the room. The padded leather headboard of the bed sits tightly up against the brick wall, and a nude painting of a woman hangs above. It displays the slope of her neck, her back, and her hips. A large masculine hand rests on her left hip. It claims her, lets you know she is taken.

It's possessive and beautiful.

The walls are a warm grey. Not too dark, not too light. Stylish lamps anchor the bed on dark nightstands. The bedding is a stark-white, fluffy contrast to the darkness of the room.

It's edgy yet elegant.

Bold but feminine.

It's *me*.

There are two doors in the room: One leads to a modest but functional walk-in closet. I must have an affinity for high-heeled boots because there are many pairs of them. The other door, closest to the entry, leads to the ensuite. Inside, a sink sits below a large vanity, and the walls command a deep golden color that contrasts the dark-tiled walk-in shower. To the side sits a large antique soaker tub.

Portia points to a wooden bench in the shower. "Coop had Walker over to put the bench in. Walker's a contractor friend of ours. I knew you'd hate one of those ridiculous plastic benches from the easy home store, so . . ." I let her trail off, understanding why Cooper had the bench put in: it's to help make things a little easier for me when I shower. Apparently I must be picky about what goes into my space. The shower would have looked tacky with a plastic chair or bench; the teak one looks as if it belongs there.

"Thank you, Portia. It's great."

She smiles and moves to the vanity. "I put the bags and tape for your cast over here. Can't get it wet when you shower." Waving a hand in front of her face, she continues. "That's all small stuff. I'm sure you're tired and ready to lay down."

I nod, wanting to explore. But as intrigued and curious as I am with the space, this is the most activity my body has endured in twenty-five days, twenty-two of which were spent in the coma—three awake in the hospital.

I follow her slowly back into the bedroom, where she already has pillows stacked against the headboard and the fluffy, white duvet pulled back. I sit on the bed and toe off the running shoes on my feet before laying back.

"This is so much more comfortable than the hospital bed," I moan.

Portia smiles at me, but it doesn't reach her eyes. "Don't I know it. We bunk in here when we get tipsy."

Hoping to bring that brightness back to her eyes, I ask her, "Like a slumber party? What about Cooper?"

The mention of her husband's name does the trick. "Cooper travels sometimes for work—"

"Which is code for, 'I'm going to Jerri's where I'll drink copious amounts of bourbon and wine—not in that order—and drunk-dial her poor husband in the middle of the night while we snuggle in bed cackling like a couple of teenage girls,'" interrupts Cooper from the doorway.

Portia throws a pillow at him. "You are so full of sh—*crap*, Cooper! You love my late night phone calls."
He smirks at her. "Close call on the curse words love, and I only love your late-night calls when you're alone. In *our* bed."
The heat in his eyes cannot be missed, and once again I find myself missing the man in my memories. I'll continue

to think of them as memories and not just fantastical dreams until I can prove myself otherwise.

I'm also jealous. Happy for them, but jealous that I'm alone. Or soon to be.

Her laughter pulls me from my misery. "And that, my dear Jerri, is code for phone sex, which I can't have with him when I'm in bed with you. But we make the most of it. Here," she says, jogging out of the room. Seconds later, she comes back with a photo album. "I know you're tired, but I'll leave these here for you to look at. There are lots of good times in there."

I nod. "Thanks, Portia, for everything. I'm gonna try to get some sleep now; that trip kicked my ass."

I give her a small smile. But from the look on her face, I know she sees through it.

The trip isn't what knocked me on my ass.

It's the unknown that's doing the kicking.

CHAPTER SEVEN

"You have to stay here, Jerri. You have to. I can't keep you safe if you don't."

His pleading falls on deaf ears. I don't want to stay here.

Not without him.

I don't want to do this alone.

"Would you listen to me, Lock? I don't want to be here without you! I'll go wherever you want me to go, do whatever you want me to do. I just want to be together," I cry.

Unfortunately, that falls on deaf ears too.

Only this time, they're not my own.

This time they're his.

"I won't tell you again, Lass. You know why I can't stay with you. I can't do what I need to do if you don't LISTEN, Jerri." He scrubs a hand down his face and squeezes the back of his neck in frustration as he looks to the sky, presumably for answers that I doubt he will find.

He continues. "Why must you be so stubborn? Why can't you trust me? Trust that I will do anything, anything"—he draws it out—*"to keep you safe. And you being with me, wherever I am, is not safe for you, Lass."*

I swallow past the lump in my throat, straightening my spine. Be it my stubbornness or my pride, I don't know, but I can't have him leave me. Not this time, not again.

Because it hurts too damn bad.

I open the door and head into my small apartment above the laundromat. It's tiny and always smells like fabric softener. And it's safe.

That's always his requirement for wherever he leaves me.

That where I stay is safe.

I go to shut the door, but his large body blocks it as he follows me into the apartment. I turn, prepared to tell him to leave, to get the hell out if he can't take me with him. To never come back.

But I don't.

Because that's the sick part of this fucked-up relationship. I can't ever leave him. And even though he doesn't admit it, he can't ever leave me.

MIND LIES

We're dependent on each other. We've needed too much from the one another other for so long that we don't know any other way. We don't know any other person.

Sure he's had others. I've had others too. But that doesn't change the fact that we always come back to this.

Him and me.

Locklin and Jerri.

And that's why when he slams my back against the door and crushes his lips to mine, I don't tell him to stop. I don't tell him to leave, get the hell out, stop breaking my heart—to never come back.

No. I don't do any of that.

I let him wrap my waist-length hair around his large fist so he can devour me.

Heart.

Body.

Mind and soul.

And when he guides my leg up around his waist, I enable him further by unzipping his jeans and releasing him from the confines of his boxers.

Because this is what we do, him and me.

We fight.

And then we fuck.

And then he does the same thing he always does, the one thing that breaks my heart more and more each time.

He leaves.

But that doesn't stop me from wrapping my other leg around his trim waist.

And it doesn't stop him from pushing my skirt up and impaling me with the force only a man of his size can achieve.

Large, strong, sure.

It doesn't stop any of it.

I moan. He's so good, I couldn't hold it in if I tried.

I shiver when he touches me because it's him, the only man who has ever brought endless goosebumps to my skin and pleasure—real pleasure—to my body.

I kiss him back., tasting and devouring, consuming everything I can of this beautiful man before he goes.

Because this will be the last time.

This time, I tell myself, I need to be strong.

MIND LIES

Not for me.

Not for him.

But for the child he doesn't know that's growing inside me.

So I push and I pull.

And when he groans into my neck, "Fuck me harder, Jerri girl,"

I do just that.

We fuck and we fight and we pull and we push.

And when his hand comes between us, his thumb making delicious circles on my little bundle of nerves, his mouth moving in rhythm with his cock, we explode.

Two souls forever, stuck together, and perhaps too afraid to break apart.

He settles me back on the ground, forehead to forehead, our heavy breath mixing together.

"I care for you deeply, Lass," he whispers across my lips.

Never, "I love you."

Never, "More."

Because Lock does not give more.

"Stay," I plead with him again. The stinging in my eyes lets me know tears are soon to fall. I won't let them, I rarely do.

But they're coming.

It's been a month since I've seen him, and there will most likely be another before he comes back again.

So I give him one more chance, one more plea, one more shot at a forever.

Because as much as it hurts me to walk away, I know this is not just about me anymore.

It's about him, or her.

It's about something greater than the both of us.

Warm, full lips press against my forehead, then my nose, last my mouth.

"I can't," He whispers against my lips.

I turn my head, duck around his body, and head toward the bathroom to clean up. I don't turn around; I just ask the other question I always want the answer to.

"How long?"

MIND LIES

I wait for him to reply. His answer will be my timeline, my countdown to when I need to have my stuff gone and moved.

"A month, possibly two. I'll text you."

I nod and close the bathroom door, knowing I won't get the text—because I don't plan on keeping the phone.

And I have no plan to see him in a month, or possibly two, because I won't be living here.

I'll be gone by then.

We'll be gone by then.

* * *

I finish in the shower. It was heavenly, with quality conditioner and soap that doesn't smell as if it came from a dispenser at a department store bathroom. After a healthy dose of moisturizer, a thorough shave which would have impressed Chewbacca, and clean pair of lounge clothes, I feel more like myself.

Or the myself I assume I should feel like.

I take stock in my appearance, trying to recognize the woman in the mirror. She has dark, thick hair that doesn't reach her shoulders. Gray eyes that look lost. Empty. Her skin is lightly tanned despite spending nearly a month indoors. Her cheek bones are high, chin small, and nose straight.

"Who are you, Jerri Sloane?" I whisper to myself.

Dr. Katherine Hope was right; she is a good looking woman. Not too tall, maybe five-foot-six. Not too curvy but not stick-thin either. I brush my fingers over the tattoo on the shoulder of a black bird in flight before leaving the mirror, the stranger, behind. Perhaps she'll have more answers for me tomorrow.

I walk out of the bathroom to find Portia waiting outside with a food tray. "You look much better, babe. Hop back in bed, and we'll get dinner out of the way."

Warily, I move back to the bed, refreshed and a little hungry. I eye the tray she brought in topped with a bowl of soup and half a sandwich before she scurries away back to the kitchen. It doesn't smell bad. It can't be worse than hospital food.

"Don't worry. It's from Junior's, the deli we like," Portia tells me.

I open my mouth to say something, but she cuts me off. "I saw that look. And trust me, you have every right to have it there. I'm not a terrible cook, so long as I pay attention to what I'm doing. It's when I don't pay attention when shit happens."

MIND LIES

I smile as she settles onto the bed beside me with her own dinner. "Like burning Cooper's dinner?" I ask.

She nods with a gleam in her eye. "Exactly that. That man can be distracting . . . trust me."

I test a spoonful of the vegetable soup. It is absolutely divine. "This is really good."

"It's your favorite from Junior's. We eat there a lot when we're working; it's a few doors down from the shop."

After eating in silence for a few moments, I broach what I feel is one of many elephants in the room. "I dreamt about him again."

Her eyes leave mine. She fiddles with her sandwich. "You wanna tell me about it?"

I lean back against the headboard, releasing a held breath. "Do you think I'm crazy?"

Soft eyes meet mine. "No, Jer. You're a lot of things, but crazy is not one of them. You're meticulous and driven. You're thorough and loyal. You've never been late paying a bill. If my hair looks like shit, you give it to me straight, and you don't give false promises. You may have lost your memory, but you're not crazy." She pauses to take a breath. "I guess the hardest thing is I feel like I've missed something, you know? Like, I've been so overwhelmed and consumed by the wedding and pregnancy stuff this past year that I feel like maybe I didn't pay enough attention."

I reach out and grab her hand because it feels like the right thing to do.

"Jer, I could be wrong, and so could you. But I'd be an idiot and a liar if I said I wasn't curious sometimes. When you go on your hunts for the shop, you're almost always still around Boston, but there are times you'll fly somewhere. There are times when I don't talk to you for a few days."

I give her hand a squeeze and gesture for her to continue. She tucks her blonde hair behind her ear and says, "Cooper and I talked last night. And please don't get upset with him because Cooper and I tell each other everything. But we talked about how you are when you come back. Sometimes, you're Suzy Sunshine, with deliveries on the way and a truck full of new treasures for the shop." She looks off, not really at anything in particular. Her eyes are glazed, lost in a moment of the past.

Softly, she says, "And sometimes, you're just *back*, with no extravagant finds, smile on your face, or deliveries coming in. Sometimes, it's like wherever you went, you forgot your happy. You'll shrug it off, sleep it off, or take the rest of the day off. I've asked—even pushed once—but I've never looked much more into it. Sometimes you'd tell me you were a little lonely. Sometimes you'd say you had the flu. And, hell, sometimes you'd say you were remembering little bits from your childhood and the loss of your family. Those memories would put you in a mood."

I contemplate before telling her, "Perhaps that is all it was. I don't know, and I can't give you the answers now."

"I know, Jer. But sometimes I wonder if I should have pushed harder. You never liked talking about your past, and we silently agreed to keep it off-limits, since I didn't enjoy talking about mine either. But maybe, Jer, maybe I should have pushed. Maybe I could be giving more answers than questions right now."

I shake my head. "No matter what, I don't think it's your fault. Nor do I blame you."

Resolute, she continues with her dinner, and when we finish, she sets the trays aside. "Do you want to tell me what you remember?"

I settle into the pillows. "Yes."

CHAPTER EIGHT

"In my memories, or dreams, whatever you want to call them, his name is Locklin," I tell her.

"I don't know anyone by that name, babe. What else you got?"

I smile. "He's big, broad shouldered. He has inky-dark hair and calls me Lass." I shoot my eyes her way. "Anything yet?"

She shakes her head. "No. But he sounds delicious. Keep going."

I do.

I tell her about the coffee shop and the ride on his motorcycle. I tell her about the questions and the time I shared with him in bed. She confirms that eggs Benny is my favorite breakfast. I tell her about his tattoos, his love for Ireland, and his accent.

I tell her about having rough sex against the door to my apartment above the laundromat.

"Wait!" She jerks upright in my bed, crosses her legs, and looks at me. "When we met, in our night classes, I told you that you always smelled good, and you told me it was because you lived above a laundromat. Everything you owned always smelled like fresh linen."

My heart skips a beat.

Once.

Twice.

I whisper, fearing to lose what I feel is the first bit of progress since I left the hospital.

"Did I have long hair then?" I ask, smoothing my short hair behind my ears.

Portia looks as though she's seen a ghost. She nods and says, "Yeah babe, you did."

We break into watery smiles. It may not be everything, but it's definitely something. It's one step higher on the staircase reuniting my past and present.

My watery smile fades as I remember my reason for leaving that apartment. "Were you ever there, or do you know where that apartment is?"

She shakes her head. "No, I don't. I remember you coming back after taking some time off. I think it was just a few days after a weekend, or something like that. You said moving took longer than you thought it would. I saw the next apartment, typical building near Draco Street, after we became closer. We didn't share much back then, Jerri. I think that's why we worked; we didn't pry into each other's lives—but we clicked," she says, shrugging her shoulders.

I silently agree with her. She's to the point. No nonsense. I feel much the same way. After only knowing her for a few days, I understand what she's telling me.

Some people work, and some don't.

Portia and I—we work.

"Portia?"

She leans back into the pillows. "Yeah, Jer?"

"I was leaving him. He was going to leave and come back after a month or two, and I was planning to be gone by the time he would have gotten back." I swallow against the impending tears. "I was pregnant."

"Oh shit."

I nod. "Yeah. Oh shit. Did I give up a child Portia? Did I lose one?"

Tears glisten in her eyes. She shakes her head. "I don't know, Jer. I don't think so. I mean, maybe you lost it? Unless you had it before you met me. But that doesn't make sense because you told me you moved when we were in class together. You said you planned to be gone before that guy, Lock, would have been back?"

"Yes. At least, that's what happens in the dream."

"Did you have a belly in the dream?" she quietly asks.

I shake my head. No.

"The only thing I can think of is getting ahold of your medical history. Who's that doctor? . . . The head doctor . . . The one who you're meeting with again?"

"Dr. Katherine Pope. She told me to call her when I was ready."

Portia agrees. "Well that's the first thing we'll put on the to-do list tomorrow. Even if you aren't totally ready, she should have your file. We'll go from there."

Feeling good about that, and our talk, I agree. There's nothing more I can do.

"I feel better, knowing that I know *something* that makes a little bit of sense."

"I get it, Jer. Well, not completely. But I'm happy something is coming together, even if I can't give you all the answers."

"Me too," I breathe out. "Now, how about you show me these photo albums before I call it a night."

She smiles and grabs the first one. "Prepare for some laughs my friend. We've captured some good moments in these babies."

So that's what we do.

We laugh.

At pictures of Portia and I dressed up as nuns on Halloween. At poor Cooper with dozens of lipstick kisses all over his sleeping form. Portia tells me his response was that she can take advantage of him anytime she wants.

We laugh at a picture of Cory—our part-time shop worker and best, gay guy friend—pleading, in the prayer position, to Cooper to leave Portia and run away with him.

She informs me this is a common occurrence and that Cory is devoted to his partner, Mark, so it's all in good fun.

I take it all in—the smiling faces, the laughter—hoping that one day I remember first-hand what is caught in this album. My past looks welcoming. It looks warm. It looks as though I enjoyed myself in much of it, even if some photos remind me that I was alone, that the man from my memories is not included.

I recall the stories Portia told me in the hospital about a man named Tom Black.

"I don't see any pictures of that guy you told me about in the hospital. Tom?"

She snorts. "Be grateful, Sweets, be grateful. I can't believe you heard me."

I nod. "I did. Even about the waxing."
She laughs. "God, we were dumb. Anyway, Tom was an asshole. Hot, but an asshole. About a year after school, we

were both still working at Ménage, which was a cross between a gentleman's club and a classy restaurant. Dancers—not nude, tasteful—worked there. Plus, the tips were killer. Anyway, he was one of your regulars."

I cut her off. "Whoa, did I dance?"

"Ha! No! Neither of us did, not that there's anything wrong with it. Like I said, not a nudie bar. Anyway, he always sat in your section when you were working. One thing led to another and then you two were dating. We were both saving money. Your dream was always the shop. Mine was always being around people and interior design. That's part of the reason why we fit so well. Anyway, you left Ménage and went to work for Tom. He's in real estate. His secretary quit. Total cliché, I know. But you really liked him. Hell, we all did, except Cooper. But Cooper doesn't like any guy who tries to get in your pants."

I laugh with her. "So what happened after?"

She sighs. "He was an asshole. Soon, you and I barely hung out. You were working twelve hours a day and were always going to dinner with him and his clients. You wore *pant suits*, which I'll tell you now is so not your style."

She gestures to the flying bird tattoo on my shoulder and my pierced nose.

I get the picture.

"He just ruled you, Jer. He tried to turn you into someone you're not. Long story short, one day you woke up, had enough, and left."

Turning my head, I ask, "Did he come after me?"

She nods. "Yes. But one thing about you, Jerri, is that once your mind is made up about something, there's no changing it. Good news is you had enough money at that point, which helped get your pride and joy started," she says, pointing to where the shop sits below this apartment.

My pride and joy.

So why do I feel so empty?

"Because I'm not with you, Lass."

His words echo through my mind. They're a stark reminder of what I have and what's not here. I tell Portia I'm tired, and she takes the dishes from the room. I don't ask if she's sleeping here.

I'm not sure if that's because I want to be alone, or because I hope she stays.

CHAPTER NINE

"Sing to me, Jerri girl."

I close my eyes to absorb my surroundings. His warm chest against my naked back. Strong arms around me. Our legs tangled in the sheets.

My heart at peace. My mind clear.

I feel the breeze filter through the open patio doors at the end of the bed. The sun is setting on the other side of the lake. I dread when it goes down, knowing it's our last night together before he has to go away again—our last night in this cabin, our meeting spot.

Warm lips kiss my shoulder and my neck before latching on to my ear. Lightly, nibbling. He doesn't wait for me, not that he ever does. He begins the song, softly singing the haunting tune about love and loss.

It's heartbreaking and beautiful.

It's everything we are.

His hand slides up my abdomen, over my naked breast, and up my neck, completing its journey at my chin. Pushing with his hand until my head is tipped back, he covers my lips with his own.

"Sing, Jerri girl." He breathes into my mouth before kissing me.

And like a sucker for punishment and agony, I do as he asks.

I sing.

*"I know you have to leave,
But let me beg you to stay.*

*This agony, you're my heart's reprieve,
I'll still love you anyway.*

*Don't make me ask,
Don't make me choose,
My soul's run down,
You're too much to lose.*

*But I'm beggin' you today,
Please, please just choose to stay.*

*I'm on my knees,
To do as you please,
Please take me anyway."*

Lock guides me down to the bed, hovering over me so he can begin his goodbye. It starts with his mouth, where he kisses my face—my cheeks, my nose, my lips, my chin. I keep my eyes closed, lost to the sensation. Sometimes it's easier, sometimes it's not.

MIND LIES

This time, I just want to feel.

I don't think I could ever forget what Lock looks like. He's too beautiful for that to happen.

My pretty and reckless.

So, sometimes, I just lose myself to the sensations. I get lost, feeling his mouth on my breasts, feeling his hands dance over my body, claiming it. I get lost listening to his Irish brogue, which is always stronger when he's turned on or pissed off.

"Tell me, Lass," he groans, reaching the juncture between my legs.

I know what he wants.

He craves my voice just as much as I crave his. "Devour me, Lock."

He groans against my wet heat before devouring me with his tongue. His fingers clench my hips. Tomorrow, the bruises will be the only evidence he was here.

Owning me.

Not just my body, but my heart.

He plays my body like a well-tuned instrument. Owning and mastering every note. Making me his own. I have no choice but to bend when he guides me. Move when he touches me.

I let out a gasp as his tongue swirls and teeth nip. Those depraved, strong hands leave my hips, allowing his fingers to delve into my body.

Forcing me to fly.

"Lock!" I cry out, trying to push him away and pull him closer at the same time.

He gives me no break. He never does. His mission doesn't stop until he leaves me.

Broken.

Bruised.

And breathless.

He pulls out his fingers, grabs my thighs, and flips me onto my knees before entering from behind.

"Shh, Jerri girl. Hold on." He groans as he wraps his left arm around my stomach and his right arm between my breasts so that he can hold onto my neck.

It's possessive.

It's bliss.

I rest my head on his shoulder, hands clasped behind his neck. All I can do in this position is hold on, take what he gives, and hope to hell he never lets go.

MIND LIES

But he will.

He always does.

"So tight, my Lass. So beautiful. Watch."

I open my eyes to see our reflection in the mirror above the dresser. His scarred, dark arms beautifully contrast my pure-white flesh.

But we fit.

We always fit.

Moving his hand from my waist to my center, I watch as his fingers complete one torturous circle after another on my already-too-sensitive clit.

"I'm g-gonna come!" I pant.

Lock's strong fingers tilt my head to the side. His mouth latches onto my neck. Kissing. Sucking. Marking. He thrusts into me hard enough that I know I'll ache for days.

But it's a sweet ache.

"Come, Jerri girl."

And I do. Like every other time, it's more explosive than the last.

He buries himself to the hilt, following me into the heavenly bliss that only he and I can create together.

It's soul binding.

It takes the breath from your lungs and the words from your mouth.

Holding me close, still inside me, Lock lowers us gently to the bed, my back held to his chest. His arms clutching. Our legs entwined.

He draws the blankets up to cover our sweat-cooled bodies before squeezing me close and kissing the top of my head.

"I care for you deeply, Lass."

I don't respond because I feel it. I never felt it with Tom; nothing I felt with him came close to what Lockin and I share.

I care for you deeply, Lass.

He's sure to tell me every time. Never, "I love you." Sometimes that I'm his water, whatever that means.

Too tired to respond, too sated to bother with questions, and too sad to know how I'll feel in the morning when he's gone, I choose to stay silent.

He'll kiss me when he goes, and I'll ask him to stay.

Like I do every time.

But every time, it's getting harder.

MIND LIES

It's getting older—and lonelier.

I fear that one day, I just won't ask anymore.

I'm sure he fears it, too.

* * *

I've just finished telling Dr. Pope—or *Katherine*, as she's instructed me to call her—all about my memories, including the parts Portia has proven were factual. It has taken almost an hour, but she has been attentive and has listened to every word. She is truly fascinated by the mind and how it works or doesn't work. And, as a plus, she's compassionate and doesn't put up with nonsense.

She's wonderful.

"So that's why I asked you to bring my medical file. I was hoping you could answer that question for me," I say.

Katherine pulls a file out of her bag and sets it on the kitchen table where we're seated. Apparently, house calls are not completely uncommon, especially with someone in my condition—it's hard to travel. It also costs about as much as half a small country, but after looking over some of my finances with Portia this morning, I've concluded that I can afford it.

Katherine shuffles through the small folder and pushes it to me. I scan the medical form before reading the Doctor's messy handwriting.

Jerri Sloane, Age 23

Brought in by ambulance. Suffered chorionic hematoma.
Patient was nine weeks pregnant at the time of miscarriage.
Kept under observation for twenty-four hours before release.
Bed rest for the following week.

Patient expected to make full recovery.

"I was pregnant."

Words blur on the pages through my watery eyes. I think of how I could have had an eight-year-old son or daughter at the moment.

They would have called me *Mom*.

The questions keep on coming. Was Lock with me? Had I left him by then? Did I call him when I was at the hospital?

"How you feeling, Jerri?" Katherine asks.

I shake my head. "I woke up this morning feeling like I had some answers, you know? Portia and I put two and two together, so when I woke up, I felt a little less crazy than I did yesterday. But now?" I bow my head and wipe under my eyes. "I honestly don't know, Doc. Was I careless? Did something happen to make me miscarry? Was anyone with me when it happened? I know Portia wouldn't have been because we weren't that close yet."

It sounds as if I wasn't very close with anyone. I have memories of Lock and proof of my life with Portia.

But who else did I have?

No one.

"It's a lot to take in. And unfortunately I can't answer those questions for you. Why don't we continue talking about what you *do* remember? That's always a good place to start." She puts her tablet and stylus on the table, ready to take notes.

"How about the apartment, Jerri. Do you remember where it was, what laundromat?"

I shake my head and reply, "No."

"Might I suggest going for a drive one day when you're feeling better to see if you can find it. Perhaps that'll jog your memory. We know you were living there while you went to night classes with Portia, so it can't be too far."

Portia reaches over and squeezes my hand. "It's a good idea, and I'd be happy to chauffeur."

Katherine thanks her. "Alright, we have a plan. What about the other places in your memories: the cabin you talked about, or the songs you sang? Any of those ring any bells?"

"The places, I don't know. There's a coffee shop, but I don't know the name. The cabin, I can only see the bed. And the song . . ." I pause, looking beyond the doctor and out the patio doors behind her. "The song I know. I can hear it, feel it, if that makes any sense."

Smiling softly, she replies, "It makes sense to you, and that's important right now. In fact, I encourage you to sing it in bed, in the shower, wherever you sang with him in the memory. Sometimes sounds bring back memories, and sometimes actions or pictures do the same thing. Like I told you, everyone is different.

"I'm trying to give you the tools I have to bring back your memory, but there's a lot of life missing here, Jerri. There's very little in your file. I'm not saying it's uncommon for someone to grow up healthy, but usually we see children with a broken bone or two, the odd hospital visit for the flu, or your regular, womanly gynecological visits. Your file is full of the regulars from age twenty-two onward. But before that, there's little."

Portia tips her head to the side. "What are you saying, Doc?"

Katherine finishes jotting some notes down on her tablet. "What I'm saying is I think the only way to get the answers is for Jerri to remember. The only reason I ever see a blank file such as this is when a patient comes from another country. When that happens, I get in touch with that country and request the information I need. Jerri's birth certificate says she was born here, in Ohio. So the only other thing I can think of is that whoever raised you didn't keep up with the standard hospital visits. Or you spent a great deal of time somewhere other than the states."

I lean my elbows on the table, head in hands. "Portia said I told her my parents died when I was younger. Is there anything about them in there?"

She nods. "There is. Sarah and William Matthews. They died in a car accident when you were twelve. Neither of them had living relatives, and neither had life insurance. You were placed into foster care at that time."

"Am I able to get in touch with the foster families?"

Katherine closes the folder and rests her clasped hands on top of it. "There's good news and bad news. An older couple looked after you. The husband passed when you were fourteen, and the wife passed when you were nineteen."

"Christ, am I the bringer of death?" I half-laugh, half-sob. In one day, I've gone from knowing little to knowing that the four people who raised me, along with my unborn child, were taken from me.

I feel the emptiness of it. I feel that blank canvas of mine, which was slowly starting to show color, begin to fade again.

Loss.

Katherine gives me an understanding smile. "I know it's a lot, Jerri. Focus on what we know for now. Go for a drive with Portia. Search through this apartment to see if something jogs your memory. Maybe sing to yourself. All of these things can help." She moves to pack her belongings into her Kate Spade bag. "Call me on my cell if you need anything before our appointment next Wednesday. And remember to be patient; you can't rush your memory."

Portia rolls her eyes. "I don't think that's a character trait she lost with her amnesia, Doc."

"Then there's hope your girl is still in there," Katherine says over her shoulder as she leaves the apartment.

CHAPTER TEN

Three more days.

That's how long it took before I could move my injured body down the stairs to get out of the apartment. Cooper and Portia have been wonderful; I couldn't ask for a better pair of friends. I'm grateful for all the things they have done for me, but I drew the line when Cooper tried to carry me up and down the stairs. It's something I needed to do on my own, and now that I can, this will be the first day I step foot in the shop.

Elegant and eclectic are the first two words that pop into mind as soon as Portia opens the door at the bottom of the stairs.

This is mine.

My eyes follow the exposed beams on the ceiling, taking in the multitude of chandeliers strategically placed throughout the room. The lighting is low, complementing the atmosphere.

Varying styles of furniture dominate the space, from heavy bookcases to low profile couches and ottomans. Throw pillows in all colors and prints bring each setting together. Low music plays in the background, and the soft rugs silence my steps as I follow my friend through the space I clearly took pride in.

There are so many pieces of furniture of different styles, and there's a shelf-covered wall filled with every type of bowl you could imagine. But somehow it all comes together. The space doesn't feel cluttered or mismatched. It just . . . flows.

"What do you think?"

I twist my head, painfully, and swallow.

"It's beautiful. Amazing."

She smiles. "You love this place. You spend a lot of time in here. Even when it's closed, you're always re-arranging furniture, making everything perfect."

I give her a small smile in return. "Sounds like my happy place."

She frowns. "It doesn't make you unhappy; it's more like your pride. You pride yourself on everything being perfect in here. Everything has to have a spot, and until you find where it goes, you're not content."

I gather much more from her words. At least they make sense at the moment, unlike my identity. I still don't know who I am and where I come from. Perhaps these feelings have resonated within before the amnesia.

"Be happy. You've just missed Mr. Grant. He came to ogle the Maserati without purchasing, yet again," a man says.

MIND LIES

I turn and am greeted by a very well-dressed man who eyes me with a mixture of hurt and sorrow. His hair is expertly coiffed, cut perfectly on the side, shinier than the hair on one of those models in a Pantene commercial. Thick-framed glasses are perched on his clean-shaven face, and a bow tie is placed perfectly below his neck. Portia explains quickly that the Maserati is the queen of our couches and that Mr. Grant is the old, moneyed fart who ogles but never purchases.

Placing a hand on Cory's arm, she continues. "Jerri, this is Cory. Ignore his whiny bitch routine. He's still upset that he didn't report you missing sooner. He feels like it's his fault. I've assured him it's not, hence the standoffish prude act he has going on right now," Portia tells me.

Cory scoffs. "Keep your opinions to yourself, Pixie. As per usual, you don't know your ass from your elbow."

She smirks. "Like I said, whiny bitch."

I smile at the well-dressed man, noting mild guilt in his eyes. Portia told me how close we all are. I was told that Cory is very much a part of our lives, and that he tends to join us for weekly dinners and holidays.

"It's nice to meet you again, Cory. I'm sorry I don't remember you," I tell him softly.

Clearly sensitive, his eyes mist before he says, "Fuck it," and places his arms around my shoulders. It's a soft embrace. His chin rests lightly on top of my head. "I know this must be awkward, but just roll with it, okay? I need you to roll with it."

I place my hands lightly on his hips and notice Portia, standing at the counter, discreetly wiping her eyes. I feel his lips touch the top of my head, and although I don't remember this obviously kind man, I feel a familiar tingle at the corners of my eyes before he leans back, keeping his hands on my shoulders.

"I guess it doesn't mean much right now, Jer. But I am so damn sorry. You gave us all time off for Portia's wedding, and I had the weekend off following that. But normally I check-in more often or stop by. I don't know why I didn't, and when I showed up on Monday and couldn't find you, I felt like the biggest prick. If I had just called or stopped by—"

"Enough of that," Portia interjects. "We've been over this. We all feel like shit, Cory, and maybe when Jerri regains her memory, she'll be pissed. But right now, let's just take the easy road, for Jerri's sake. She's got enough going on as it is."

"Pixie—" he says.

I place my hand on his, resting on my shoulder, and say, "She's right, Cory. No hard feelings. I don't remember anyway. And right now, that's all I want to focus on. Remembering."
He shakes his head. "Fine. That doesn't mean I can't still punish myself though. By punishment, I mean that I've already booked you in with Marcus and have given half my

paycheck to pay for it. Portia said you're feeling better, so you're getting the full treatment. Our treat."

I tilt my head. "Marcus? Like Mark, your partner?"

Portia snorts. "Cory will only call Mark by his full name. He's prissy like that."

He shoots her a look. "*Mark* is such a nineties abbreviation of a great name. *Marcus* is a very good name, and he deserves the full of it."

"Oh, he likes the *full of it* alright," she laughs.

Cory straightens his glasses and wags a finger in her face. "We both know your jabs at my gay relationship slide right off my shoulders, wench; besides, I watched you avoid sitting on hard surfaces before the wedding. I've seen Cooper in the showers at the gym, so I know where he stuck it—and it's wasn't between the flaps."

I bark out a laugh and watch as Portia simply raises an eyebrow and shrugs her shoulders in a way that says, "I love my husband, and I'm not ashamed." Clearly these two have a very open and friendly relationship, judging by the amount of banter.

"As I was saying," Cory continues, "you'll be primped and preening like a peacock. I booked all your favorites: nails, face, hair, and of course a massage."

I shake my head, a little lost for words and slightly taken aback. It feels incredibly overwhelming to have strange people remind me of my favorites, likes, and dislikes, from the soup and sandwich Portia fed me bought from my favorite deli to the spa treatments I prefer. It's one thing when I'm wandering around upstairs in a foreign place I once called home. For the most part, I can treat it like a semi-vacation, a place that's more than comfortable, a place where you find yourself pausing to take in the view from a window. It feels like seeing the colors on a particular painting you don't remember seeing before.

However, being down here, in this shop I call my own, in a place with people who know more about me than I care to think about, it just makes me feel more lost. There's no getting-to-know-you faze. It's awkward and empty, and I feel like more than a third wheel. I feel more as if I'm the giant fucking elephant in the room, and regardless of how much these people care about me, I'm starting to feel incredibly uncomfortable.

Stepping foot in *Eclectic Isle* was just part of the journey today, a way for me to see my so-called pride and joy before continuing on the hunt for my memories with Portia. More than ready to end the awkwardness and empty feelings taking over my battered body, I say, "I appreciate that Cory, thank you." Looking at Portia I ask, "Do you mind if we get going now? I usually get tired in the afternoon, and I'm hoping we can cover as much ground as possible today."

Portia and Cory share a glance. "Sure thing, lady. Let's go. I'll call you later, Cory."
"Wait," I say. "I feel like an ass now. What's happening with this place? Am I supposed to work? Should I close

this down for a bit until I'm well enough to continue working?"

Portia loops her arm through mine and continues pulling me toward the door. "It's all good right now, Jerri. Cory's working a little overtime, and we have a part-timer art student who we just moved to full-time while she's on spring break. Everything's taken care of."

I clear my throat, avoiding the sting, and kick myself for earlier "ill" thoughts regarding these caring people, who obviously just want what's best for me. The afflictive feeling in my gut has not completely abated, but I choose to focus on what's important and where we're headed. My feelings can be dissected and analyzed later when I'm in the haven of my bedroom.

Once in the car, Portia types "laundromat" into her GPS. It lists fifteen laundromats within a ten-mile radius, so she says we'll start with the one closest to where we went to night school and branch out from there.

Looking out the window, I watch people on the street pass by, going about their lives. A mother tries to catch up to her son, a toddler, who chases a pigeon. A man in a suit pulls angrily at his tie as he argues into his cell phone. All these people take for granted the moments surrounding them, the moments that make you feel whole at night. They take for granted the importance of remembering.

The significance of smells, the influence of a breathtaking smile, and the value of those closest to you are all the things that should make your days feel significant. But once you lose that time, it has the power to break you.

I notice that Portia's tiny frame and short blonde hair does make her look like a pixie. Caught in that train of thought, trying to place my mind on more important things, I tell her, "I appreciate you doing this with me." I clasp my hands together, squeezing them hard enough that my knuckles turn white. "The fact that I can't remember a single thing about you, and yet you're still doing this with me—well, just . . . thank you."

She turns down the radio and adjusts her hold on the steering wheel. "Nine years ago, I showed up at school with a busted lip and a black eye. I made a stupid decision, one of many. His name was Matt. We hadn't known each other very long, but you were the first to see past my bullshit excuses. You offered me a place to stay. You may very well have saved my life, Jerri."

She clears her throat, shaking off her emotions before continuing. "Regardless of what you did for me then, I would still be here for you now. But *because* of what you did for me at that time in my life, there is no way in hell I *couldn't* be here for you now. I was at a really low point, and you helped pick me back up." She gives me a small smile. "I'm not picking you up as you did with me; I'm just holding your hand, babe. That's what family does. We hold on."

Nodding, I quietly agree. "We hold on."
* * *

MIND LIES

"Five times the charm?"

"I hope so, Portia. I really do."

The first four laundromats where a bust. Three were single-story buildings—no apartments above. The fourth was at the bottom of a ten-story building that looked nothing like the one from my memories.

Rounding the street corner, Portia parks the car beside a two-story building. I sign out front reads, Ming's Coin Wash. As we start on the sidewalk, the low heel of my boot catches on the concrete, causing me to stumble. Luckily, I right myself as my vision starts to blur.

"Don't leave me here, Locklin. Please! I can't stand it anymore," I beg. Strong fingers tighten around my arm, catching me as I stumble on the concrete walkway heading toward the back of the building.

"I'm sorry, Lass. I truly am. But this is safest place for now. Trust me."

My laugh is harsh when I reply, "I'm so fucking done with safe, Locklin. I love you, and you leave me. Every damn time. I'd take unsafe with companionship over safe, lonely, and empty. I can't keep doing this, Lock. I can't."

"Jerri!" Portia's harsh voice snaps be back to the present. We're still at the side of the building. The cool, grey concrete against my back feels better than the sweat accumulating on my temples. Taking a deep breath, I open my eyes to meet Portia's concerned ones.

"This is it. It's up there." I nod toward the red, rusted staircase to my left. I feel relieved, and scared, that we've found it. On one hand, I've confirmed that I'm not completely insane. But on the other, I worry about the constant references in my memories regarding my safety.

What did I need to be safe from?

Better yet, from who?

The side door opens, and a tiny Chinese woman with greying hair exits carrying a bag of garbage. Tossing it into the bin, she turns and looks at us with a mixture of shock and happiness. "Miss Jerri, you back! You see sign, apartment for rent," she says, pointing to the stairwell.

I did not see the sign.

I feel slightly shocked that this woman recognizes me. Portia takes the lead. "Hi! I'm actually the one apartment hunting. I'm Jerri's friend Portia," she says, smiling kindly, reaching for the little older woman's hand.
"I Ming. You come. I show you," says the woman known as Ming. She starts dragging Portia by the hand to the staircase. Hanging onto the railing, I follow at a much slower pace, still cautious of my healing body and cloudy mind.

"Miss Jerri live here one year. Always pay rent. Last man no pay, so he go!" Ming jabbers on as she leads Portia through the door to the apartment. I pause on the landing to take a deep breath before crossing into the apartment. Memories continue hitting me.

MIND LIES

"Would you listen to me, Lock? I don't want to be here without you! I'll go wherever you want me to go and do whatever you want me to do. I just want to be together."

I begged him to stay right here in this very spot, in an apartment he put me in to keep me safe. Taking a few more steps inside a place that smells like fabric softener, I come to the wall that separates the kitchen from the entry way—the same wall he passionately fucked me against while I was pregnant with his child.

The child I miscarried.

Where is he?

Waiting for something to hit me, another memory, a clue that could help me figure out why I left, I blindly follow the two through a place I once called home.

"So, the apartment comes with the furniture, Ming?" I hear Portia ask. I feel bad for the kind woman taking her time to show us an apartment we have no intentions of renting.

"You bring own bed. Everything here stay for you," Ming tells Portia as she bobs her head up and down.

"I believe it's time to christen the new bed, Lass," Lock groans in my ear as he pulls the dress off my shoulders.

Glancing toward me where I lean against the wall, Ming adds, "Miss Jerri no look good. You come." She waves her hand at me, shooing me toward the bathroom, and I blindly follow. Wetting a cloth in the sink, she stands on her toes and presses it against my forehead.

"You need rest in condition, Miss Jerri." She tells me, waving her hand up and down my body. I nod, taking a few deep breaths to calm my head and stomach.

"I'm just a little light headed. Thank you, Ming."

I take the cool cloth from her hand as Portia squeezes my shoulder. "We should get you home, Jerri."

Approving, Ming nods before pointing at my flat stomach. "Too much for baby. Must be boy. Boy make tired very early."

I smile a little, lifting my hair and pointing to the stitches in my head. "I'm tired because of my head injury, Ming. No baby." I'm sure she noticed the ugly bruising on the side of my face; perhaps she was just too kind to say anything. She simply shrugs her shoulders and mutters, "Boy make tired," before wiping down the sink with a towel.

"Ming?" I ask. She looks at me. I continue. "Do you remember the man who lived here with me?" She shakes her head. My shoulders deflate.
"Man no live here with Jerri. Man come after and ask where you go. I tell him Ming not know." She gives me wide eyes as if to say that even if she did know the man, there would be no way in fuck she would tell him where I had gone.

MIND LIES

"Do you remember what he looked like?" Portia asks. Ming shakes her head and points to my hair. "Hair dark. He tall." She raises her hands above her head, flicking them to indicate "much taller," and shifts her eyebrows up and down in a way that suggests she very well may have liked the way this tall, dark-haired man looked.

I watch Portia pressing her lips together in an attempt to stall a laugh. "Thanks so much, Ming. I really should get some rest," I say.

Portia adds, "I'm hoping to find a two-bedroom apartment, Ming. But if I change my mind, I'll definitely call you."

We follow her out of the bathroom, and as we pass the beige couch in the living area, I pause and grab onto the back of it as a memory takes over.

With my hands braced on the back of the couch, Locklin sweeps my hair over my left shoulder, exposing my right. He starts to place kisses along my skin. His teeth graze my ear lobe. He whispers, "Sing, Jerri girl."

Leaning my head back against his shoulder, I do just that.

Sing.

"Let's get home, girl." Portia says, oblivious of my aching heart.

CHAPTER ELEVEN

"I know what we need to do."

Rolling my head to the side, I stare at my good friend lying next to me on my bed. I collapsed as soon as we came in the door, but I haven't fallen asleep yet. With too much on my mind, and so many unanswered questions, it seems like an impossible feat.

"What's that?" I ask.

She sits up, twisting her hands together trying to find the right words. "You've had two memories now about the song he asked you to sing to him, right?"

I nod. "Yes. It seems really personal. I don't know who the artist is or anything. I googled the words, but nothing came up."

"You're always humming and singing to every song on the radio, Jer. So I'm going to preface this by saying you have a beautiful voice," she tells me with a straight face.

"I'm sensing this is where you drop the bomb?" I ask her with a raised brow.

She confirms. "Not a bomb per say. I was just thinking that if I record you singing whatever song it is you sang to him, I could stick it on YouTube, and maybe it might bring us some luck, you know? Maybe this Locklin guy will see it. If he doesn't see it, maybe someone who knows him will and pass the message along."

I frown. "What message?"

She shakes her head. "That you're trying to find him. We can add that message to the video. There's tons of shit like this that gets posted on YouTube. People are hit sensations overnight."

I cut her off. "I don't want to be a hit sensation, Portia."

She places her hand on mine. "I know you don't. You'd hate all the attention. We don't need to put your face *in* the video. But we could put your face in profile or something and attach a message to the song. Cooper can help."

It feels so personal.

Like an invasion of my privacy.

From what I remember, each time I sang that song to Locklin, it was in the middle of a passionate moment, something I feel should only be experienced between the two of us, certainly not with the world.

But what other choice do I have? I don't know what else to do to find him. Going to the apartment didn't help me get any closer to finding him, and other than the coffee shop and the cabin, which I have very little memory of, I've run out of places to look.

I guess I have to consider how badly I want to find him. But maybe I should be asking myself whether or not he wants to be found.

"Let me sleep on it, okay?"

Reassuring me with a kind smile and understanding eyes, she tells me, "Take as long as you need, Jer. It's just a suggestion."

I nod in thanks before she heads home to her husband.

* * *

"Run, Jerri!"

Tripping over the loose gravel of the driveway, I do my best to stay on my feet. There's blood running down my leg, and my hip is on fire. Locklin's grasp on my fingers tightens to the point of pain as he pulls me off the driveway and down the hill.

My bare feet, now torn from the gravel, slip on the damp grass, and I stub my toe on a sharp rock. I cry out, only to be silenced by Lock as he pushes me to the ground, one arm banding around my waist, his hand tight on my mouth.

Silent tears stream from the corners of my eyes. He tries to comfort me. "Shh, Lass. I won't let anyone hurt you, but you need to be quiet."

MIND LIES

I nod, understanding, grateful he's here for me.

I shiver at the thought of what may have happened if he wasn't.

Lights reflect off the water, and Locklin uses his body to shield my own as they skip over the hill, narrowly missing us. The headlights of the car continue around the bend before they disappear from sight. "We're travelling to the far dock over there. Do you see it, Lass? Not far."

I take hold of his hand. He pulls me up off the ground, steadying me as my legs shake. Whether they shake from fear or from blood loss, I don't know. Closing my eyes, trying to gain what little strength may be left, I swallow down every emotion and focus on survival. Steadily, I place one foot in front of the other, wanting desperately to be far away from this part of hell.

I should never have been here this late.

I should have listened to my gut and left a long time ago.

My vision begins to blur despite my best attempt to stay upright. The blood loss is too great. The cool breeze on my leg confirms that it's wet from hip to toes with blood. I wobble as we near the dock, swaying slightly while clinging to Locklin's hand. Sensing my struggle, he puts one arm under my legs and another behind my back. Easily, he cradles my body in his arms as he briskly walks toward the boat.

"Hang on, Lass, I've got you."

"Don't leave me, Lock, please." I mumble into his chest as I begin to lose consciousness.

Placing a kiss on the top of my head, he replies, "Never."

* * *

Jolting awake, I rip the sweat-soaked sheets from my body and clutch my chest.

What the hell were we running from?

Swinging my legs over the side of the bed, I head for the bathroom. I flick on the vanity lights and turn on the taps, repeatedly splashing water over my heated face. Reaching blindly for the towel, I clean myself off, still panting from the shock of my dream—or memory. I almost hope it were a dream; if it were real, I'm afraid to know what it was about.

"Think, Jerri, think," I mumble to myself.

Turning to exit, I bang my hip on the counter, the same hip bleeding profusely in my dream.
"Dammit."

Lifting up my nightshirt, I glance down at my left side to look for any type of scarring. I see nothing out of place, but I'm determined to prove the dream wrong, or perhaps to prove myself wrong, to confirm that my dreams are not a product of my amnesia-filled mind. I *need* it to be real. Flipping on the bright overhead lights, I pull down the side of my boy shorts and twist toward the full-length mirror on the wall behind me.

"Holy shit."

There.

It's there.

A three-inch scar sits on the back of my hip in a spot that would normally be covered by the waistband of my jeans. It's not raised but is actually rather smooth, suggesting it was probably a clean cut. It had happened some time ago; either that or a well-to-do surgeon did a good job ensuring it healed properly.

I stare between the cut and my ghostly white face in the mirror. A mixture of fear and shock sends me to my knees. Quickly, I crawl to the toilet and empty the contents of my stomach. I heave until there's nothing left.

I'm completely empty.

Who am I?

Not knowing is literally killing me inside. If I had led a normal life or had a friend who could explain my thirty-two years, the not-knowing pill would be a little easier to swallow. If these dreams are in fact memories, I can't help but feel pain, knowing that I have literally alienated Portia, my best friend, from the first few decades of my life.

And for what?

If the dream is real, if Locklin is out there, why hasn't he come for me? He saved me from whatever the hell happened in my dream. If he's a good man, why hasn't he been here with Portia—with me?

If he isn't a bad man, if he made me safe all those years as my friend, lover, and protector, why haven't I mentioned his name to Portia? Why have I kept him a secret?

In one of my dreams, it was mentioned that he and I would stay in contact by cell phone. Portia had replaced my missing cell the other day, and although the picture file on *that* phone is empty, the contact list is full. Rushing into my bedroom, I unplug the phone from its charger and open the contacts folder. Eighty-seven contacts. Furniture vendors, art suppliers, upholstery specialists. No Locklin.

"Damn it!" I huff. "Alright, Jerri Sloane. If you had something to hide, where would you put it?"

I sit down on the side of my bed and start checking the nightstands. They're an obvious place to start. And seeing as I have no idea where anything is—and the only place I had rummaged through, as per Katherine's suggestion, was the desk in the living area, which only revealed paperwork and finance reports—I figure that I have nothing to lose.

MIND LIES

The contents of the top drawer include lip balm, sleeping pills, an e-reader, and hand cream. Opening the bottom, I find a few books and a decorative box. Opening the box's lid, I can't help but smirk. "Well, Jerri, you're nothing if not resourceful." I chuckle as a return the box filled with every gadget guaranteed to get a woman off.

The nightstand on the other side of the bed has nothing of help, but I'm determined. My need to find something helpful is more important than my need to breathe. Rushing to the closet, I erratically pull shoe boxes off the shelves. I dump their contents at my feet, wondering if something useful could be inside.

I dump it all with no remorse for the mess I create.

I pull coats off their hangers and fling socks from drawers. I empty it all as if I were a jealous woman searching for evidence of a husband's betrayal. No drawer remains full, and no coat pocket is left turned in. Receipts and loose change litter the small space once everything has been ransacked.

"Fuck!"

Collapsing onto the floor with my head in my hands, I finally allow myself to weep. More is lost than just my memory. I'm just a shell of a woman, lost in a ransacked closet with nothing but sobs to keep me company. There is nothing valuable about the expensive footwear and clothing surrounding me.

No.

The only things worth any value are those of which I can't remember. Those that are lost. I have no man to keep me company, no mother to hug and tell me this too shall pass. I have no idea what makes me happy or what brings me peace.

I don't know where I've been or where I came from.

I. Have. Nothing.

So I let myself weep on the floor of this closet. I shed tears for everything I may have had and what may never come back to me. I weep until long after the sun rises and Portia finds me. She finds me with silent tears still streaming down my face. She falls to her ass beside me without saying a word. We're connected from shoulder to hip on the floor. She takes my hand in hers and leans her head against my own.

No words.

Just silence and understanding.

It almost makes it hurt more.

She knows who Jerri is. She's aware that words weren't going to fix this breakdown, so she didn't bother to speak them. There is no "I'm sorry" or "Don't worry, Jerri. It'll get better soon." There is just silent support in an unwavering form. It's one woman, literally leaning on another—as if she is saying, "I won't let you do this on your own."

MIND LIES

I have no idea how long we sit on the floor in the closet. The sun is higher in the sky, and my shoulder is damp from mixed tears. My mind has been running in circles, processing the little I know, trying to process what I don't know and the many things I still wish to find out.

I have nothing left to lose.

Recalling Portia's idea from the previous day, and coming to the conclusion that things can't get any worse before they get better, I make the decision.

Clearing my throat, I softly tell her, "Let's do it, Portia. Let's make the video."

She squeezes my hand.

CHAPTER TWELVE

Staring at the window, eyes squinting from the brightness of the sun streaming through, I adjust myself on the ottoman while waiting for Portia to find the perfect spot behind me. After leaving the closet, we talked over coffee and came up with a plan. My desire to remain somewhat anonymous is very important to me. Portia confirmed it would have been important to the old Jerri as well.

We set the ottoman up for me to sit in front of an east-facing window. The light is nearly blinding for me, but it's perfect for Portia to use. The exposure creates a glow around my body, blurring the edges and concealing my face.

From her view through the camera, I'm angled slightly to the right, wearing an off-the-shoulder tunic so that only one of the characteristics that defines me is shown.

The raven tattoo sits on my shoulder, taking flight toward my neck. I recall our earlier conversation regarding said tattoo as I wait for her to make final adjustments on the camera.

"I think we should keep something that defines you as you in the video, such as your tattoo," she told me.
"I noticed it in the mirror the other day," I replied. "Do you know when I got it or what it stands for? I don't feel

like someone who would just tattoo something random on her body without an explanation."

She shook her head. "You wouldn't and you didn't. You've had the tattoo for about six years. You went with me to a tattoo appointment and decided to get one for yourself. You said you'd been planning it for a while, just hadn't took the plunge yet. When you came out and showed me, I asked what it was for." She paused, heading to the sink to rinse out her coffee mug.

"What did I tell you?"

Leaning her back against the counter, she said, "That it was time to fly solo—to carry on with your dreams."

Apparently I purchased the building for the shop the following week, with Cooper as an investor and Portia as a manager.

"Okay, Babe. I'm ready when you are," Portia says from behind.

Looking over my shoulder at the camera, I will my nerves to settle as she gives me a small but encouraging smile. There are no instruments playing in the background; it's just going to be me and my voice, singing to the man from my dreams to come back to me. Turning away from her and recalling the fullness in my heart when he was with me, I close my eyes and picture Locklin. I take a deep breath, imagining his scent filling my lungs and his warm, hard body holding mine.

"This song is for the man from my memories. Maybe I've imagined him, and maybe my amnesia is fiercely playing cruel tricks on me; or maybe, just maybe, I've lost my fucking marbles." I laugh softly. "If I haven't, please prove me wrong. Prove that my mind doesn't lie. Come back to me."

"I know you have to leave,
But let me beg you to stay.

This agony, you're my heart's reprieve,
I'll still love you anyway.

Don't make me ask,
Don't make me choose,
My soul's run down,
You're too much to lose.

But I'm beggin' you today,
Please, please just choose to stay.

I'm on my knees,
To do as you please,
Please take me anyway."

Carrying the last note until my lungs are robbed of breath, I end the song softly. I sang with everything I had, everything I wished to have, and the last bit of hope that takes up residence in my empty heart.

I don't bother to wipe the tears from my cheeks when Portia sits down beside me. "That was heartbreakingly beautiful, Jer." She sniffs and shakes her head. "I don't even know what else to call that. It was just . . . wow."

I close my eyes and nod my head. "I *feel* it when I sing that song, Portia. I feel *him*." I cough out a humorless laugh. "The fact that I can't remember, *and* the fact that he's not here, makes me feel empty, or maybe even stupid—"

"You are not stupid, Jerri," she interrupts.

Grabbing my hand, she continues. "Don't beat yourself up for not remembering; clearly, you had a strong connection to Locklin because even a deaf man would feel what you put into that song." Her determined eyes meet mine. "People kill for that feeling, Jerri, and if at the end of the day all you end up remembering are these feelings you shared with him, you need to remind yourself that *that* is more than what some people feel in a lifetime."

My chin quivers before sobs break free. She crushes me in her arms, holding together what's left.

"I'm so happy I didn't wake up in that hospital to a shitty best friend," I mumble into her sweater. She laughs as she cries with me. "You're stuck with me for life, Lady."

A throat-clearing breaks us apart, and Portia smiles over my shoulder. "Hey, babe."

Wiping my eyes, I address them both. "This is the second time today someone has come in without knocking. Do I have an open door policy or something?" I joke.

Cooper answers, "Portia texted and told me to be here around one. I knocked but you didn't answer. As for Portia, she has no respect for closed doors."

She scoffs. "That's not entirely true, Coop."

He gives her a stern look. "The only door you don't open is the one to the toilet."

She smiles. "See, not entirely true. I don't need to walk in on people having their morning constitutional. I have boundaries, you know."

He shakes his head before sitting down on the couch. "How are you, Jerri? Portia said you had a rough night. Let me know if there's anything I can do to help."

I smile at him, but Portia speaks. "You're already helping, babe." She turns to me and continues. "Coop's going to upload the video for us through a bunch of different something-or-others and tag, or tap it, to YouTube to get it lots of views."

I frown at her, and Cooper shakes his head in defeat. Clearly Portia does not understand the ins and outs of computers, and it's not worth the energy to explain it to her, so I just say, "Sounds good."

"Speaking of rough nights, you didn't tell me what last night's dream was about before we got started. I assume it must have been big since you decided to follow through with the video idea?"

I nod. "Yes. It was big."

She places a hand on my knee. "You don't have to share if you don't want to, Jer."

I shake my head and reply, "No, I do." Taking a deep breath, I tell them about my dream of Locklin carrying me to a boat. I tell them about the blood dripping down my thigh, about my heart racing in fear just before passing out. A round of "Holy shits" and "What the fucks?" are whispered as I pace the living room recounting the terror.

"You think that one's real?" Cooper asks.

Solemnly, I nod my head as I reach to undo the button of my jeans. Turning around, I pull them down a few inches and hear a gasp from Portia.

"Oh my god. Why haven't I seen that before?" she asks.

Shrugging my shoulders in a way that says, "I don't know," I pull my pants up before facing them. "There's something else," I say, watching the color return to their faces. Portia has moved to the couch beside Cooper, who has his arm around her, holding her close.

Sitting down on the ottoman, I clasp my hands between my legs as I tell them, "In one of the memories, I asked

Locklin where he would go if he could go anywhere in the world, and he told me he'd go back to Ireland because to him it always felt like home."

Portia says, "You told me he had an accent and he calls you Lass. Maybe you went there with him. I guess you could have gone since we met, as well. When we first became friends, we didn't keep tabs on each other as much as we do now. Going a week without speaking wasn't uncommon," she reasons.

I shiver, goosebumps pebbling my flesh, as I deliver the rest of the memory. "Those boats? The dock he carried me to before I passed out? . . ." I pause, waiting for them to acknowledge they're listening. "There was writing on them. It wasn't in English."

I let go of the breath I was holding.

"It was Gaelic."

We are enveloped in silence for a few minutes. The three of us are lost in our own thoughts, trying to piece together the snippets of my previous life. I place my head in my hands, running everything through my head: the past, the present, and the unknown future. "Oh my god," I whisper, shaking my head.

"I didn't tell you," I say to both of them. "I didn't tell you. If this is true, if I'm not nuts, if I haven't lost my fucking marbles, this is why."

Portia frowns. "Why what, babe?"

Cooper's eyes light. I think he's coming to the same conclusion I am, and we silently acknowledge why when we lock eyes. "You, Portia," he tells her.

She frowns, confused, and looks back and forth between us. "Me what?"

Cooper squeezes her shoulder. "If Jerri's right, and this shit did happen, she didn't tell you because she didn't want to put anyone else in danger."

Portia scoffs. "That's ridiculous. We work together, Cooper. We've lived together for a very short time, and"—she pauses to make eye contact with me—"no offense, Jer, but I was literally your only friend when we met. If someone wanted to get close to you, no matter what I do or don't know, they would assume I did. I've been the only person close to you for ten years."

Cooper says, "That may be true. But think about it; she didn't tell us about this Locklin guy, and she didn't make any other friends other than you, myself, Cory, and Mark. When she was with Tom, she never really got close to any of his friends. She just hung out with them when she had to for his sake and for work."

"I get that, but she's a private person who doesn't like a lot of people. I don't like a lot of people either," she replies.

Cooper smiles. "You like me just fine, and you'll still talk a stranger's ear off. Jerri won't. She avoids personal questions like the plague."

I rub my temples, feeling a headache coming on. Listening to people talk about me in the past tense and digesting all this information is enough to make my head spin. "It sounds like I'm not the only one with more questions than answers," I huff.

"I'm sorry, Jer. We're not trying to make you upset. We're just as confused as you are," she says.

I highly doubt that, but I nod in agreement.

"How about we get this video up and see where that takes us?" Cooper throws in.

Portia adds, "Come home with us, Jer. You've been held up in here long enough. We'll have an early dinner, and you can have a final look at the video before Cooper puts it up."

I want to decline.

I want to go back in my room, curl up in my bed, and pull the covers over my head. I want to block out the world and burrow under the safety of the blanket.

That's not how you get answers.

Don't be a coward.

Reluctantly accepting to go home with Coop and Portia for dinner, I clean up and follow them across the street. "You're not cooking, are you?" I ask, attempting to make light of an incredibly serious afternoon.

MIND LIES

Her laugh precedes me as I walk out the door.

* * *

One thing to know about software developers: they're loaded.

Cooper and Portia's apartment, which makes up the entire third-floor of the building across the street, is divine. Portia had once mentioned her love for interior design, and with Cooper's unfoldable wallet, she has achieved creating a spectacular home.

Modern meets comfort in the edgy space, which is complete with lights that turn on when you speak to them and couches you could easily fall asleep on.

"Did you quit taking your pain meds?" Portia asks from the other side of the island before sliding a glass of wine my way.

"Pretty much. But I took one last night before bed because my legs were bothering me after all the walking we did. Why?"

Cooper answers, "Because they're not good to mix with alcohol."

I frown. "Why'd you give me the drink before you asked?"

Portia smirks, and Cooper slaps her on the ass. "Because she would have given you the booze no matter what your answer was. And she's assuming new Jerri would do the same as old Jerri, which is drink it anyway."

I smile at them both. It's a small smile, but it's there. They know each other so well, and I envy that. "You ready to see the finished product, Jer?" Cooper asks. Taking a sip of my wine, I nod.

He swipes something on his phone, and the TV to the right of the kitchen comes to life. Then the video starts. The east-facing window did its job beautifully. The bright sunlight gives my silhouette an ethereal glow as I begin singing. It looks beautiful. But it hurts to watch. The sound of my voice singing the haunting tune is at odds with it. I almost want to redo the video in a dark basement somewhere—no light, just shadows.

Greys and blacks.

But it would hurt too much to do it again. I guzzle my wine, nearly emptying my glass as the song comes to an end. The words, my callous intro, and the emotion are enough to make me finish it off. I noticed that Cooper attached a web address to the bottom of the video. He clicks on the link, which opens to a question:

You never use the words I love you. You say:

If my memories are true, and if Locklin responds, it will say, "I care deeply for you, Lass."

Cooper tells me there will also be a spot beneath the question to put in contact information, including name, phone number, and email. I hope to hell he sees it. I hope the video reaches him and he finds me. But I dread the thought of him replying the appropriate answer and not leaving contact information.

How cruel would that be?

Reminding myself I'm already broken and have nothing left to lose is the only thing that shakes me out of my misery. I give Cooper a small, uninspired smile. "It looks great, Cooper. Thank you."

He nods as he moves to the stove. "It's the least I could do, Jerri," he mumbles, stirring the pasta sauce he's making to have with dinner.

"Cooper?" Portia asks with a small scowl on her face.

He shakes his head before dropping the spoon back in the bowl. Rubbing his hands over his face, he turns to face us. "I'm sorry, Jerri. I have the resources to help. I should have asked you . . . but I'm not sorry for what I found."

I look between them.

"Asked her what? What did you do Cooper?" Portia asks accusingly.

He moves to my side of the island and takes the stool beside me. He's such a handsome man; he carries himself with confidence you can definitely notice. "While I was uploading the video, I did a search for your old cell phone to see where it's been used over the past few months."

I frown. "Why are you sorry about that? Did you find it?"

He shakes his head. "No. But I'm still invading your privacy, and I have no intention to stop."

"Cooper!" Portia scolds. He simply raises a hand and gives her a stare that says, "Shut your mouth, Woman." If I weren't so confused, I could see how that would turn her on.

"As I was saying, I'm not stopping. If this shit's real, Jerri, I know the old you as well as the new wouldn't want anyone to be in danger. Not only am I trying to protect you, but I need to protect my wife as well."

I melt a little at his determination and love for his wife. He continues. "It was one thing when you had your memories and knew what was going on, but since we don't, we need answers. You obviously did a good job keeping this separate from your life with us before, but now we're blind. We know nothing, and unfortunately I think that might do you more harm than good right now. We need to find out where you used to go, Jerri. The phone is what I started looking into without your permission, but I'm asking you now to dig deeper into other areas."

"I cannot believe you hacked her phone records, Cooper."

MIND LIES

He squeezes his eyes shut, searching for patience, I think.

"It's okay, you guys," I tell them. "I'm lost. I know nothing. And I need to know something. Dig wherever you have to; I don't care where or how you do it."

Placing his hand on mine, he asks, "Are you sure?"

I nod. "I'm sure. Wait, isn't that illegal? Like hacking or something?"

He smirks. "Hacking is half my job, Jer. Don't worry. I won't get caught."

Portia rolls her eyes. "The almighty hacker's ego doesn't need to get any bigger. Don't encourage him."

I ignore the warnings in my head, hoping to hell he doesn't get in trouble, and ask him if he found anything useful. Sobering at my question, he replies, "Brockton."

"That's the town I was near when I crashed my SUV, right?"

He nods. "It is. Your phone has also pinged off towers there more times than is normal over the past few years."

"What do you mean, 'more than is normal'?"

He sighs. "Your accident actually happened somewhere between Plymouth and Brockton. When you phone or text someone, the signal pings off the nearest tower to get to the recipient. I searched through your text history with Portia, trying to find a common denominator."

I nod and wave my hand for him to continue. He solemnly looks at me before saying, "For the sake of speed, I narrowed the text history down to the texts you and Portia shared while you were in that area. You two are like a couple of old women and talk too much through text, considering you see each other almost every day."

Portia cackles like an old hen before he tells her, "By the way, I figured out where my brown leather bomber jacket went."

She sobers quickly. "Son of a bitch."

He snarls at her and says, "I liked that jacket, Portia."

She scowls back. "Suck it up, computer geek. It was hideous."

I raise my hand, mildly curious about the coat fiasco. "We're getting off topic."

Throwing another scornful gaze, he continues. "In one chat history, Portia asks if you had anything promising in the North that week and you replied, 'No, heading south to you tonight.'"

"Okay . . ." I mumble.

He shakes his head. "You weren't in the North, Jer. You were in Plymouth, which is south. You would be heading north to get home, not south. But you told her otherwise."

My shoulders sag. "I'm sorry for lying to you, Portia."

She waves her hand. "This is like an episode of Colombo. I'm too interested in the clues to be upset with you for lying to me. You had your reasons, Babe. Possibly life or death ones. No worries, we'll figure it out."

God bless this understanding, straight-shooting woman.

"Okay, Coop, what else have you found?"

"I found a parking ticket near Whitman, which is also just off the highway from where you had your accident between Brockton and Plymouth. Closer to Brockton."

His information is sobering. "I've only put a few searches in, Jerri. This is the tip of the iceberg, so to speak. I've only had the past hour to run a few things. Who knows what else we'll find."

Ain't that the truth.

I've learned a lot about my secretive past-self. It's frightening to think that one person could be so reticent, and I'm still wondering why I was forced to be that way.

Our talk moves to lighter topics as Cooper serves us an informal dinner of pasta, salad, and bread. It's definitely the comfort food I needed, and the fact that I'm only running on a few hours of sleep, thanks to last night's revelations, means the food hit heavy, and it hit hard. Add in the two glasses of wine I drank, and I'm ready for bed at seven on a Thursday night.

Portia offers to walk me home, but Cooper tells her she's on clean up duty and he'll do the honor. "I offered to help clean up," I repeat to him, but they both wave their hands at me, shooing me out the door.

When we reach street-level, he asks again, "Are you sure you're not pissed at me for digging into your past?"

I arch a brow and reply, "Would you stop if I said yes?"

He chuckles. "Probably not."

I nod. "That's what I thought. For what it's worth, I appreciate it. God, I feel so lost some days. Most days."

"For what it's worth, Jerri, I almost hope this isn't real. You're my wife's best friend, and regardless of how much she lets on she's not hurt from your reticence I know once it all sets in, she's going to take it hard."

I gasp. "I'm sorry, Cooper. You have no idea how sorry I—"

He clasps my arm to guide me across the street, cutting me off. "No, Jerri, you don't have anything to be sorry for. If you lied to protect her, which is what I believe you did, I get it. Hell, I even respect it. My point is I hope it's not real because of the potential danger involved, for you and my wife. But mostly I hope it's not real because I dread what might happen if it is, where you might go."

"I don't understand," I tell him.

"Think about it, Jerri. If this guy is real, if your wish is to go to Ireland together, to run away, if it's all true, what will happen if the danger is gone? What will happen if he does come back?" He pauses as he runs a hand down his face. "What if this is just a pit stop, Jerri? What if this 'safe place' is exactly that, just someplace safe you settle in until the shitstorm blows over and you go back to wherever it is you came from?"

It all sinks in.

He's not just worried about the danger. He's not only worried about me. He's worried about what will happen if this is a pit stop, what will happen to my relationship with Portia when it's all over.

Stopping once we reach my side of the street, I set my hand on his arm and wait until his eyes reach mine before I speak. "When I woke up in that hospital bed, it could have been anyone there to greet me. But I didn't get just anyone; I got the best damn friend a girl could ask for. She could have run out on me. She could have left me to fend for myself, but she didn't." I shake my head. "I have no family, no aunts, no uncles, husbands or babies. I don't have a goddamn person in this world who gives a shit about me enough to come and stand by my bedside, except for her. I woke up with nothing, but so far, Cooper, she has given me everything.

"I may not remember her, but I can't imagine doing this without her. I can't thank either of you enough for all you've done. But bottom line, Cooper, regardless of where this takes me, I will not throw away what she's given me. She's been completely selfless since she found me a few weeks ago, and if that's the kind of person she is, I'd be a fool to not realize the past ten years with her haven't been as important."

Mid-rant, Cooper's eyes soften, but I continue, speaking from the heart, telling him all I feel for his lovely wife. Hooking my neck in his elbow, he pulls me close and kisses the top of my head before walking us toward the back of my building. "You're a good friend, Jerri."

Smiling, I say, "As are you, Cooper."

When we near the steps, Cooper puts his hand on my shoulder. As I raise my eyes to ask him why, I note the man standing at the door leading to my apartment above the shop. He's ringing the doorbell.

"Can I help you?" Cooper's voice is much stronger than it normally is. He's on alert and hasn't let go of my shoulder. The man is dressed similarly to Cooper and is matching in size with similar wide shoulders and narrow waist. He's wearing dark jeans and a dark long-sleeve shirt beneath a dark jacket.

"Looking for Jerri Sloane," he says, his striking blue eyes trained on me. He obviously already knows who I am. "Who's asking?" Cooper replies.

Pushing his coat aside, the stranger shows a badge hanging like a dog tag around his neck. "Boston P.D. Detective Bryan O'Shaunessy."

Cooper asks, "Don't you guys usually travel in pairs?"

Boston P.D. guy smirks and points to the blacked-out SUV on the side street before asking, "Can I have a few minutes of your time, Ms. Sloane?"

Confused and curious, I nod. "Yes, but Cooper stays," I tell him.

He nods as if he doesn't give a shit and asks, "Got somewhere we can talk?"

Cooper replies, "If it won't take long, we can talk right here."

Boston P.D. shrugs and leans against the building. "I came to the hospital a few weeks ago, but you were still out. Took a bit to track you down. I came the other day as well, but nobody was home."

No, I wasn't, because Portia and I were at Ming's Coin Wash, where the earth fell from beneath my feet.

"Anyway," he continues, rubbing his bald head. He's fit, is maybe late-thirties, and has a distinct Boston accent. "I need to ask what you remember from the night of the accident, where you were headed and coming from. Blood results came back quickly. They determined that no drugs or alcohol were at play, but I need your side of the story."

"Was there another side?" I ask.

He shakes his head. "No, there was not."

I frown. "If it were a single car accident, I don't know why my comings or goings are important."

Standing up from the wall with his hands clasped in front of him, he says, "It usually isn't, but in this case it is. Anything you tell me could be helpful."

Cooper takes the words from my mouth when he asks, "Why in this case?"

Boston sobers. "Do you have any enemies, Ms. Sloane? Anyone who might want to cause you harm?" The blood drains from my face, but I do my best to respond truthfully. "I don't know." It's not a complete lie. If my memories are true and someone does want to hurt me—I don't *know* who they are.

"Why?" Cooper asks.

"Because the brake lines on Ms. Sloane's SUV were cut," Boston soberly replies.

I gasp, and Cooper's hold on my arm keeps me upright. He guides me toward the outside steps so that I can sit down. Breathing deeply, head in hands, I ask, "Why are you just telling me this now? It's been a month!"

He clears his throat. "I wasn't at the scene when the wreck took place. The officer who was made note that there were no skid marks on the road. Normally that would mean the driver was impaired or fell asleep at the wheel, but you came up clean. I tried to see you in the hospital, but you were still in a coma; and, as I said, I came to see you the other day, but you weren't home. So this is me following up."

Cooper huffs and sits down beside me. "She can't help you."

Boston takes a bolder stance, clearly agitated. "And you are?"

Cooper looks him dead in the eye. "Cooper Gray. My wife and I are Jerri's close friends."

"I can see that," Boston replies, his tone insinuating we're more than friends. I hold my hand up, cutting Cooper off before he unleashes. "I was just at the Gray's for dinner, and Cooper walked me home. To be honest, I'm grateful he did because your presence at my back door is a little intimidating." I wave to his brick wall of a body. "And I can't help you because I don't remember," I grudgingly add.

"You don't remember the accident? Maybe you can tell me where you came from at one in the morning?"

I shake my head. "I take it you didn't speak with the doctor who released me?"

He shakes his head. "I was informed when you woke up, but I was out of town. By the time I got to the hospital, I found out you'd been discharged."

I scoff. "I wouldn't have been able to help you any sooner. I don't remember because I have amnesia, Detective, which means I remember nothing. I don't remember what my car looked like, much less how the accident happened. The only reason I know my birthday is because I read it in my medical file. So as I said, I can't help you. I wish I could, but I can't."

He softens instantly, the blood draining from his stark but handsome face. "I'm sorry, Ms. Sloane. I wasn't aware."

"Clearly," Cooper mumbles, earning him a scowl from the detective.

"And where were you on the night of the accident Mr. Gray?"

Cooper scowls back. "In the Cayman Islands, on my honeymoon." The Detective still looks skeptical, so Cooper adds, "My wife and I live in the building across the street. She can confirm we were there. You can also look at my credit card statements. Go ask the resort staff and the pilot who flew the damn plane."

Reluctantly, he nods, placated by Cooper's response. "Did you remember this man and his wife when you woke up, Ms. Sloane?"

MIND LIES

I shake my head, tired of the conversation. "No, I didn't. But his wife and I run this store together, and there are hundreds of photos of us together in my apartment, so I'm pretty sure they can confirm we know each other," I respond sarcastically.

"I hope your memory returns, Ms. Sloane. The cut brake line was no accident. I'm gonna leave my card; if you remember anything, please call me." He hands me his card and asks, "Are you driving again?"

Stuffing the card in my pocket, I reply, "No, I haven't replaced the old vehicle yet, and to be honest I'm not ready to. I'm not sure I would remember how to drive properly, let alone know where I'd be going."

Stuffing his hands in his jean pockets, he speaks as he steps back to his truck. "I'll be in touch, Ms. Sloane. Stay safe."

Not yet knowing who I need to be safe from, I simply wave lightly and hang my head.

Do you have any enemies?

Your break lines were cut.

"Shit just got a whole lot more serious, Jer."

I nod, watching the SUV with two occupants drive away.

"It sure did, Coop,"

CHAPTER THIRTEEN

"Did you think I wouldn't find you, Lass?"

I freeze as I pull the key from my apartment door. It's not the old apartment above Ming's Laundromat. It's the new one a little closer to night school, the one I moved to so I could get away from the man currently parked on my couch in the living room.

Locklin.

It has been four months since I last saw him, four months since I packed my few belongings and moved into this tiny, low-rent apartment. It has only been two days since Portia left, and I'm grateful she's not with me tonight; I have no idea how I would explain Locklin's presence.

I had offered Portia my couch to sleep on after her horrible on-again-off-again boyfriend gave her a black eye. I still don't know her very well, but I knew enough that no woman deserved that sort of treatment, and I also knew she needed a safe place to lay her head at night. The arrangement only lasted a few weeks while she waited for an apartment to open up. She left the other day, and I can truly say I miss having her here.

You don't realize how lonely you are until the sound of silence truly sinks in.

MIND LIES

Locklin has broken that silence, and for the first time since we met, I can honestly say I am not thrilled to see him. I spent weeks, maybe months, lost in myself and the grief over losing our child.

Lost and alone.

His presence now is a kick in the teeth.

"I don't recall inviting you in."

Even in the dark, I know he has that stupid smirk on his face, the one that says, "I'll go where I want, do what I want, and see who I want, and not a damn thing will get in my way."

"You left me, Jerrilyn." The deep timbre of his voice, and the use of my full name, lets me know exactly how pissed off he is. "No forwarding address at Ming's. No text. No calls. Why?"

His Irish brogue, which is more pronounced when pissed off or turned on, sends shivers down my spine. Much to my dismay, it still and probably always will affect me. Regardless of his wants, I need to put myself first. We've been doing this back-and-forth for years now, and no matter how much steel I put around my heart—sometimes to keep him in, sometimes to block him out—I know it's time.

Closing the door, I finally turn to face him. The bulb over the stove casts a faint light on his face. The dark hair flopping over his forehead casts shadows over the angles of his cheekbones. I drop my purse on the counter and lean back against it. I have no intention of taking a place next to him on the couch. I can't think, let alone speak properly, when we're that close.

Folding my arms over my chest, I prepare to say what I've planned from the moment I left Ming's. I knew he would find me eventually. Stupidly, I had hoped for more time.

"I'm done running with you, Locklin."

His fingers clench into fists as he replies. "I've kept you in the same place for more than a year. That's hardly running."

I shake my head. "I know. I guess what I mean is I'm not running again. And if you need to, I won't be coming with you. I'm staying here, Locklin."

Leaning forward, he places his clenched fists by his thighs and flexes them. Mockingly, he says, "I had no intention of moving you. Boston has proved to be safe, so I don't understand the theatrics and you running from me. If you wanted a new apartment—by the looks of it, a much shittier one—you could have talked to me first, and I would have helped you fucking move." His voice raises with each word. "Because you wouldn't talk to me, I had to track you down like a goddamn dog. THEN, I have to wait for days until that woman from school leaves your apartment. What the hell were you thinking, Jerri?"

MIND LIES

I move from the island and stand on the other side of the coffee table, holding onto what little patience I have left. "What was I thinking? I'll tell you what I was thinking, Locklin—"

"Please, fucking do!" he yells.

I calmly say, "I was thinking that I'm done hiding in an apartment with no life and no friends. I was thinking that if and when I'm not in school, I'm going to get a job. I'll be twenty-four soon, Locklin, and I'm done hiding away while life passes me by."

He throws his hands in the air in frustration and stands from the couch. "In case you've forgotten, hiding keeps you safe!"

"Oh, piss off with the safety bullshit again, Locklin. What do I do all day, huh? Up until YOU decided night school was safe, I spent my days held up in an apartment. The only thing I had to look forward to was when you would finally show up." I curse the crack in my voice, but I power on. "It's not just about school or getting a job, which I plan to do. It's the fact that the only purpose I've had for the past few years is to sit . . . and wait . . . for you. My life revolves around you, Lockin. My days became, 'How many weeks until Locklin returns,' 'How many days will he be staying,' and 'How many days until he comes back'? I'm sick of it, Lock. I can't do it anymore." Wiping the tears from my cheeks, I shake my head when he starts to move closer. "I don't want to do it anymore, Locklin."

He staggers, and when I have the courage to face him, I raise my wet eyes to meet his confused ones. Shaking his head, he says, "You don't know what you're saying, Lass."

I nod. "Yes, Locklin, I do. I'm done waiting months on end for you to come to me. I'm done waiting weeks before I get a text letting me know you're alive. I'm done being your temporary resting spot."

"You were never temporary. WE are not temporary!" he says, slicing his hand through the air to emphasize his point.

"It's not your choice, Locklin. I won't sit and wait for you anymore. Either you're here or you're gone. I've given you two years to settle this, and you haven't. I'm done waiting, Locklin."

Pushing the coffee table to the side, he curses. "This is bullshit, Jerri! You cannot make me choose. I'm not ready to take them down yet; I need more time!"

I knew that's what he would say. "That's fine, Locklin. You go do what you need to do, but just know I'm not in it anymore."

Skirting the coffee table at speed, he grabs onto my shoulders. "You can't do that to me, Lass. I'm still here because of you! I'm doing this for y—"

"Don't you dare." I nearly growl the words at him. "Don't you dare, Locklin. You're standing in this

apartment because of me, but the reason you're gone for months on end and won't let this go is because of her."

Shaking his hands off my shoulders, I move to the island and retrieve the small black-and-white photo from the back of the drawer. Locklin watches me, running a hand through his thick hair. I stop in front of him, admiring his rugged beauty for what may be the last time before I hand him the photo.

Tentatively, he reaches out, holding the corner of the image with care before angling it toward the light in the kitchen. He frowns, and then his jaw goes slack when he reads "Baby Sloane" in the top right corner. The image of the unborn child is but a blob, but it still holds weight—the weight of something he and I created together..

"Jerri girl," Locklin whispers. He looks from the photo to my stomach, surely not having read the date on the image, which was taken many months ago.

I shake my head and speak softly. "Do you remember what I asked you when you left Ming's last time?"

"Same thing as always, Lass: for me to stay, and when I'll be coming back," he answers.

I nod. "That's right, Lock. I asked you to stay, and you told me you can't. And I asked how long you'd be gone, and you said maybe two months. Do you want to know why I wanted you to stay so badly that time? Why I was so upset?"

He shakes his head. "You're always upset when I go, Lass, as am I. But we make it work. We've done this a long time, and we know each other better than any other, do we not?"

I frown. "No, we really don't, Locklin. I asked you to stay because I was two months pregnant with your child."

"Was?" he rasps, but I put my hand up to keep him from speaking. "Two months, Locklin. I asked you to stay because I was too scared to do it on my own. I didn't want to do it on my own, but if I had to I would. I would have done anything." I whisper vehemently, getting angrier with the loss that's coming. "But you know what happened days after you left, Locklin?" I let the tears pour down my cheeks as I tell him. "I suffered a chorionic hematoma—a miscarriage."

Grabbing the sides of my face, he wipes his thumbs over my wet cheeks before asking, "Why didn't you tell me? Do I not have the right to know? Why would you keep this from me?"

I sigh. "Because it wouldn't have made a bit of difference."

"How can you say that?" he angrily replies.

"Because it's true," I tell him. "Would you have stayed? If I had told you about the baby that day, would you have stayed?"

MIND LIES

The sound of silence is his answer, and it confirms what I already know. He will never give up, and until he finds complete justice for her, *I will always be second fiddle.*

No woman or child will change that.

As much as I admire his determination, his drive to complete a goal, I remind myself it's not conducive to a relationship, let alone a family.

I squeeze his wrists and lower them from my face. "I'm done being alone, Locklin. I was alone when I was rushed in an ambulance, praying our baby was alive. And I was alone in the hospital bed when I was told I was losing our child. And I was alone when I called a taxi, not a loved one, to take me home." I wipe my eyes and whisper, "I'm done being alone, Locklin."

He too has shiny eyes, and he stubbornly shakes his head. "You won't be alone."

Letting go of his wrists, I tell him, "I already am."

"No!" he argues. "You should have told me! You could have called me; I would have been there!"

I scoff. "Where were you a few days after you left? The harbor? On a ship to Ireland? Where, Locklin?"

"It doesn't matter. I would have come back, Jerri. You lost a child for fuck's sake. Our child. I would have made time!"

Shaking my head, I ask him, "And would you have stayed?"

"Yes, I would have stayed!" he shouts.

"For how long?" I quickly reply.

"Until you were well!"

"Exactly!" I shout back. "You would have stayed until I was well enough to be alone, and then you would have left again. What if that baby had survived? Would you have stayed with me then? Would you have helped and been here for the birth and raising of our child?"

"Don't, Jerri. You act as though people don't travel for work."

"This is not work, Locklin! It's revenge! There's a big fucking difference."

He sighs, nostrils flaring. "I would never leave you on your own, Jerri. I would have helped you when I could, and I would have been there for our child."

"Yes, when it was convenient for you. I won't live like that, Locklin."

"No, you're choosing not to live like that, there's a big fucking difference there too, Lass. Have the past few years meant nothing to you?"

MIND LIES

"Don't you dare turn this around on me. Your silence has been deafening, Locklin, and I'm not going to feel guilty for wanting more. Do you know how badly it hurt knowing that while I was losing our child you were out avenging her? I've been patient and understanding for years. That meant everything to me, Locklin. You had been my everything. But for nine short weeks, it wasn't about you or me; it was about the baby. It was during that time I realized that there are more important things in life than avenging death. Those nine short weeks of embracing the life we created were proof of that."

Before I even get the last sentence out, I'm in his arms. His hand holds firm at the back of my neck, and my face is buried in his chest where I breathe in his scent. "I'm so sorry, Jerri girl. I know words don't help, but I am sorry." His lips move where they are pressed against the top of my head. Locklin doesn't process emotions instantly. He'll quickly analyze the facts (which he's done) and argue the logic, and afterwards, which could be a few hours or a few days, the rest will set in.

In this case the rest is the loss of our child and the ramifications for his actions. He truly does mean what he says. I know he is sorry, most likely for a lot of things. But the kicker is it won't change. He won't change. I've been doing this dance with him for long enough, and she *will always take precedence over what happens between us. And another thing about Locklin—he never makes a promise he can't keep.*

He made her *a promise, and if it takes him 'til his dying day to fulfill, so be it. He won't stop.*

A long time ago, I made peace with that, peace with the way he is. But today? Post-pregnancy loss, I can't.

These are the famous last words that I never thought I would be the one repeating. I hate those two words, the two that break my heart every time he leaves. But it's time now.

Pushing against his hard stomach, I lift my head off his chest to look at his face. He places another kiss in my hair before he too leans back. I run my hand up his chest until I reach his jaw. I rest my hand there, absorbing the warmth and energy that radiates from this powerful man.

"You're not going to ask anymore, are you, Lass?" he asks.

I press my lips to his chin and whisper, "I can't."

Holding my face close, he tells me, "This is not goodbye, Lass. I won't let you tell me goodbye. I care for you deeply, so I'll give you some space."

I give him a squeeze. "I know, Locklin. But don't expect me to wait."

And then I let go.

CHAPTER FOURTEEN

"Here you go, Love. Saltines and ginger ale."

Yet again, when I woke up from my dream this morning, I flew straight to the toilet. The memories bring me closer to Locklin but have yet to give me answers. The only thing I'm getting is the feeling of emptiness and pain, slight dizzy spells, and nausea, of course.

I'm still trying to piece together the timeline of memories as Marcus settles me into the chair at his salon and spa. He's a beautiful man, nothing reckless or rugged about him. He has long, floppy, straight hair at the top of his head, but it's nearly shaved on the sides. The blonde hair and bright blue eyes combined with his height give him a Norwegian appearance. Of course, his skinny jeans and bedazzled purple scarf detract from the Viking persona.

Marcus is yet another member of the fabulous group I wish to remember. I've been in his company for an hour, five minutes of which were spent with my head in the toilet, and he still makes me feel as if I've known him for years.

I suppose that's true.

It's just a pile of years I don't remember.

I take small bites of the saltines, sipping on the ginger ale as he begins the process of trimming my hair. "Portia promised to cut off my balls if I do anything too drastic."

I frown at him. "Pardon?"

We make eye contact in the mirror when he says, "I saw the contemplative look on your face. I've always wanted to try something new with this lush, thick hair of yours. I love this feisty, mid-length bob thing we have going on here, but I've tried to talk you into something sassier. Portia told me no sass today or she'd have my balls.

I smile. "She is a bit of a ballbuster, isn't she?"

He gives me wide eyes. "Hunny, you have no idea. Remember when I gave her fuchsia highlights?" He waves his hand. "Of course you don't, my bad. Anyway, Pixie wanted viper-red. I told her repeatedly it would not blend well with her blonde, so I did what I thought looked best. I'm the best stylist in town, so my best is the law around here," he deadpans.

"So what happened?" I ask.

He scoffs. "She knew it looked great, way better than viper-red. Bitch still stole my bedazzler."

I fight a smile. "I take it this BeDazzler is important to you?"

He raises a brow. "Do you think this scarf would look half as entertaining and stylish without the jewels?"

I'm serious when I reply, "I don't think it would."

He raises his arms. "There you have it. BeDazzled always wins. Now, enough about the ballbuster. Tell Marcus all about home life and how you're getting on. Your eyes are sad and dull and your hair is flat."

Since Marcus sees that sad eyes and flat hair are clearly signs for distress, he gets to work while I try to explain.

I nonchalantly tell him, "I suppose when you don't know who you're looking at in the mirror every day, the windows to the soul tend to lose a little life, ya know?"

His face softens. "No, Love. I don't know."

I shrug my shoulder in an effort to ward off the uncomfortable feeling of talking to a stranger who knows me so well. "Well, it is what it is I guess. The harder I try to remember, the more tired I get."

He nods. "I'm sure the walk here helped with your fatigue. But until Cooper has Portia's car looked at since she parked on the street yesterday—because, you know, the whole brake line thing—looks like you two are walking or cabbing." I frown, and he says, "Cooper told Portia about the visit from Boston PD. Portia told Cory and then he told me. Now we're all double checking vehicles before driving you anywhere."

"Not much stays a secret around here, does it?"

"Was it supposed to be a secret?" he asks.

"No. I guess it's just confusing."

"What's confusing?"

I sigh. "Everything."

Marcus grabs the scissors. "Well, Love, one thing that is not confusing is how fabulous this hair is going to look when I'm done. We'll save the blow-dry for when you're done with the massage. Let's get you clipped, painted, and primped, and you'll be feeling like your fabulous self in no time."

I sincerely doubt that, but since I look a little worse for wear and have nothing pressing going on at the moment, I sit back and let him work his magic before he ushers me to the massage room.

"It smells fantastic in here," I tell him, eyeballing the diffusers in the room and the cozy heated bed in the middle.

"Strip and get comfy, Love. Sarai will be here in five."

I smile over my shoulder. "Thank you, Marcus."

He kisses the top of my head. "Anything for you, Love."

When he shuts the door, I proceed to strip down to my birthday suit and get under the blankets. When Sarai comes in and introduces herself, as though we've never met before, I'm grateful. She says a few kind words and tells me she'll be gentle around the swelling in my knee. When she asks about other symptoms, I tell her about my slight dizziness and nausea.

I remember her telling me to breathe deeply before I promptly passed out on the table.

* * *

"Ms. Sloane? Can you hear me?" an unfamiliar voice asks.

I grumble in reply, wanting to go back to one of the best sleeps I've had since I came home from the hospital.

"Ms. Sloane, I need you to open your eyes for me, okay?"

Doing as the unknown woman asks, not because I want to, I open my eyes to many concerned ones. Marcus and Portia are both wide-eyed, holding each other's hands. Sarai stands near my feet where I'm still laying, naked but covered in a sheet, on the table, and an unknown woman with foils in her hair hovers over my head with her fingers around my wrist, checking my pulse.

"What happened?" I ask.

"Sarai said you wouldn't wake up," Marcus tells me.

"Have you eaten today, Ms. Sloane?" the woman asks.

"A piece of toast this morning," I weakly tell her, then add, "Peanut butter."

She nods. "Good. I'm Dr. Webber by the way, one of Marcus's clients." I nod toward the foils in her hair in a way that says I already figured that out.

"Your friends here told me about the head trauma you recently sustained. I'm going to recommend you get dressed and call your doctor at the hospital." I gape at her, but she continues, "Light dizziness and nausea can be normal, but it's been over a month now since the original accident and almost two weeks since you've been out of the hospital. Marcus said you were sick this morning?"

I shake my head. "A little. Usually happens after a memory hits me."

She places my arm back on the table and stands. "It's still unusual and too frequent. I'm sure your doctor will want to do a round of blood work and run some tests to make sure everything is normal."

"Don't argue, please, Jer. Cooper's already on his way to take you," Portia says.

I have no desire whatsoever to go back to the hospital, but from the worried looks on their faces, I grudgingly accept Sarai's and Portia's outstretched arms to sit up so I can get dressed and head to the hospital.

"Whoa," I mumble, trying to stand up. Dr. Webber and Marcus left the room, and Sarai's arm around my waist helps hold me steady as I weave.

"Take it slow, Jerri. I was only massaging you for about fifteen minutes, but I think you were out cold for all of them," Sarai tells me. It takes some work, but once I'm decent, I make it to the back door and into the waiting car with Portia and Sarai's help.

"How you doing, Jer?" Cooper asks once I'm settled into the back seat with Portia at my side. I give him a small smile before closing my eyes and resting my head against the window. "Had better days, Coop."

It's silent for what feels like minutes before he says, "It's been less than twenty-four hours since we uploaded the video." I open my eyes and meet his in the rearview mirror. "It's already gone viral," he adds.

Portia gasps next to me, and even though I don't remember much, I know that this is huge. "What? How is that possible?"

"I'm sure it's a combination of the story behind the song and the high-traffic sites I uploaded it to. #LoveLocklin will be trending by tomorrow."

Portia adds, "Has anyone responded to the question yet?"

Unfortunately, Cooper shakes his head. "Not the answer we're looking for."

I close my eyes again, and Portia takes my hand. "He'll see it, Jer. We'll find him."

All I can do is nod even though I'm not sure I agree with her. I hate to be negative, but how much shit can be dumped on one person? Between the cop last night, my messed-up memories, and my journey back to a place I never wanted to go back to, well, I guess I'm having trouble trying to view the glass half-full.

* * *

"Can I get dressed now?" I ask the nurse.

"Best wait until Doctor Havan comes back. He should be here any moment," she tells me before leaving the room. I stay on the bed, and Portia adjusts the sheet before taking a seat in the chair beside me. "You think they give courses on shitty bedside manners at nursing school?" I snort. "I haven't met a kind one yet."

I laugh at her observation before a knock sounds at the door. Dr. Katherine walks in. "Good morning, Jerri." I frown and look at the clock, noting it's only 11:30 a.m. It feels as though a lifetime has passed since I showed up for my ten o' clock appointment with Marcus. I mumble a "good morning" back to her, and she moves to stand at the side of my bed.

"Aside from the obvious, how've you been doing?"

I like that about her, her bluntness.

Taking a breath, I tell her, "I'm tired, Doc."

She pats my arm in a friendly manner. "I could probably tell you about twenty different things that contribute to your fatigue, but none of them will make you feel any better. I don't recommend sleeping aids with the recent head trauma either."

"The pain pills knock me out. I've only taken them a few times, usually at night. It helps a bit but not much."

"I think it's more the pain meds allowing you comfort enough to sleep, as opposed to actually putting you to sleep. Are your memories still coming back when you go to bed?"

I nod. She already knows about the laundromat apartment, the miscarriage, and Locklin, but I've refrained from calling and telling her about the incident in which Locklin and I were running. I haven't told her about the scar on my hip, either. For some reason, I figure the less people know about that one the better. After all, if there is danger out there with my name on it, I hope to keep the people that it may impact to a small handful.

I'm not sure if she knows about the detective yet or the brake lines that were cut on my car, but the door opens with Dr. Havan entering through it before I get a chance to ask.

"Ah, good. You're here," Dr. Havan says to Dr. Katherine. Portia and I share a look before Katherine says, "Dr. Havan asked me to be present, Jerri. What we've talked about in private is between you and I, and Dr. Havan understands that I know a lot more about you than he does. That being said, he thought I might be able to help today."

Still confused, I wave for them to continue.

"Alright, Ms. Sloane, your blood work came back. I'll admit I was worried with the frequent nausea and dizziness. I wished you had come sooner, but I'm grateful the issue does not seem to be related to your brain trauma."

I let out a breath I didn't know I was holding. "That's good, right?"

He gives me a thin-lipped smile. "It is. However, we've discovered the reason for these symptoms." It's so quiet you could hear a pin drop when he says, "You're pregnant."

My hand somehow wound up in Portia's, and she's squeezing it.

Hard.

Katherine is on the other side of me, prepared as any head doctor would be to help me navigate the news.

I'm pregnant.

What if Locklin is the father?

And worse, what if he's not?

MIND LIES

"Oh my god," I whisper, squeezing my eyes shut. I have déjà vu; a barrage of images flash in front of me like a movie reel.

I wake up in the middle of the night. My sleep shirt is soaked. My hands are slick with . . . blood. I try to dial 9-1-1.

I'm lying in the hospital, battling the depression that tried to sink its claws into me after I realized what happened to my baby. I realize I'll always be doing this on my own.

My child would only have a part-time father, if he lived long enough to take on the job.

Locklin's words echo in my ear: "You left me, Jerrilyn."

"Jerri, are you alright?" Katherine asks, snapping me out of my memories.

"Do you have my file in that bag?" I ask her. She says yes and proceeds to pull it out. I waste no time in grabbing it from her, placing it on my lap and flipping furiously through the pages.

"What are you looking for, Jerri? Perhaps I can help?" she says. I ignore her, reading the top of every page until I'm satisfied. I then go back to the page that mentions my miscarriage. I pull it out and wave it at Dr. Havan. "Is this going to be a recurring problem? Will I carry this baby to term? Am I high risk?" I ask.

He looks over the page before setting it back on the bed. "From what I understand, Ms. Sloane, you should not have any problems carrying to term; however, you'll need to speak to an obstetrician to be certain. I already paged the one on-call if you wish to find out exactly how far along you are and what to expect."

I shake my head. "Yes, send her. I need to know." He gives me an affirmative nod before heading to the door. "If the dizziness persists, please come back and get looked at."

I barely acknowledge him as he leaves, not because I'm rude but because I'm too overwhelmed with the news of the pregnancy.

"Do you think it's him, Jerri?" Portia asks. I sigh. "I don't know. I have no idea who the father of my child is. Jesus." I laugh. It's a humorless one, but it's there. How many people can say they got knocked-up, suffered from amnesia, and then forgot who got them pregnant?

Me. That's who.

"We'll work through this, Jerri. What were you remembering earlier before you asked for your file?" Katherine asks. I wave my hand in dismissal. "Just the note that mentioned my previous miscarriage."

Thankfully, the obstetrician chooses this moment to enter, saving me from lying anymore to Katherine. I don't want to lie to her. She's a wonderful woman and a great doctor; however, there are some things that need to be kept to myself.

MIND LIES

"Hello, I'm Dr. Ranier." She offers her hand, and I mildly shake it, watching the nurse roll a portable ultrasound machine into the room. "I've been briefed about your condition, Ms. Sloane. I understand you have worries, maybe a few questions?"

That's an understatement, but I say, "I do. Were you told about the first miscarriage?" I wait for her to confirm before I continue. "Will it impact this one?"

She proceeds to set up the machine, moving on autopilot. "Unfortunately, miscarriage is common thing, but it doesn't always mean the mother will have difficulty carrying again. I'm sure you fit into that category, Ms. Sloane. But to be safe, let's go in and have a look, okay?"

Dr. Katherine slips into the hall while Dr. Ranier instructs me to lie back and relax.

"This is very early, Ms. Sloane. I'm sure you conceived around the time of your accident, give or take a few days, which puts you at about four weeks pregnant." She points to a tiny dot on the screen. "It's not much to look at yet, but there he or she is."

I fight back the few tears that gather in my eyes. "And how does everything look?"

Portia holds my hand in both of hers. "Everything looks great so far," Dr. Ranier says. "We'll schedule another ultrasound for a month from today just to be on the safe side."

"Thank you. I have one more question."

She nods. "Shoot."

"Would being in a coma or on any of the medication I was given effect the pregnancy?" She flips through a few pages of my chart sitting at the end of the bed before shaking her head. "Honestly, in most cases, it would be considered too early for something to happen. We'll run a few extra tests at the next ultrasound, but I don't think you have anything to worry about. Priority number one now is taking care of you so you can take care of baby. I'll leave a prescription at the desk for your pre-natal vitamins and folic acid. I also want you to make sure you're eating properly. Your blood sugar levels were quite low today, as were your protein and iron."

I tell her, "I haven't had much of an appetite after the accident, but I'll make sure that changes."

"Good." She smiles before wrapping up her machine. "I'll see you in four weeks."

CHAPTER FIFTEEN

"What were you really looking for in that file, Jer?" Portia asks in the car on the way home. After I told Katherine I would call her in a day or two once I got some rest, we beelined out of the hospital as quickly as my tired body would allow.

"My name," I tell her. She frowns, so I elaborate: "In my last memory of Locklin, he called me Jerrilyn. It wasn't a nickname. It was like when someone's pissed off at you and chooses to use your full name to let you know how serious they are."

"Was he pissed off?" Cooper questions.

"Yes. He was. It was when he found me after I left the apartment above Ming's laundromat. He was waiting for me in my apartment the day after Portia moved out."

Cooper says, "This isn't a bad thing, Jerri. I can look into more with that name, see if it helps me find anything new."

"I want to go to Brockton," I tell him. "I want to see where I got that parking ticket, maybe find out if the coffee shop he and I went to is there. I want to see where I got into the accident as well."

"Whoa, Lady, that's a lot for one day, don't ya think?" Portia says, clearly more worried about my well-being when all I'm worried about is getting answers and finding the father of my child.

"No, Portia, I need to do something. If you guys are busy, take me to a car service place or something, I need to—"

Cooper cuts me off. "We'll take you, Jerri. Portia's just worried after what happened this morning."

I give Portia a kind glance and tell her, "Thank you, and I appreciate it. But either I can sit at my apartment or sit in a car. And right now I'd rather sit in the car on our way to potentially finding some answers as opposed to sitting on my ass doing nothing."

"You're not doing nothing, Babe. Hell, look at the video; it's up to one point four million views already. Coop said there's already a following of people rooting for you to find your man. We're bound to get some answers from that alone."

"I can't bank on just that, Portia. I can't sit and wait. I'm pregnant!" I fume. "And I have no idea who the father is or who tried to *kill* me last month."

I hear her muffled "Okay, Babe" from the front seat, and the car remains silent for the rest of the drive.
"Hey, Jack, could you send me the exact location of where the parking ticket was issued as well as the site of the accident? Thanks," Cooper says into his phone.

MIND LIES

"Who's Jack?" I ask.

Cooper's phone beeps a few times, and he plugs the address into the GPS before answering, "He works with me. If you're worried about more people getting involved, I'll tell you now I trust him with my life."

We already passed the sign for Brockton, and I pay close attention to the streets and businesses as we're driving. Cooper finds a spot near a book store and points across the street. "That's where the parking ticket was issued, Jer. There's no overnight parking on the street. That's why you got the ticket."

I nod before pulling on the handle to get out of the car. "Small town, huh?" I don't wait for them to answer; I just start walking toward the unknown.

Portia falls into step beside me and loops her arm through mine. "I hope you don't think I was trying to talk you out of coming here. I'm not," she says.

I squeeze her arm. "I know you're not. And I'm sorry for losing it a little in the car back there, but I'm just so frustrated. I'm fucking pregnant, Portia. How messed up is that?"

She leans into me. "It's not messed up. You'll be a great mother, Jerri. And we'll do whatever we can to help you find him. Just be prepared that I may not be so forgiving in the future. Yes, you're pregnant, but after almost losing you once, and the scare we had this morning, I'm going into over-protective mode because I don't want anything to happen to you."

"Look up, Jerri," Cooper says from behind me. I glance up the street and see a steaming coffee mug on the overhang of a storefront. My steps falter. I practically drag Portia behind me until we reach the front door. Swinging it open, I let the scent of coffee beans assault my nose before taking in the decor.

Red loveseat by the window.

"This is it," I whisper. "It's the same. I mean, the couch is the same from my memory, even the layout." I look to Portia with wide, hopeful eyes before the young male barista behind the counter in front of us asks, "Latte and blueberry muffin?"

I don't recognize him, but I ask if he recognizes me. "I remember orders, not names," he says.

I cock my head to the side. "And I always get a latte and a blueberry muffin?" He looks at me like I'm a little crazy before Portia turns on her megawatt smile and says, "My friend here had a bit of an accident and is suffering from amnesia. So I'm taking her around to all our favorite places to help jog her memory."

Barista guy nods and says, "I don't recognize you, she's usually in here with her husband. Plain black coffee." He makes a face as he says it, as if black coffee is hazardous to your health. Portia keeps the smile on. "She sure is. We were supposed to meet him here, but we were running late. Of course he forgot to charge his phone again." She shakes her head at me and adds, "He always forgets to charge it. Was he in here already? If not, we'll take his coffee to go and meet him at home."

Barista shakes his head. "Nope. Haven't seen him in a few days."

Hope.

That's what I feel when he mentions that Locklin was here: deep-to-my-bones hope. As Portia orders a round of coffees, including Locklin's, I squeeze her hand so hard I think I might leave nail marks. I ask for a to-go tray before we haul ass out of there.

"Oh. My. God," she exclaims when we get out onto the sidewalk. I'm too stunned for words as she and Cooper jabber back and forth on the way to the car; Cooper about hacking the coffee shop's financials to see if he can find a credit card receipt with Locklin's name on it, and Portia for solving the smoking gun that proves Locklin is indeed more than just a man from my dreams.

We pile into the car, where Cooper proceeds to tell us we're going to the impound lot that has my vehicle. I remain silent, nodding along when I'm supposed to and staring out the window as we drive to our next destination.
Locklin was here, in this town, a few days ago.

Hope.

* * *

"First row at the back," the impound attendee tells us. "Detective O'Shaunessey's back there now having another look."

We all glance at each other before walking toward the back of the impound lot. "Why would he be here again?" Portia asks. "Didn't he already say he was here?"

Cooper shakes his head. "He never confirmed he was here exactly; he just told us the brake lines had been cut."

"Yes, but why would he need to look at it? Isn't that what the mechanics are for?" I ask. Cooper doesn't answer because at that point the detective and his partner, standing at the side of a white Chevy Tahoe, come into view. They're leaning close, clearly arguing about something. But they stop their hassling when they hear approaching footsteps. Both their heads turn at the same time; Bryan O'Shaunessey's bald one and his partner's dark-haired one. As soon as I get an eyeful, I realize they must be related. They have the same tanned skin, muscular build, angular jaw, and thick eyelashes as one another. Bryan is clearly an attractive man, but his partner is beautifully rugged. His two-day stubble suggests he doesn't give a shit what people think of his face, and his hair, which is a little too long, tells you he has more pressing matters than getting to the barber.

"Ms. Sloane," Bryan addresses, nodding at me before glancing to his partner. They share a look, words unspoken but a conversation had. Bryan continues, "This is my partner, Detective Cavanaugh." He gives us a chin lift, striking blue eyes—the same as his partner's—fixed on me.

I break eye contact first to address Bryan. "A message was left for me a few days ago at the shop. It asked me to clean out my belongings before the truck gets sent to the wrecking yard."

Bryan nods. "Go ahead. We're pretty much done here. The vehicle was already printed; there was a partial on the undercarriage, but since it wasn't that close to where the brake lines were cut, I'm not holding my breath."

My shoulders sag a little as I was hoping for better news. "Well, thank you for trying anyway."

He moves away from the driver's door and asks, "Have you remembered anything yet? About the night of the accident or otherwise?"

I shake my head as I move toward the door, hoping to find something that will give me a clue. "Unfortunately, the answer to that question is still a big fat no." I try to open the door but it won't budge, due to the completely smashed front end. Moving to the back door, I have better luck, but Cooper kindly pushes me to the side and offers to clean out my belongings.

Turning back to the detective, I ask, "You found anyone who wants to kill me yet?"

"Jerri!" Portia scolds, interrupting detective Cavanaugh as he opens his mouth to speak. "Can you not talk about someone wanting you dead with such a cavalier attitude?" she adds.

I sigh before rubbing my temples. "I'm sorry. As I said earlier, I'm just frustrated."

She leans against the truck and says, "I get it. It has been an eventful day. But let's keep the killer talk to a minimum."

"Eventful day?" Detective Cavanaugh rumbles. The timbre of his deep voice is enough to give me goosebumps—not necessarily the bad kind. O'Shaunessey gives him a look I can't decipher and pipes in, "Anything you want to share, Ms. Sloane?"

I shake my head and wave him off. "Wasn't feeling well this morning, but I'm fine now. Just a little tired."

Placing his hands on his hips, he says, "I don't have any leads yet, but I can promise you we're still looking into it. I meant what I said about remembering. Even if you think it means nothing, it could mean something."

I give him a tight-lipped smile. "I know. But nothing yet. I have your card; I'll call you if something comes to me."

Promising to call if they find something, they both stare at me for a moment before saying goodbye. I'm not holding my breath at the moment either, but I say thank you none the less.

"All set," Cooper announces. He retrieved a hobo bag from somewhere in the vehicle and filled it with everything he could find. No memories or flashbacks come to me, and since nothing looks familiar, I follow them back to the car.

After we're all seated and buckled, Cooper drives for a few miles to the site of the accident. I don't even bother to get out of the car. The road is unfamiliar. The tree I hit clearly sustained no lasting damage aside from a few broken limbs, and the glass that would have littered the highway over a month ago is long gone.

"Anything?" Portia asks, and I just shake my head. The slight curve on the road suggests I was travelling at full speed and was unable to break enough before hitting the tree. I eye the cars we pass, partly thankful that I don't remember the head-on collision at fifty miles per hour.

"On a lighter note, you didn't tell me how delicious the detectives were," Portia says, smiling.

Cooper scowls. "Portia!"
She gives him an innocent look and says, "What? It's true. Cavanaugh is like that silent, broody type you always love, Jer. He couldn't take his eyes off you."

I run my fingers through my messy hair, which never did get blown out by Marcus this morning. It feels like a lifetime ago. Yawning, I tell her, "He was not hard to look at. I agree with you."

She nods. "They have to be related. Those eyes?"

I silently agree before leaning back against the headrest and closing mine, all the while contemplating how I can get to the coffee shop every day to hopefully run into Locklin.

Would I even recognize him?

My heart tells me yes, but my mind argues no.

CHAPTER SIXTEEN

"Easy, Lass. You need to be still."

Locklin calmly runs his hand over my head, massaging the back of my neck in an effort to calm me. I'm half on my side, half on my stomach as I bite back the cry that wants to rip free from my throat. The pain when Locklin applies pressure to my hip is excruciating. I was blessed to have passed out for a while, but when he transferred me from his arms to this small cot, my fortune was over.

"Where are we?" I ask in an effort to take my mind off the blood that continues to soak through the towel. No cut should bleed this much. It confirms that it's less of a flesh wound and more of a stab wound.

I feel the light rocking motion as the boat he brought us onto moves through the water. I know Locklin would protect me from harm, but that doesn't mean I'm not curious as to where he brought me. Squatting in front of the cot, he leans his face close to mine. "You're safe, Lass. No one can hurt you here." I jump when I hear a thud on the upper deck of the boat. Shaking his head, he says, "An old friend of mine. This is his fishing boat."

I nod, feeling more assured, and cringe as he changes the towel. "I'm getting tired, Lock."

A pained look crosses his face. "I know. Paddy will be down when it's safe to stitch your wound."

Closing my eyes and tucking my chin into my chest, hoping that the past few hours will be expelled with the breath I release, I breathe deeply through my nose and out through my mouth. When I woke up this morning, I prayed yet again that I would get to see Locklin today, but never in my wildest dreams would I believe it'd be under these circumstances.

When I started this job six months ago, he caught my eye immediately. Ever since then, it has been a cruel game of cat and mouse. I chased him. I had him, and then he acted as though he'd never met me. It was a bruise to my ego until I began ignoring him right back. I quit saying good morning. I no longer went out of my way to bring the guy's pastries, and I pretended his handsome face wasn't hard to look at each time he wandered into our building. I told myself that maybe the age difference bothered him—his twenty-six to my twenty—and left it at that.

Then he cornered me in the file room and fucked me hard against the wall.

"I'll make sure you don't forget me, Lass. Because you'll feel me for days," he'd rasped in my ear.

That was three months ago.
Our relationship—if you can call it that—consists of random fucking at random times. Sometimes he shows

MIND LIES

up at my flat, in the file room at work, or at the cafe I frequent to screw me in the supply closet.

It's not glamorous.

It's definitely not romantic.

But for some insane reason, I never tell him no. I feel alive when I'm with him, as if I can breathe again.

I know little about him, but it doesn't stop me, especially when we near the end of our trysts and he tells me how he can't wait to see me again, how I'm his water (whatever that means), and how redemption may be his after all. Many of the things he says make no sense, but the tenderness in his eyes, and the way he cleans me up and looks after me when we're done, tells me I'm not just a random fuck for him.

I've awakened in the middle of the night to find him sitting in the chair by my window, watching me sleep.

There have been nights when I've dug through my dinner menu drawer after a long day, usually Tuesdays, too tired to make anything. On these nights, a knock usually sounds at the door, a delivery man waiting on the other side.

A delivery man I didn't call.

One rainy morning, I woke up to a flat tire and had to take a taxi to work. When I came home prepared to change it on my own—it was already done.

I once asked Locklin about the random acts of kindness, and his response was, "Quiet, Jerri girl," before proceeding to stick his head between my thighs, effectively cutting me off.

So although I'm on this boat, with the man who spends more time fucking me than talking to me, I know I'll be okay.

I know he will look after me.

Actions speak louder than words after all.

I hear the clanking of chains and a splash in the water. The loss of the boat's momentum suggests an anchor was dropped. "Paddy will be kind to you, Lass," Locklin tells me before a man enters the small cabin. Dressed in navy-blue work pants and a plaid overcoat, the burly man resembles one who has spent many days on his fishing boat. His stubble has grown into a beard, and his grey hair flops out from underneath his hat. At a glance, he seems intimidating—that is until you look at his eyes.

Light sky blue, surrounded by crow's feet. Combine those with the wrinkles on his cheeks and you know this is a man who has laughed or smiled for much of his life. The lines between his brows could be from contemplation or anger, but I choose to think the former as he helped me escape what could have turned into a lifetime of hell.

MIND LIES

"Ye sure know how to make a hames a' me boat," Paddy complains to Locklin. In turn, Locklin shakes his head and Paddy swings his kind eyes back to me. "A brick short of a full load since 'e was a wee bairn." He jokes, waving a hand toward the blood-soaked towels on the floor and the trash bin outside.

"More pressing matters, Ol' Man," Locklin scolds while waving at my hip. Paddy grabs a bag from under the cabinet and settles himself on a chair at my bedside. "Ye dinnae get thick with me, Lad," Paddy grumbles, his accent an odd mixture of Irish and Scottish.

Setting the bag between us, he pulls out bandages, a syringe, and what looks to be a sewing kit. "Stitched me deck hands up fer years, Lass. No need tae be white in the face."

I'm about to tell him the whiteness of my face is most likely due to the blood loss, but I think he's messing with me. His English is thickly accented, so I have a little trouble understanding what he's saying, being that I'm less than one hundred percent coherent.

"This'll take the bite off," he exclaims as he prepares a syringe with what I hope is a severe pain killer. Within moments, a calm settles over me. The fire in my hip dulls considerably.

"Thank you," I dreamily say, and he gives me a kind smile. Locklin rests his hand on my shoulder as Paddy dons gloves and threads a needle. "You're soft as shite, 'ol man," Locklin tells him before placing a kiss on my

head. "I'm going to keep watch. Paddy will look after you."

I simply nod and watch him go.

"He was always a quiet bairn," Paddy says, shaking his head. He adjusts the towel covering my bare bottom, exposing the gash. "But when he speaks, 'ye listen. Wise lad," he goes on, stitching me up. "But ya dinnae tell him I said so."

I give him a small, tired smile. "My lips are sealed."

He tips his head in thanks and carries on. "Ain't ne'er seen 'em with a lass since Siobhan. Ye must be special to him, Lass. He hasnae asked for help in ages—not 'til he met the likes of you."

I'm not sure what to say to that. Clearly Locklin cares for me, which warms my heart in a beautiful way. I settle on asking, "Who is Siobhan?"

He shakes his head and replies, "It's nae my story, Lass. He'll cop on, or I'll be cursin' to high heaven." He's pressing a clean bandage over the neatly stitched wound when Locklin returns.

"What filth are you puttin' in 'er head, Ol' Man?" he asks.
Paddy scowls at him and grabs his bag, "You'd wantae know. Nessa be waitin' fer us. Time to ship off."

Locklin sits in his vacated chair and begins stroking my back in the same calming way he did earlier.
"Nessa is Paddy's wife. They're going to look after you for a few days."

"Why can't I go back to my flat?"

"I'm sorry, Lass, but it's no longer safe. Nessa and Paddy will be good to you."

I frown. "You're not staying, are you?"

He shakes his head. "I can't."

* * *

"Have you thought about the offer yet?" Cory asks from the other side of the shop counter. It's my third week back at work, and although the first few days were a little rocky, I've caught on rather quickly. Dr. Katherine explained that some things are truly as simple to remember as riding a bike. Since waking up from the coma three months ago, I have remembered the mundane things, such as brushing my teeth, how I like my coffee, and now, apparently, how to run my shop.

The invoicing was a little tricky at first, but when it came to staging and purchasing, I took to it like a baby to the bottle. I enjoy having something to put my energy into, enjoy having a purpose other than obsessing over my past and trying to find the father of my unborn child. The almost-daily trips to the coffee shop to find Locklin were a bust. Regardless, I started keeping a diary to write my memories and questions in, and one day I hope to write the answers.

I never told either of the detectives about my memories of Locklin. If they have seen the video that has gone viral on YouTube, they haven't mentioned it. Of course you can't see me in the picture to make a positive ID, but as they're detectives, I had a feeling they might have figured it out.

They haven't. If they did, I'm sure they'd be here questioning me about my memory.

It has been almost four months since the accident, attempted murder, whatever people are calling it, and I haven't seen the detectives since the afternoon at the impound lot. I got one follow-up call a week later, and since then it's been radio silence.

Cory's question about the offer spikes my heart rate and brings me back to the present. A popular band, which is originally from Boston, came across the video some time ago. Apparently, they not only fell in love with my story, and want to help, but they have also asked me to open for them. They want me to sing that song at their upcoming show.
Right here in Boston.

The Theater will be a more intimate venue, and although it's not televised, it still scares the shit out of me. I have no desire for people to see who I am, but I also feel as though I'm running out of time. Since Cooper's company is filtering all the responses that come in, I have the benefit of not seeing what people write to me. Portia assures me ninety percent of it is good and supportive; it's the other ten percent that's filled with whack jobs and haters I have no desire to find out about. Cooper still continues his search for the ghost of a woman I was.

All this time and she's still just that.

A ghost.

Sighing, I tell him, "I don't know, Cory. I want to if it will get me better results. But let's be honest; that video has been up for about two months now. If he hasn't seen it yet, I don't know how singing at the theater is going to help, unless he's in the audience. But I highly doubt that."

He shrugs. "What have you got to lose, Jer? Ask them to keep the stage lighting low so people can't see your face. Somebody is bound to film it, so it's going to end up all over the internet again. I guess the only question to ask yourself is how badly do you want to find him? And what would you do to make that happen? If the answer is anything, then I say you go for it."

He straightens his bow tie and gives me a questioning glance.

How badly do I want to find him?

Pushing the invoices aside, I lean a hip against the counter and whisper, "What if he's already seen it?" I take a deep breath. "What if he doesn't want to be found, making all of this work Cooper has done for me worth nothing?"

Cory leans across the counter and takes my face in his hands. "What if it's for something? Because that, Dear Girl, could be everything."

A single tear rolls down my cheek. "Damn you and your logic, Cory," I reply, laughing. "And damn these hormones!"

"Hands off the lady!" Marcus shouts in an English accent as he enters the shop. The chandelier lighting reflects off his bedazzled orange scarf as he struts toward the counter. Cory sternly says, "How many times must I ask you to keep your voice down? This is a respectable business, not your gossip-ridden hole down the street."

Marcus slaps his ass as he rounds the corner and takes me in his arms. "Don't be a bitch, Cory. I know you love my hole." Air kissing my cheeks, he asks, "How are you today, Love? Is my lesser-half bothering you? Hmm?"

Smiling, I lean into him. "He's been fine, Marcus. My hormones are all over the place. Tell me, did I cry this much before?"

They both shake their heads. "I think the only time I have seen you cry was when Pussy Galore got stuck in the dumpster out back and you had to go in and save her," Cory replies, referencing the once-stray cat that now lives in the shop in her own little cat house. She's a long-haired, sassy little beast, who sits in her carpeted tower people-watching all day long. Marcus says she's not watching—she's *plotting*. The cat doesn't like to be touched and hates people, so I can't say I disagree with him.

Portia scoffs as she rounds the corner. "The only reason she cried was because it was onion-peeling day at the deli next door, therefore the dumpster was full of them. Who'd cry over a cat anyway?"

Cory lifts a brow and crosses his arms. Portia gives him a look that says, "don't you dare, or I'll spill all your secrets too."

Cory remains silent.

"What'd I miss anyway," Portia asks. "You been crying again, Babe? Are the gays getting on your ass again?"

Marcus snorts, "Pun intended," while Cory says, "You walked right into that one, Pixie."

She scowls at them both. "Just say the word, Jerri. I'll strangle this bitch with his bowtie and beat the other with his BeDazzler."

One thing about this beautiful space I call my own, there's never a dull moment.

"No strangling or beatings are needed," I tell her, shaking my head.

She purses her lips. "Fair enough. We still on for Tequila Tuesday?"

"It's Wine Wednesday, you twat. Can't you keep your days straight?" Cory asks.

She shrugs. "I missed Tequila Tuesday. I'm cashing in my rain check. You in, Jer?"

I shake my head. Although I've been doing my best to participate in these outings, being pregnant is starting to suck my energy. "No, I've got a hot date with a baby book and a cup of decaffeinated herbal tea."

Portia leans into the counter. "I can sit this one out, Babe, if you want some company."

I wave her off. "No. You guys go ahead. Have a drink for me."

Cory whispers, "She definitely needs one."

Marcus adds loud enough for me to hear, "What she needs is a good pounding." Cory slaps the back of his head as they walk to the door, Portia in tow yelling she loves me and she'll see me in the morning.

CHAPTER SEVENTEEN

"Silence at last, Miss Galore."

Talking to the miserable cat somehow makes me feel better after everyone leaves. I love the banter between the group, the camaraderie. It's humble and heartwarming, and I'm incredibly grateful to have them in my life. But that doesn't mean I don't appreciate the silence when they go.

Gathering the bag of shredded paperwork from behind the counter after I've locked the front door, I make my way to the back, turning the lights off as I go. There's a comfortable lunch room between the front and the delivery bay, and I swing by to grab the trash there as well. Exiting the building, I cross the large alley and toss the bags in their appropriate bins before heading back. I double check the shop door, making sure the self-locking mechanism is engaged before rounding the back of the shop to my apartment door.

The man standing on my steps takes me by surprise, but out of fear—or sheer stupidity—I shout, "Hey!" and the man shoots off the steps like a bullet and takes off around the corner. Reaching into my back pocket, I pull out my phone and edge closer to the building. The light over the delivery bay door is on, but the bulb above my front stoop is out.

"Shit!" I exclaim, clutching a hand to my chest. No part of town is completely safe, but it's not quite dark yet, and the man is long gone. I pull up my contacts as I walk, debating whether or not I should call 9-1-1, Cooper, or one of the Detectives.

The door to my apartment is still shut, and turning the knob proves it's still locked. There's paint missing on the door where the lock meets the door jam. "Son of a bitch," I curse. I punch in the code to unlock the door and fly through as soon as it's open, locking it behind me.

I quickly scan my surroundings before flipping on every light at the base of the stairs and heading back into the shop. With all the lights on, and Pussy Galore to keep me company, I feel a little safer.

Plopping down onto a couch, I take a few deep breaths before dialing Detective Bryan.

"O'Shaunessey," He answers. I calm my hoarse breathing before replying, "That's a mouthful, so I'm just going to call you Detective Bryan, or Bryan, from here on out."

He's silent for a few moments. Then he answers, "Ms. Sloane?"

I nod, but when I realize he can't see me through the phone, I say, "You seriously recognized my voice?"

He replies, "No, I have call display."

MIND LIES

Smacking my hand on my forehead, I say, "Right. And it's Jerri. Please, just . . . call me Jerri."

He clears his throat. "What can I do for you, Jerri?"

"I think someone was trying to break into my apartment," I tell him.

"What? When?" he asks intensely, nearly shouting.

"About one minute before I called you."

"Where are you now? Are you safe? Is the intruder gone?"

I roll my eyes and reply, "I'm in my shop with all the lights on. I'm pretty sure I'm safe, and I watched the intruder run away when I spooked him."

"Why didn't you call 9-1-1?" he asks.

I sigh. "Because I focused on getting somewhere safe first. It seemed stupid to call 9-1-1 after he had already left. It could be random, but what if it's connected to whoever cut the brake lines on my truck? If that's the case, wouldn't someone end up calling you anyway?"

"I'm not sure whether to call you clever or crazy, Sloane. Keep your phone on you; I'll be there as soon as I can." I'm about to hang up when he adds, "And don't touch anything around the door!"

Setting my phone beside me, I lean forward with my elbows on my knees and my head in my hands. I debate calling Cooper and Portia since they're just across the street, but then I remember Tequila Tuesday and Wine Wednesday and decide I won't bother. Someone holding my hand isn't going to calm the storm inside me. It has been months since the accident, and I'm sure it was just a randomly attempted break-in.

Knocking sounds from the back of the shop. Pussy Galore hisses in that direction but doesn't bother getting down from her tower. Walking slowly with my phone in hand, I head toward the door and stand on the tips of my toes to look through the peep hole.

The lighting outside the door is bright; therefore, it's easy to make out the unforgettable man on the other side.

Detective Cavanaugh.

Unlocking the door, I swing it open. "That was fast."

He nods and replies, "Was in the area." The deep timbre of his voice doesn't fail to give me goosebumps. "Why didn't you ask who was on the other side of the door before opening it?" he asks.

I remain silent and point toward the peephole on the door. When he looks in that direction, I take the opportunity to study him.

MIND LIES

Same black jacket he was wearing the last time I saw him. A tight grey Henley underneath paired with dark jeans and motorcycle boots. He looks familiar. Then I think of the dirty books Portia has introduced me to; I'm pretty sure this man is on the cover of half of them.

Not waiting for any other reply from me, he turns and heads toward my apartment door. I follow him, feeling safer in his presence, and watch as he pulls a flashlight out of his pocket.

"This light out, last night?" He asks, nodding toward the large marine-style lamp above my apartment door. When I shake my head, he reaches up inside the lamp and gives the bulb a few turns. It comes back on again.

"Broken glass makes noise," he mumbles.

"Pardon?" I ask.

Squatting down in front of the locks to look at the scrapes on the door, he says, "If they broke the glass, stepping on it would make noise. Turn it, no light—no noise."

Leaving the stoop, he walks back toward the shop door. "Needs to be finger-printed. Let's make sure they didn't enter the apartment."

A man of few words.

I unlock the rear shop door again and lead him into the building. Turning to head upstairs, he puts a hand on my arm, causing more goosebumps and halting my steps. "Stay behind me."

Frowning at his request, I do as he says and follow him upstairs. Cavanaugh flips on the lights as he goes, darting around furniture with far too much grace for a man his size. I wait near the island in the kitchen, watching as he flits in and out of the closet, looks under the bed, and pauses to stare at the erotic photo above.

I still love that picture. The man's hand possessively placed on the bare hip of a woman. The curve of her naked back is smooth and flawless in contrast to his lightly scarred working hand.

Shaking his head mildly, he quickly checks the bathroom before coming back to the kitchen. "I'll check the terrace," he mumbles as he walks past me, opening the patio doors to the small rooftop terrace at the back of my apartment. It's not huge; it's only about a fifteen-by-fifteen-foot space holding a small outdoor sectional, a small grill, and a narrow table with chairs.

"All clear," he tells me, closing and locking the patio doors.

"Jesus!" I jump, startled when something touches my leg. Looking down, I see the cat—who has never come upstairs—sitting pretty, as they call it, shooting her evil eyes at Detective Callaghan, who has rushed to my side.

MIND LIES

Holding my chest to calm my racing heart, I mumble, "It's just Pussy."

I nearly get lost in the Detective's bright blue eyes when he bends down to my level. Closing my eyes against the rush of attraction, I take a moment to collect myself as he asks, "Come again?"

"Come, Lass. Again!" Locklin shouts in his deep Irish brogue as he pounds me into the headboard.

I gasp, opening my eyes, cursing these pregnancy hormones, which are making me hornier than a cat in heat. "Nothing," I mumble. "The cat." I laugh lightly, pointing to the floor. She hisses again when Cavanaugh looks at her. He simply scowls back before nodding.

"No intruders," He tells me.

I nod back and repeat, "No intruders."

We stand in an awkward silence. He's staring everywhere but my eyes, and I'm wondering if I'm supposed to offer him a drink or something. He breaks the silence when he says, "You shouldn't be alone."

I cross my arms, nearly offended, and reply, "Plenty of single women live alone and manage just fine, Mr. Cavanaugh."

He does a shitty job of holding back a scowl and says, "Until the man is caught, you shouldn't be staying alone. Maybe you can stay with friends?"

I shake my head and move to the stove. Grabbing the kettle, I take it to the sink and begin filling it with water. "I'm not going to impose on my friends' lives. Wouldn't it be counterproductive to put more people's lives in danger if someone is in fact trying to get to me?" Placing the kettle on the stove, I add, "And it's been almost four months since the accident. Tonight may not even be related to that. Don't you think if someone wanted to hurt me, they would have done it sooner?"

Crossing his arms against his broad chest, he says, "Or they could be waiting for the appropriate time to strike."

I laugh condescendingly and shake my head. "That's insane. What do I have?" I ask, waving my arms around the apartment. "I may have a hefty savings account, but surely it's not worth killing someone over."

His face goes from frustrated to pissed off, and in two seconds he's in my face, piercing blues aimed right at me. "Perhaps you saw something you don't remember seeing. Maybe you pissed someone off and have no memory of it. The possibilities are endless, Ms. Sloane. Is there something you're not telling me?"

I swallow and shake my head. "Nothing."

He studies my face as I push my hair behind my ear and shakes his head as though he's not sure whether he believes me or not. "I'll be outside," he mumbles, close enough to my face that I can smell the mint on his breath. Breathing deeper, I inhale the scent of fresh laundry and man. It's not the woodsy scent of the man in my dreams, but it's an aphrodisiac none the less.

Cursing my quivering body and hardened nipples, I shake off the attraction and ask, "Outside?" Not my most clever moment, and I swear he almost smirks before his scowl moves back into place.

"Outside. Parked near the alley. Make sure the doors are locked behind me. Someone will be here soon to print the door." He turns toward the stairs and adds, "Won't need you down there for that."

I watch his retreating form, stunned, until I hear the slam of the door downstairs.

"What an odd man," I mumble to myself, the kettle starting to whistle on the stove. After making my decaffeinated tea, I take a seat on the sofa and stare out the window at the SUV parked on the street.

Cavanaugh was true to his word: when I go to bed hours later and wake up in the middle of the night, he's still parked there.

* * *

"What's up with your partner?" I ask Detective O'Shaunessey the next morning. He came into the shop to tell me there were no prints to be found on the door other than my own. Obviously the intruder was wearing gloves.

Can't say I'm surprised. Anyone who has watched CSI or any other crime show in the last ten years wouldn't be stupid enough to not wear gloves.

He scowls before responding, "What do you mean?"

I shrug. "He's odd, barely speaks, and has a seriously shitty attitude."

Bryan coughs, trying to fight a smile, and replies, "He's not much of a people person. Never has been."

I nod, as if that answers the question. I suppose it doesn't matter. If he's good at his job, who cares what kind of attitude he has? I blame the fascination on my libido, which is currently off the charts, and continue rearranging the new dinnerware that just arrived on the shelves.

"Well, thanks for your time, Sloane. I'll be in touch," he says as he heads out the door. I don't bother responding because I don't have too much hope that he'll find anything. If Cooper, who has been able to hack just about anything, hasn't found any answers yet, I don't have a lot of hope for the Detectives. Cooper was able to find every woman in the world who goes by the name Jerrilyn, and we still don't have any solid idea of who I am.

It's frustrating.

Some days it pisses me off more than others. Days like today, when I'm tired from a lack of sleep and my hormones are running high. I obviously haven't been laid since I got knocked-up. Top that with all the other drama happening in my life, and my lack of patience is wearing thin.

Or thinner, I suppose.

"It is a nice piece," says Mr. Grant, the eyeballer of the Maserati couch. "Would look great—"

"In the reading room next to the oak credenza. I know," Cory mockingly interrupts.

Mr. Grant scowls at him. Cory scowls right back. I don't blame Cory for being short with him. The old man comes in a few times a month to eye the couch that never sells because it's so expensive. He then *always* tells anyone who will listen the story of where it will go and how good it would look if it was his.

But he never buys it.

Even though he could buy out half the businesses on this street.

Apparently, the Maserati, as we call it, is better to be admired on my shop's floor and never in his house, even though you know he wants the damn thing.

"I don't appreciate the back talk, young man," Mr. Grant haughtily says. Cory rolls his eyes.

"Oh for Christ's sake. Buy the damn couch! Life is short, and sometimes memories are shorter. You want it? Buy it!" I shout before heading toward the break room.

"Thought you said she has amnesia?" the old man grumbles to Cory.

Apparently, Jerri was a bit of a firecracker pre-amnesia.

Post-amnesia, she's just tired and impatient.

"Cory!" I shout. "We're doing the theater. Tell Marcus I need a dress."

Sometimes the best decisions are made under pressure.

CHAPTER EIGHTEEN

"You sure about this, Love? You know I don't like when you're upset," Marcus asks me as he fastens the back of my strapless dress. I thought he would have come at me with glitz, glamour, and BeDazzle—I couldn't have been more wrong.

"This isn't a celebration," he said. "You're practically in mourning. Whether he comes or not, you still feel as though you lost something. That something could either be your memories or him, but either way, we're not here to celebrate. No. We're here to weep over a divine man who planted that beautiful little creature in your belly."

"What if it wasn't him, Marcus? What if I slept with someone else?"

"You didn't, Love." He answers, and when I scowl at him, he firmly adds, "You. Didn't."

I regard the black, strapless, floor-length dress. It's really stunning. Tight in the bust. Layers of chiffon and silk flowing over my hips in wispy waves before touching the floor.

It's lovely.

"I'm not upset, Marcus. A little nervous, maybe. I'm glad they agreed to keep the lighting around me and not *on* me. But just because they can't see my face, clearly doesn't mean I won't see theirs." I huff out a breath. "I guess I just don't like the idea of feeling exposed."

Grabbing me by the shoulders, he turns me to face him. "Not a soul out there is here to think ill of you. You're lucky none of them know who you are and where you work because I'm sure the shop would have been bombarded with fan people all rooting for the love story of Jerri and Locklin. People go crazy for that shit."

He's not wrong. After the millions of views, Portia had informed me that the unwavering support from people across the country was astounding. The hashtag #LoveLocklin is still going strong, and I admit that the backing from these people warms my heart at times. It's the other times, when it's cold at night and my bed is empty that hurt.

"Correction, it's not shit. But you know what I mean." He flaps his hands around, fixing my hair. "You're a vibrant woman, Love. If he's worthy of that, he'll find you."

I give him a light smile before shaking off the nerves threatening to overtake me. I seem to have been making a lot of last-minute decisions lately, this being one of them. I waited weeks before saying yes to do this . . . two days ago, which gave me little time to prepare— little time to back out.

MIND LIES

I go back and forth between being desperate to find Locklin, and being so pissed off at him that I can't be bothered. Sometimes, I lie in bed, lonely at night, wishing for him to find me. And at other times, I spend endless hours in the shop, doing anything I can to take my mind off him.

I now get what Portia told me months ago: The shop is not my happy place. It doesn't bring me joy; it makes me content to have a purpose. Perhaps that's what I've done. I've drowned myself in work, fallen into old habits, even though I'm not necessarily sure what those habits are. It feels familiar, though. They give me the feeling that this is what I've always done when I'm lost or without him.

Drown myself in work.

Keep myself busy enough that I forget, even if for a short amount of time.

"Five minutes," the stagehand tells us, poking his head into the dressing room. I briefly met the band when we arrived. The lead singer of the rock band—Scarlet Towns—gushed with me about my story, telling me that when the band does their signature shot of whiskey before taking the stage, it will be dedicated to Locklin coming back to me, not their usual play hard salute.

I told her I was grateful; for them to change-up their toast is like asking a baseball player to change his lucky socks.

"Deep breath, Love," Marcus mutters in my ear as he guides me from the room. He plants a kiss on each of my cheeks before being escorted to his seat with the rest of the crew.

I stand awkwardly in the hallway behind the stage. Closing my eyes, I take a few more deep breaths and smooth my dress over my small baby bump. I'm happy Marcus chose a dress that was flowy and loose in the waist. The last thing I want is someone calling attention to my pregnancy. I've had enough drama to last a lifetime, and answering questions about the pregnancy would bring more.

"Ms. Sloane?" A deep voice rumbles behind me. Opening my eyes, I turn slowly to see both Detective O'Shaunessey and Detective Cavanaugh.

I frown. "What are you doing here?"

"You cannot go up there," Cavanaugh grumbles. O'Shaunessey adds, "Sorry, Ms. Sloane. I know this is coming a little late, but considering we still haven't found the person who wanted to harm you, we don't think it's a good idea for you to put yourself out in the open like this."

I laugh humorlessly, shaking my head. "You're joking, right?" Their faces remain stoic and emotionless. "I've been driving. I've been working. Hell, I even go out at night by myself when the craving for greasy drive-through food hits me. I've been *exposed*. I've put myself out there for months, and now you're telling me, at the last minute I might add, that I shouldn't put myself out there? You're telling me I could be putting myself in danger?"

O'Shaunessey remains quiet, but Cavanaugh nods and says, "That's what we're saying."

I scoff. "Give me proof. If you have some proof, I will think about not going out there. But if you don't have anything, you can turn around and quit wasting my time."

They share a silent conversation with looks and chin-lifts before O'Shaunessey says, "We have reason to believe someone's been following you. Although he hasn't tried anything yet, there have been reports of someone lurking around your neighborhood on and off for the past week."

I shake my head. "And do you have an arrest? Proof that it was me they were after? Because I can tell you right now I'm alone. A lot. So if someone wanted to do something, they've had ample opportunity."

Cavanaugh tightens his hands into fists, and O'Shaunessey flares his nostrils. "This could be very serious, Ms. Sloane, if this person is following you, especially if he's the one who cut the brake lines on your Tahoe."

"Time to take your place, Ms. Sloane," the stagehand reminds me. I nod to him and turn back to the Detectives. "If what you're saying is true, then he's probably already here. Too little, too late, Detectives.

I'm going on that stage, with . . . or without your consent."

"We assumed you were here for the show; we didn't expect to find you back here. What are you here to do exactly?" Cavanaugh asks.

Straightening my shoulders, I give them one last look. "Saying goodbye."

* * *

"I'm sure many of you are familiar with the woman about to take the stage," the lead singer, Scarlet Towns, tells the audience as she seats herself on a stool, acoustic guitar in hand. "You all know my shitty history with love and loss . . ." She pauses, allowing everyone in the small theater to remember her soulmate who was tragically killed.

Clearing her throat, she continues. "So I guess you could say I'm desperate for one with a happier ending." Giving a hollow smile, she tells the crowd, "The woman attached to the trending hashtag #LoveLocklin is about to sing for us. This woman, who prefers to remain in the shadows tonight, has fought one hell of a battle. She woke up in a hospital room a few months ago with amnesia, and sadly, or perhaps fortunately, the only memories she has are of him."

I stand in the shadow, the only light on stage beaming down on Scarlet as she finishes my introduction. "I could drone for hours about this woman, how much I'm rooting for her, and the man she can't seem to find. But instead I'm going to let her finish off this intro and grace you with the soul-crushing song that literally makes my heart ache."

The light on her dims slightly, and the one behind me brightens. The crowd's attention shifts to where I've been standing the whole time, lost in the shadows. It's fitting, it seems. And as they focus on my over-exposed form without being able to see my face, I have the urge to tell them that's exactly how I feel every day.

Overexposed.

A blurry image that won't seem to focus.

Perhaps the blur at this moment is the wetness in my eyes, but I ignore it and settle on a random face in the crowd, preparing myself for what I feel will be the final goodbye.

* * *

"This is the last time," I tell them.
Tears fall freely down my cheeks, but my voice is steady.

Clear.

Definitely not strong, though.
No.

Because I'm breaking.

What they see on the outside: the beautiful dress, shiny hair, squared shoulders, and perfect posture. I stand poised like a woman who has her shit together on the small stage . . .

It's a lie.

A ruse.

A wolf in sheep's clothing.

A gift, the packaging far prettier than what's to be unwrapped.

I feel like a fraud, but I don't tell them that. I feel as if I'm dying, as if all these cracks that have continuously hurt my heart are ready to crumble.

Ready for it all to fall apart.

I'm ready, to fall apart.

They don't know what it's like to stand up here, calling out to the love of your life, crying to him for months, begging him to find me. To hold me and shelter me and put me back together.

But he never comes.

MIND LIES

He never crushes me in his strong arms and tells me I'm not crazy, that he's here. He never shows up to tell me he loves me, he needs me, and he'll never let me go.

He never comes.

He never shows up.

The crowd begins to boo. Not because they don't want to hear me, but because they don't want me to give up the fight. They don't want me to let go.

I'm not a quitter, but sometimes you need to know when to stop, when to toss in the towel, because no matter how many times you cry your heart out, the end result is always going to be the same. Always going to end the same.

With me.

Crying my heart out.

Alone.

Not with the man I'm supposed to share my life with.
I take a deep breath, reciting pretty much the same thing I have every time I sing to him. The only difference is that this time the crowd is much larger. This time, it's not Portia aiming a webcam at me while I search for my soulmate.

The one nobody knows.

The one who could very well be a product of my overactive imagination due to my amnesia-filled brain.

Lies.

But I know in my heart he's real.

I know he's out there.

Because I can *feel* him.

Giving a light smile, the same one that never reaches my eyes, I tell them again, "This is the last time. I don't think I'll be able to speak after I do this, so I'm going say what I need to now, and I hope you'll listen."

I watch them all, those I can see clearly, as they settle into their front row seats with their eyes trained on the stage. I wait for the hushes and murmurs to die down, all eyes on me, before I continue. "I can't thank you all enough. What started out as an idea and a YouTube video riding on nothing but *hope*—you all clicked *view* or *share* and turned it into something viral overnight."

Applause and cheers echo throughout the theater. I absorb the positivity in the sound, the vibrations filling me before I adjust the mic to continue. "If it weren't for people like you, and my best friend's support, we wouldn't be here. And if we weren't here, he might not hear me call for him."

MIND LIES

I pause to swallow past the lump in my throat. "That video-gone-viral gave me hope." My voice breaks on the word "hope," but I power through. "It gave me hope that the man in my memories would come back to me. It gave me hope that after so many of you shared that video, I wouldn't be without him. Millions of people have watched it, and I was sure that he'd be one of them."

I blink, letting the tears roll freely before giving them another empty, watery smile. "But he's not here," I softly say.

Shaking my head, I sigh. "I can't keep doing this, singing the last song we sang together, to the man I remember. I *can't*. Not because I'm giving up, but because it hurts too much."

Wiping my cheeks, prepared to give them my signature line, I lift my head. "Maybe I imagined him. Maybe my amnesia is fierce, playing cruel tricks on me. Or maybe, just maybe...." I pause, waiting for them to say it with me: "I've lost my fucking marbles."

My hollow laugh joins more boisterous ones. I watch as a few tissues are drawn from purses, people discreetly wiping their eyes. They've followed this love story as I have lived it. They've watched me cry my heart out for the man I used to know.

The man in my memories.

The one who never comes.

"So this is it, Ladies and Gents. This is the last time. Not because I don't love him, not because I don't think of him often, but because it hurts too damn much."

Squaring my shoulders, I face my cheering squad with little determination and a lot less hope. "So, to the man with dark hair and beautiful bright blue eyes who I remember, . . ." I pause, letting that term hang loosely because I'm a woman with amnesia who remembers nothing aside from him. They chuckle. I finish, saying, "Who goes by the name of *Locklin*. This is from me, to desperately missing you."

The lights in the theater dim, the spotlight above remaining lit while I sing to the man I love.

Whether or not my mind lies, I give it all I have: my heart, my soul, my love, singing to the man from my memories, begging him to come to me.

One.

Last.

Time.

CHAPTER NINETEEN

"I know you have to leave,
But let me beg you to stay.

This agony, you're my heart's reprieve,
I'll still love you anyway.

Don't make me ask,
Don't make me choose,
My soul's run down,
You're too much to lose.

But I'm beggin' you today,
Please, please just choose to stay.

I'm on my knees,
To do as you please,"

The mic cuts out prematurely, as does the power in the theater.

"Oh my god."

"What the hell?"

Rounds of shocked gasps and murmurs echo through the space, and when the emergency lights kick on, you can clearly register the surprise and fear on everyone's faces after being left in the dark.

It's amazing how silent it is when the lights go out, both literally and figuratively.

"Come," is barked in my ear before a strong hand grabs onto my arm and leads me toward the side of the stage.

"What the . . . ," I mumble before realizing the hand belongs to Detective Cavanaugh. Doing my best to keep up with him in the four-inch heels I'm wearing, I take advantage of his support on my arm until we reach the hallway backstage where the lighting is better.

Steadying my hand on the wall, I try to jerk my arm from his grasp. "Jesus Christ, Cavanaugh. What the hell is going on?" He reaches back quickly as I try to remove my arm. My arm returned to his grasp, he leans down into my personal space.

Soap.

Musk.

Man.

I ignore the shiver running down my spine and focus on his stark-blue eyes. He rasps, "It's time to leave."

I flap my mouth a few times before being dragged again but manage to spit out, "You're making no sense!

If someone wanted to hurt me, they'd have done it already. I don't know why you're so hell-bent on getting me out of here." I trip over a power cord but manage to right myself and add, "What happened to the power?"

Having had enough of my questions, Cavanaugh turns around and fumes, eyes blazing. "It's not safe here!" he replies harshly before leading me toward a back exit.

It's not safe for you here, Lass.

Listen, Jerrilyn! It's not safe here. I cannot stay with you.

My mind remaining hazy, I stumble through the back exit and onto the pavement as my heel catches on my dress.

"Jerri!" Cavanaugh shouts. It's loud, piercing, and sends sharp pains shooting through my skull like lightening crackling through the sky.

"Get down!" someone, O'Shaunessey, I think, shouts. Suddenly, I'm tackled to my side. Pain flares through my hip, and the hard ground gets closer to my face before it's saved by a leather-clad arm.

My face is pulled into Cavanaugh's chest. His body jerks atop mine, arms tightly surrounding my body, like a vice grip.

Safe.

"I've got you, Jerri, hold on."

Locklin's voice echoes through my ear before the memory takes over.

Crack! Crack!

My body remains still as Cavanaugh's jolts with the impact before I let go.

Before I let the memories take me away from my failed attempt at calling for the man I love to come for me.

Blackness creeps in. My mind lies take over.

But this time, they don't bring me hope.

Just soul crushing pain.

CHAPTER TWENTY

Mindlessly playing with the frayed edges of my dress, I listen to the soothing sound of the heart rate monitor. Normally, anything with an incessant beep would drive me insane. But in this instance, it's a reminder.

We're alive.

The beeping is not as comforting as I would have hoped.

No.

In fact, it's a giant fucking kick in the teeth.

Who would have thought it would have come to this?

Who would have imagined, in their wildest dreams, that I, the woman with amnesia, had all the answers I needed right in front of me?

Every answer to every goddamn question I ever had was ready and willing for me to take. For me to learn and remember and know?

A mild cough startles me from my internal rant.

I've had ten hours to fume.

Ten hours to sit in this beautifully tattered dress, calm my shit, and rehearse my speech to the man who could have given me everything.

But instead, he kept it all.

I stand from the uncomfortable chair I've been sitting in. I move to fix my hair before I get closer to the bed, but then I remember it doesn't matter.

Nothing matters.

Because if I wasn't worth enough at my best, surely my messy hair, torn gown, and filthy body covered with dried blood—me at my worst—will change nothing.

"Jer—"

"Don't speak," I interrupt, holding up my hand, voice raspy.

I watch his face fall. His weary eyes shut in pain. Not pain due to his injuries. Not pain due to four hours of surgery.

No.

Pain due to heartache.

MIND LIES

We've come full circle. Only this time the emotional pain doesn't belong to Portia, who watched her best friend wander lost in her mind.

This time—it's *him*.

He knows.

Placing my hands on the bedrail at the foot of the hospital bed, I take in the man in front of me.

The bastard.

His clean-shaven jaw grew with stubble overnight.

Dark hair, not as long and shaggy as I like. Clearly he's been back to the barber.

I follow the plains of his solid tattooed chest and the wisps of dark hair on his tanned arms, and only when I'm ready, only when I'm brave enough, do I finally meet his piercing blue eyes.

"You lied," I strongly tell him, my voice deep and full of emotion. I softly raise my hand when I see he wants to speak again, but I know it hurts. I know the tube that was down his throat did some damage.

I continue, ignoring my blurry vision from tears that threaten to fall. "When I woke up in the hospital four months ago, I wanted one thing," I pause, choking back my sob, "just one thing."

"Jerri . . ."

I shake my head, eyes closing, tears falling free. I face him with all of it. Screw strong. I let him see it all: the hurt, the agony, and the heart-crushing pain that comes with not knowing.

The anguish that comes with not being wanted.

"You," I whisper. "I just . . . wanted . . . you."

Opening my eyes, I watch as the light leaves his. Any hope from waking, any wish he had to be alive, healthy, and happy when he had woken up is shattered.

Just like my heart.

"Do you have any idea what it's like to wake up and not know who you are?" I ask him.

The selfish prick remains silent, but I press on. "Do you have any idea what it's like to constantly dream of a man, to constantly ache for him, only to find out he's not there? That he may very well be a product of your amnesia-filled mind?"

I don't wait for him to answer before adding, angrily, "Do you have any idea what's it's like to yearn, sing, and beg the love of your life to come back to you? Only to find out he doesn't want you?"

"I ca—" he rasps incoherently.

MIND LIES

I speak louder.

Push harder.

"It's death! It hurts so goddamn bad you want to curl up, fall asleep, and never wake up again." I shake my head, ignoring the determination in his eyes. His hands remain clenched at his side, the restraints having been put on after surgery to ensure he didn't remove the chest tube when he had woken up.

"I wanted you so badly, I didn't sleep. Barely ate. I would fall asleep just so I could dream of you. Because no matter how amazing Portia and my friends have been, I only wanted *you.*"

I laugh at myself mockingly. "But you never came. I hoped, I dreamed, I prayed, and I even fucking sang, clearly making a fool of myself, because I was singing to someone who didn't want to be found in the first place!"

Fed up, he talks back as much as his battered throat and gunshot-wounded chest will allow him. "You should not have shared our song," he rasps. "That . . . was . . . ours."

The convicting tone in his rugged voice does nothing to deter me.

We've been here before.

And, as always . . . "I was never enough for you, Locklin. I won't *ever* be enough."

"Not true," he whispers in agony.

Shaking my head sadly, I tell him, "You've left me, over and over again. But while I was lying in that hospital bed, like you are now, you truly and utterly departed. I don't mean enough for you to console, and I don't matter enough for you to ever stay.

"I had so little, and I was so desperate I would have given *anything* for an answer, let alone to have you by my side." I pause, unable to control the sobs that wrack my body.

"Come here, Lass."

The whimper leaving me will be the last one. I vow right now that I will not let myself mourn after this.

This is it.

It's over.

"I've never had the option of leaving you, Locklin. I always chose to hold on and never let go." I nod. "But it's time. What you've done in the past was forgivable. But this," I wave my hand between the two of us, "this, what you did and how you left me, is not forgivable. There's no coming back from here. Because for once in my life when I truly needed you the most, you left me behind."

"No, Lass. Don't say that."

I ignore the sign of tears that cloud his beautiful blue eyes. I ignore his outstretched fingers reaching for mine. Instead, I wipe the tears from my cheeks with the back of my hand and move to his bedside.

He tilts his head to the side, and I give in to the urge, running my fingers through his silky, dark hair. His eyes close briefly, soaking up the affection.

My touch.

"At one time, you meant everything to me. I would have gone to hell and back just for a fraction of your attention, your love." Leaning down, I place a kiss on his chapped lips and recognize the feel of him, the smell.

The taste.

"That time is gone."

Pressing the piece of paper into his hand, I stand and imprint the shock on his face to memory. The agony, despair, and disbelief.

Everything I felt ten hours ago.

"My mind lied, Locklin. I thought the man in my memories was the love of my life. But that's not true." I shake my head in defeat and add on a whisper, "Because he never loved me back."

I leave. I turn from his bedside with my shoulders as straight as my tired body will allow and force my feet to walk, away from his bed, out through the door, and into the hallway. I don't even stop at the nurses' station in the ICU; I just speak loudly and clearly as I pass by, ignoring the shouts from his room as he desperately calls my name.

Calls me back to him.

"Jerri!"

Clearing my throat, I make quick eye contact with the head nurse before saying, "Mr. Cavanaugh is awake."

* * *

LOCKLIN

When her sweet lips touch mine, I know she means it.

She's gone.

My Lass wants to go.

No.

MIND LIES

Not go.

She already left.

"Jerri girl," I rasp. Fuck, my throat hurts. My chest is on fire. I know I was shot; where, and how many times, I do not know.

"Jerri," I try again, pulling with my wrists to sit up, but the damn arm restraints are strong. All I manage to do is wrinkle the paper she put into my hand before she walked out of my room.

Out of my life.

Using my fingers, I twist it around and angle it toward me so I can see it better.

"No," I whisper.

"NO!"

She can't.

She cannot leave now!

"Jerri! Come back!" My Irish brogue is thick. I allow it, although I hated trying to sound like a native Bostonian in hopes she wouldn't recognize me.

Remember my voice.

My shout goes unnoticed, and I ignore every pain piercing through my body as I fight to sit up and remove the arm restraints.

I need to get to her. She has to come back. She needs me!

"JERRILYN!"

A hand lands on my shoulder. "Sir, I need you to calm down."

"Jerri!" I shout.

"Push ten milligrams of Haloperidol," the nurse says moments before my body becomes lethargic.

"She can't leave," I mumble to no one in particular as I stare at the black-and-white photo that has today's date on it.

Baby Sloane

Age: sixteen weeks.

I fight the darkness. The damn drugs they shot into my system are threatening to put me to sleep.

I'm a dad.

I'm a bastard.

She's a mum.

MIND LIES

She bloody well fucking hates you.

I'm alive. The bullets didn't kill me.

I'm as dead as they come.

Why?

Because she's gone.

CHAPTER TWENTY-ONE

"Does the scar on my hip bother you that badly?" I ask him.

Whenever we're in bed, his hand always gravitates to my scar. I'm thankful I don't see it every day, resting on the back of my hip, but each and every time we have been in bed together lately, it seems like it's all he sees.

"It feels like I've failed," he grudgingly answers.

I look over my shoulder at his crestfallen face. This man carries so much on his shoulders.

Pain.

Loss.

I've tried to make it better. But no matter what I do, no matter how many times I go over what happened that night, no matter how many times I reassure him that the outcome could have been worse had he not been there, he still takes the blame. He still struggles to carry the weight of it, as though he were a prisoner dragging a ball and chain.

"Then fix it for us," I tell him.
He sighs. "I'm trying, Lass."

MIND LIES

I shake my head. "No, I had a different idea."

I pass him my camera, which is filled with beautiful shots from the lake we're currently staying at. He eyes me with confusion. Once he takes it, I say, "No pictures together. No real names. No phone calls from traceable phones."

He nods. "Our rules."

"That's right. But so long as our heads aren't in the picture, I don't see any issues with this."

"Issue's with what?" he asks.

Laying on my stomach, his left hand still possessively placed on my hip, I say, "Your hands, Locklin. They can heal and can cause pain. Use them to heal."

He looks from the camera to my naked hip. "I'm not sure what you want me to do, Lass. How will a picture help?"

I give him a small smile. "I'll never forget what you look like, feel like, or even taste like, Locklin. But sometimes, I miss how good it is to be together. Give me this: something of us together."

His thumb moves in soothing circles on my hip. "Us, together. No faces," he confirms, and I nod.
No faces.

Just his hand claiming me.

Owning a part of me that was almost stolen.

Protecting.

And soon, hopefully, loving.

* * *

"How you doing, Babe?" Portia asks from the doorway to my bedroom. I'm frozen solid as I stare at the portrait above my bed, the same one that captivated me from the moment I stepped foot in this room.

The portrait with Locklin's strong hand placed possessively over the scar on my hip.

A scar that now reminds me of a frightful time in my past, a time when I learned evil truly existed.

A time when, had Locklin not been there, I would have been raped.

Just like *her*.

Worse, I could have been killed. But that's something I try not to think about.

Abandoning the picture, I return to my duffle bag. I don't plan on taking much since most of my clothes have become too tight to wear. I'll need to buy everything new.

Zipping the bag shut, I turn and tell her, "I will be. I just need to get out of here for a while."

She squints, confused. "Is this because you remember him, Jer? He'll still be in the hospital for another few days."

I shake my head sadly then walk to her. I don't waste time in hugging her fiercely, not because I don't think I'll see her again but because she is truly the best woman a girl could ask for in a best friend.

"It's not just remembering him," I breathe out. "It's remembering everything."

"When did it all come back exactly? Did it happen all at once?"

I smile sadly and nod. "When the shots went off."

She wipes a few tears escaping her eyes and says, "Thank god. At least you have your answers, and for that I'm happy for you, Babe." Shaking her head, she continues. "I still can't believe what happened. And how unfortunate is it that you and Scarlett look similar? Jesus, Jer. I almost had a heart attack when they locked down the theater."

I nod in agreement. The sick, twisted man who waited at the back of the theater for a glimpse of

Scarlett is indeed a psychopath. His plan had been to take out the bodyguard and kidnap Scarlett. I don't know all the details. All I know is he was waiting in a delivery van, and when he saw someone who looked like her, he started shooting.

"You and me both," I tell her. "I thought he was coming to finish me off."

She smacks my arm. "I told you not to say shit like that."

I side-hug her and then grab my bag from the bed. "Sorry."

She sighs. "So if you remember everything . . ." She trails off, and I look at her with a raised brow.

I cut in. "It means that I remember you still have my Gucci boots and you have yet to clean the shop like you promised."

She laughs, not as boisterous as usual. But it offers a little light on this semi-dark day none the less.

Sobering, she asks, "You sure you wanna do this, Jer?"

Nodding toward my bag on the bed as I pick it up, I answer, "Yes. I'm sure."

I can tell she's upset, but her stubborn pride won't let her tell me that. Linking my arm with hers, I walk with her out of the bedroom. "I feel like I have to, Portia. Now that I remember him, I know he won't stop coming here. He's ruthless, stubborn, and definitely doesn't like being told no. He'll show up the minute he gets out of the hospital, and honestly," I pause, breathing deeply through tears still wanting to come when I think of him, "it hurts too bad. If I see him, if I give in to him like I always do, well, let's just say my body can't take anymore hurt at the moment."

She leans her head on my shoulder for a moment before adding, "Speaking of hurt, O'Shaunessey is downstairs."

"Shit."

"Yeah, sorry to be the bearer of bad news. You really that pissed at him too?" she asks.

I nod. "Yes, I am."

Reaching the bottom of the steps, I square my shoulders before opening the door to the back alley. Brian stands next to his suburban, hands tucked into his pockets, head down.

That's right. Feel guilty, you bastard.

Hearing the door slam shut behind us, he looks up, blue eyes filled with remorse.

"Jerri . . ."

I shake my head at him in disgust. "Save your breath, Brian."

Taking a few steps toward me, he says, "It wasn't my call, Jerri. It was his."

I scoff. "And you always do exactly as cousin Locklin says—don't you?—even though he's technically your informant and you're the detective. Tell me, does your superior know that your informant, *your family*, is a lying bastard posing as a cop?" He goes to speak, but I keep on. "Better yet, are you able to sleep well at night, knowing you lied just to please him? You lied so that I could remain lost in my head. You knew the whole time who I was, and you damn well know exactly who's trying to kill me. So tell me, Brian, while I tossed and turned all night, desperately trying to figure out who I am, how did you fucking sleep?"

He swallows heavily. Then he replies, voice rasping, "I'm truly sorry, Jerri."

I look to the sky, clearing my head of his remorseful face before telling him, "I'm sorry is an admission of guilt, not an apology. You lied about Locklin, neglecting to tell me he wasn't your partner. You knew all along who was out to kill me when I asked, and you lied when you looked me in the eye and told me you were working hard to find out who it was."

MIND LIES

He curls his lip around his teeth and says, "You lied too, Jerri. You told me you had no memories; you remembered Lock the whole time."

I shake my head at him. "I remembered a man, not who he was. I also remembered someone trying to kill me, but I wasn't sure who I could trust. Apparently, my instincts were right when I chose not to tell you." His face falls at the jab, and I add, "I once respected you, Brian, but that ship has long since sailed. Because now? Now you're nothing but a liar, just like your cousin."

Opening the back door to Portia's car, I toss my bag in the back seat, ready to leave this place behind for a little while. I love my friends. I love my shop, and my home has been comforting to me these past few days. But I feel antsy, knowing Locklin could show up at any time. For the first time in my life, I can truly say I want nothing to do with him.

How does a woman say that about the father of her unborn child?

I've asked myself that question many times over the last twenty-four hours, and the simple answer is that it's easy when said father is a lying bastard.

I'll never keep him from his child. If he chooses to leave the danger in the background and wants a life with his child, he will have it.

A life with me, however, is not in the cards.

He solidified that when he left me, lost and broken.

He chose that future, or lack thereof, when he chose vengeance over what we had together.

"He's hurting, Jerri." Brian solemnly says before I sit down in the car and close the door. The window is open, so he hears me when I reply, "Not as badly as I am."

I can tell he wants to say more, but I ignore him and the pain that comes with speaking to a man who now reminds me so much of Locklin.

Cousins.

Brian was raised in the States, whereas Locklin was raised in Ireland. Their fathers were brothers; Brian's father was a kind man who was unfortunately killed in the line of duty, and Locklin's father was a gambler, a man made of lies who lived off the thrill of the bet and the rush of the money. Fortunately, the bet and the money both caught up to him. He died of a severe heart attack at the age of fifty-three.

Bryan was the first person Locklin introduced me to when I arrived back in the States. I hardly saw him. Maybe a few times a year. But I always knew, as per Locklin's promise, that if anything were to happen, or if I were ever in danger and he weren't around, I was to contact Bryan.

I won't say he was a close friend. We never hung out enough for that to happen. But I respected him and his job with Boston PD. I also respected him for the simple fact that he was a relative of Lock's and truly a good, honest man.

Honest.

Another kick in the teeth, considering he has done nothing but lie to me for over four months.

It seems at the moment that's what my life has been built upon.

Lies.

I laid it all out for Portia and Cooper last night. Absolutely everything. From the moment I took the job overseas to the attack and the past ten years of lying through my teeth to them about everything from my family to my past.

There were tears.

Cooper did a lot of pacing.

And I, well, I felt like a piece of shit.

I understood why I lied to them for so long. I truly did. Whether it was the amnesia, the pregnancy, or learning the truth about my past that called for me to lie, I'm not sure. But what I do know is that it is time for a clean slate with the people who have been nothing but supportive and one hundred percent honest.

How could I go on, feeling equal in our friendship, *our family*, if I didn't return the favor? There's no way I could continue to leave them in the dark; not because it wasn't fair, but because I owe them that much.

"We're here, Jer." Portia softly says from beside me.

Looking out the window, I take in various boats and ships resting at the docks. The smell of the ocean bringing back memories of the first time I was here.

Ten years ago.

How things have changed since the last time. Yet I'm still here, back where my old life was left behind, where a new one is ready to take its place.

Grabbing my bag, I get out and meet Portia at the front of the car. This is the end of the road for her and the beginning of the unknown for me. All I know is I need time, space, and a familiar old family to make me feel partially whole again.

Wrapping my arms around my best friend, I hold her close. I am grateful my memories have come back, and I am grateful for her.

"I love you, P." I whisper.

MIND LIES

She sniffles. "Love you too, Jer. Call me soon, okay?"

I nod, giving her one last squeeze before walking toward my past—and, hopefully, a brighter future.

"Ye' lost?" asks the older man untying the giant ropes holding the vessel to the dock.

I shake my head, looking for the tattoo on his left hand. Once I spot it, I tell him what Paddy told me to say—my ticket onto the small ship.

"Heading home to see Nessa," I softly tell him. Straightening, he tosses the rope and gestures with his hand to come along. "Ye don't waste time. Come, Lass."

My heart pitter-patters when he says lass, but I swallow my hurt and follow him onto the ship.

"Home is nae where ye sleep, Jerrilyn. Home is where ye heart is full."

Nessa's words from the past echo through my head as I head toward the first place I ever felt at home.

The first place my heart became full.

CHAPTER TWENTY-TWO

"Deep breath, Jerri."

I don't make a habit of talking to myself, but when I work late and few people are around, I can't help it.

It's creepy.

As are many of the men working out of the warehouse-side of the building.

O'Doyle Imports has been my employer for half a year now, and if I wasn't so dedicated to my job as head of the purchasing department, I wouldn't stay here so late.

I enjoy my work. Not just because I hope to own my own store full of treasures one day, but because this job gives me extensive knowledge when it comes to the importing and exporting of goods and the purchase and acquiring of foreign treasures.

This job is exactly what I need to help develop my business sense for when I open my own shop.

Moving to Ireland for the job was a big leap, but considering I had left little back home in the States, it was an easy choice to make. Having arrived almost a

MIND LIES

year ago, I've had plenty of time to settle in and learn the lay of the land, so to speak, before starting work.

I have no regrets.

I absolutely adore it here. The people, the smell, the beautiful landscape. It's welcoming and makes me feel at peace, even though I only know a few people . . . including the man who continues to screw me silly on a semi-regular basis.

Locklin.

Opening the door to the warehouse, I smile a little as I think of the dark and broody man who left my bed this morning. Several shipping containers came in today, hence the reason for me working late, again.

It's dark outside. The warehouse is dimly lit. I search for shipping tags and content forms on the large desk in the back corner. Usually, all the paperwork would be on my desk by now. But someone has been getting sloppy lately because this is the third time I've had to come and search for it myself.

Shuffling through bin for today's imports, I crane my neck when I hear muted voices. Yet another reason I hate working late.

As I said, creepy.
I find the papers I need and begin reading them as I walk. Then I note, yet again, that a container or two is unaccounted for. This has been at least the sixth time

since I have worked here that this has happened—and it has become a real pain in the ass. When I get frustrated enough to contact the higher-up, they always take care of it. But the bottom line is I hate not being able to sort this out myself.

I make a quick cruise along the back wall of the warehouse, checking off container numbers, getting closer to the voices.

"Hello?" I ask, walking closer to the end of the space where the larger containers are held. I shiver, feeling like the idiot in a horror movie, when a Russian accented voice from behind asks, "Late workin'?"

I spin around, hoping to find the quiet security guard who occupies the booth out front.

But I'm not that fortunate.

I've only seen the creep behind me twice, but I'd have been happy not to see him again. He's the type with the dead eyes and constant leer that instantly puts you on edge. One of the women at reception had said he's probably harmless, but the look on his face has suggested otherwise to me in previous encounters.

Calming my racing heart and clutching the paperwork to my chest, I give him a small nod before responding, "Just finishing up. Someone forgot to bring the receiving papers to my desk today, but I found them."

MIND LIES

He stares blankly at me, and I move to make my way back to the office when he moves slightly to the right. "You were talkin' to someone?" he asks.

I shake my head. "No. I thought I heard people talking." I let out a dry laugh, hopefully excusing myself from this awkward conversation. Unexpectedly, a banging noise from behind causes me to jump.

"Help. Help us," moan voices from behind. I spin in that direction, forgetting the creep in front of me.

"What the?" I mumble. Heart racing, I speed toward the container making the noise.

"Would not do that if I were you," the creep says from behind as I swing the latch on the container next to a big bay door. But before I can get it open, he grabs my hair, hauling me backward with so much force that I lose my footing and land on my tailbone.

I cry out in pain and reach behind me, scratching any exposed skin I can find on his arms and hands.

"Bitch," he grunts, hardly fazed from my attack. He hauls me roughly by the arm and slams me face-first into the metal shipping container containing god knows who.

"Get off, you son of a bitch! Help! Help me!" I wail, and my heart breaks when at least three voices sounding much weaker than mine holler back.

"Help us!" a few women cry, and not only in English.

A cry for help in what I assume is also Russian comes from the container.

He slams me face-first into the hard, unyielding metal of the container. "Who the hell are you?" I grunt.

"Let us go!" the women howl.

I kick my sandal-clad foot behind me into his shin. He grunts and then presses his erection against my hips. I swallow the bile quickly rising into my throat and open my mouth to scream again.

Forcibly grabbing my jaw and twisting my head to the side, he cuts off my cries.

"Not someone you want to meet in warehouse at night," he grunts into my face, his accent thick.

"Let us go. We won't tell anyone," I meekly say, my one-hundred-and-twenty-pound body continuing to struggle against his two-hundred-plus one. He doesn't answer but roughly twists my arm behind my back instead. "I don't get paid to let merchandise go. But perhaps I get bonus for extra."

My entire body shivers, and I struggle against his firm hold on my arm and scream as loud as I can, kicking and losing my sandals in the process.

MIND LIES

"Help m—"

"Quiet!" he commands, flashing a knife in front of my face, touching it to my cheek.

I shake my head lightly. "Please, no. Please."

"Nosy bitches not good for business," he says before licking up the side of my neck.

Gagging, I try to shift away, but I feel the knife at my waist. "No! Please don't!" I wail, twisting my body away from the blade. He slams me forward again, my head crying out in pain. He lets my arm go but then grabs the waistband of my shorts.

I scream when his fingers pull the waistband away from my body. I try to pull away from him, feeling the knife slice through my belt.

I'd rather die.

That's all I can think of as I fight, which only seems to anger him further. I feel the breeze of the night on my lower back; he has succeeded in cutting through my shorts. A pain unlike anything I have ever felt shoots through my body as his knife pierces my hip.

"Agh!" I cry in agony.
Suddenly, the man disappears from behind me, and a muted thud follows.

I spin around, leaning against the container for support. As I try to flee, strong arms surround my shoulders.

"No!" I push my arms out before a soothing voice says, "Easy, Lass. I've got you."

Choking out a sob, I look up into stormy-blue eyes. "Lock?"

His jaw ticks before he bends down and places a forceful but gentle kiss on my lips. "We need to run, Lass. Okay? I'll keep you safe, but we need to run."

I nod. "The women?" I mumble, pointing to the container. I hear a clang behind me, jumping at the noise. A man dressed in black, who had arrived with Locklin, opens the door. To my horror, there are three women huddled into a corner.

Their faces are dirty, and the stench of human waste is strong. They look from me to the man who opened the door, to the evil man out cold on the floor.

"We don't have much time. Come," the dark man tells the women. They remain in the corner and look at me with wide, scared, yet hopeful, eyes. Locklin steadies me with his arm and says, "Tell them, Lass. They'll be safe, but they need to go. Now."
I nod, ignoring the tears pooling in my eyes; seeing the woman in huddled in the container is a difficult sight. One is no more than a girl. "You'll be safe, but you need to hurry!" I emphasize, using hand gestures

MIND LIES

Surprisingly, they trust me, perhaps recognizing me as the woman who was screaming a moment ago. Perhaps their trust is based on pity; surely they can see the blood pouring down my face and leg, that I'm hurt.

Breathing through my mouth to avoid the smell in the container—God knows how long they were kept in there—I watch as they exit the container, taking slow painful steps with the man dressed in black guiding them.

That could have been me.

I give each woman a nod and a small smile, telling them with my eyes that I hope to high heaven they remain safe and untouched for the rest of their innocent lives. The young girl, who can't be much older than sixteen, has tears streaming down her little heart-shaped face as the other two hold her up, like support beams on either side of a weak structure.

That poor girl.

All have bruises or welts on their wrists.

All have pain in their eyes. I'm afraid to know how it got there.

"Come, Lass," Locklin softly says as he guides me to the side of the building. The man in black waves the women toward a green van labeled as a seafood delivery van. "They'll be safe, Lass. I promise."

With a wave toward the van, I numbly nod and give a small smile to the women as they pile in.

"Danke," the oldest, a blonde woman, whispers before guiding the others to safety. She has true appreciation in her eyes.

The van speeds off seconds later. Locklin goes still in front of me.

"We need to run, Lass. Now," he grumbles, dragging me by the arm. Headlights shine across the front of the building.

"Run, Jerri!"

Tripping over the loose gravel of the driveway, I do my best to stay on my feet. There's blood running down my leg, and my hip is on fire. Locklin's grasp on my fingers tightens to the point of pain as he pulls me off the driveway and down the hill.

He'll keep me safe.

I know he will.

CHAPTER TWENTY-THREE

Jolting awake, I take in my surroundings and ground myself for a moment before swinging my legs over the side of the small twin bed. Light streaming through the porthole in my room tells me it's late morning as I get up and head to the small ensuite for a shower.

Travelling on a freight ship across the Atlantic is not glamorous, but it's not filthy or gross either. Paddy ensured I got my own room down the hall from the captain's suite. The rooms are simple—white and steel. But they're clean and relatively quiet, save for the roaring of the ocean and the hum of the ship.

After my shower, I dress in a simple pair of jeans and black sweater before leaving my room and heading to the mess hall for something to eat.

Three meals are served every day, and I've missed breakfast again, which leads me to the fruit counter. Grabbing a banana and making a piece of toast, I wrap up my breakfast in a paper towel and head to the main deck.

It's my fourth day here, and in a couple more days, we'll dock in Belfast. I can't say it has been an uneventful journey. It has been quiet, and if I'm not engaged in mind, I'm occupied by sitting in this plastic chair, which is bolted to the deck, watching the men below me move to and fro as they do all the things that require keeping such a large vessel afloat.

Leaning back with my feet planted on the railing and breakfast in my lap, I think back to the women I saw that night, the innocent women I used to think of constantly before my memory was gone.

After Locklin rescued me and helped me get settled with Paddy and Nessa, he assured that his friend, the man in black, got them to safety, that no one would hurt them anymore. His details were vague, much like the man in question, but there was no doubt in my mind that he spoke the truth.

Locklin is not a man who would harm women, or allow harm to come to them.

To my surprise, it would be almost a month later before he would tell me about his front as an exporter of fish and seafood in Ireland.

Was it an actual business?

Yes.

It was a longtime family business passed down to Paddy from his Scottish grandfather. That's how I met Locklin. He'd come into our office to set up shipping, but these visits became more frequent; he wanted to initiate contact with me. Soon these interactions became our unconventional relationship.

Locklin worked for Paddy for many years before the business became more of a front for him to uncover what I now know was human trafficking, which is something Locklin holds close to his heart after what happened to *her*.

Siobhan.

It would be almost a year after my attack before he would finally tell me about her as well.

"Miss?"

I turn, seeing a kind man, Flynn, behind me. "Yes?"

He smiles kindly, his gray hair blowing against the ocean wind. "Phone call for you outside the captain's deck."

I smile back and follow him through the maze of portals before taking a seat at the small table in the hallway and putting the phone to my ear.

"Hello?"

"Ye sea sick yet?" Paddy's voice heartily grumbles down the line.

I smile and reply, "Not yet. It has been a smooth cruise."
He laughs. "Flynn says the seas are smooth until ye reach the port. Nessa's nearly dancin' awaitin' ye to git 'ere. . . ." He trails off.

"I can't wait to see her either, Paddy. It has been too long."

"Aye, Lass, it has," he grumbles. He begins to speak again but hesitates.

"What is it, Paddy?" I ask.

He sighs. "Ah, Lass. I don't like lyin' to me boy. I know ye said it was important. But I'll tell ye he called today. I dinnae know if I ever hear him so hurtin'. Says he made a poor choice, but he's workin' on fixin' it. He would nae tell me what it was."

Swallowing past the lump in my throat and ignoring the fact that a hurting Locklin still hurts me as well, I say, "I'm very sorry, Paddy, but over the phone is not the way to discuss what happened. Two more days, please?" I say softly.

Clearly, he hears the sorrow—pain—in my voice as he replies, "Ye know I'd do anythin' for ye, Lass. Two more days."

I sigh. "Thank you, Paddy."

Hanging up the phone and settling an internal restlessness I can't seem to shake, I pace the hall with no destination in mind. Locklin was right when he told Paddy he made a poor choice, but there will be no fixing it.

MIND LIES

How do you fix the heart you broke? How do you take back leaving someone behind? How on earth do you make a hurting woman's heart whole again when she knows you didn't want to be the one to hold it together in the first place?

When she knows she wasn't important enough to hold onto?

To keep?

There's only one answer: you don't.

"Excuse me, Ms. Sloane?"

I turn and greet the captain's right-hand man, Colin. He's in his early forties and has been very kind. His wife Laura works on the ship as well, and although I haven't quite made friends, I've had tea with her.

"Hey, Colin. How are you today?"

He smiles. "Good, thank you. I don't mean to be a burden, and if you would like to say no, that's entirely fine. However, the chef has come down with the flu, and I was wondering if you're interested in taking over the kitchen for dinner? There was a small leak in the boiler this morning, so we're shorthanded." He fixes his hat before adding, "Feel free to say no, but you seem a little restless, so I thought it was worth a shot since Laura told me you like to cook."

He smiles sheepishly at me. I return the smile before asking, "How many people do I have to feed?"

Standing taller, he says, "Twenty-six, including yourself. Everything you need is in the big fridge and freezers."

I nod slowly. "You know what, Colin? I think that sounds like a good way to occupy my afternoon."

He nods. "So I got myself a chef for the night?"

I nod back, feeling a little lighter knowing I have a purpose for the day. "You sure do."

* * *

The men sure like their beef on this ship. The past four dinners have consisted of burgers, spaghetti and meatballs, Swiss steak, and Irish stew, of course. Staying with the curve, I had grabbed three large prime rib roasts from the fridge and paired them with grilled root vegetables, large baked potatoes, homemade Caesar salad, and au jus.

"Paddy speaks highly of ya, but he hadn't told us what a fine cook you were," the Captain tells me from the head of our table as he devours his dinner. Forgoing the regular buffet lineup, I had placed platters of food on every table and had one of the deck hands help me set them.

"I'm glad you enjoy it, Captain. Thank you. But there's a catch," I tell him with a raised brow. He returns a raised brow, signaling for me to continue. "If I cook, I don't like to clean up. Perhaps some fortunate eaters can help clear the plates and load the dishwashers when we're finished."

Chuckling, the Captain, an older man, hollers, "The lady fed ya. That means you fishy-smellin' bastards are in charge of cleanin' the kitchen."

There are hollers and "Hear! Hears!" followed by palms landing heavily on the tables. For the first time in days, I laugh. I'm grateful they enjoyed my dinner and am happy I don't need to be on my feet anymore. My back is killing me; and, lately, my growing baby has been forcing me to have at least one nap a day.

I know the men on the ship have noticed my bump, though only a few have mentioned it. Regardless, the men have been considerate and respectful, either because they're fine men or because Paddy gave the ship a tongue-lashing and a warning.

I'm leaning toward the latter.

Settling into bed that night, I place my hands on my full stomach and pray for peace. I hope Ireland provides me with much-needed shelter and perspective. I haven't thought about children in years—having my own that is. After what had happened the first time, of course I am hesitant. Once I began my relationship with Tom, I went in with the hope that one day I would have a child, but it didn't take me long to know that it would never be with him.

Or anyone other than Locklin.

How do you picture having children with anyone else when for the past twelve years you've been in love with only one man?

I think it's a blessing.

It's as if the universe is telling me that even though I don't get to have *all of him*, I still get to keep a *part* of him.

"Two more days," I whisper to myself before swiftly falling asleep.

CHAPTER TWENTY-FOUR

Closing my eyes, I breathe in the crisp, clean Irish air before walking off the ship. Once my home, this place brings back many memories, good and bad. But I focus on the good ones and smile when I spot the lovely couple below.

"Dear girl!" Nessa beckons, nearly weeping. She rushes forward and crushes me in her arms. "Oh, Dear, how I 'ave missed ya!"

I blink past the growing, happy tears in my eyes and hug her back, nearly as hard. "I've missed you too. So much."

She stiffens. I know she has felt the bump at my stomach. Leaning back, she looks into my eyes. Hers are so light and blue and full of hope as she looks to me for an answer. Her perfectly coiffed white hair frames her round face, and I simply give her a small smile and say, "We'll talk when we get settled, okay?"

She wipes a few stray tears from her cheeks and nods. "Yes, okay."

Paddy picks up on what's happening and pulls me in for a bear hug. "Been too long."

Very few words for a man of so many. It's been three years since I've been back; we have survived only on a few phone calls on holidays here and there to get us by. You would think we would have much more to say, but now that we're here, together, the moment causes us to hesitate. It's strange how that works.

"That it has, old man," I say cheekily. "Miss me?"

He laughs. "Aye, now get your smart arse in the car. Nessa's got a feast waitin'."

Looping my arm through hers, I follow the burly man through the port to his waiting vehicle. I enjoy listening to them speak. Nessa and Paddy both have a mishmash of Irish and Scottish accents, depending on their mood. Both were born in Ireland but spent their formative years in Scotland where their parents worked during that time.

As usual, she asks me a hundred questions on the walk and the drive, from how my shop is doing to how Portia and Cooper are. We talk about everything and anything other than the giant elephant in the car:

Locklin.

***

Paddy and Nessa brought me to the cabin on their country property: a small two-bedroom abode resting nearly a mile down the path from their house. It has as much charm and character as the landscape surrounding it and is complete with a large stone fireplace, an open-concept living area, and a small kitchen with a table for four positioned under a window. There's a small porch on the back with two rocking chairs that overlook a tiny lake, much like the one in my dream of Locklin and me. I hate that it brings back memories of him before I've even settled in.

Back when I stayed here, recuperating from my attack, I lived with Paddy and Nessa in their large country home. I chose to stay with Nessa since Paddy travelled a lot at the time for work, and at the heart of it, I wasn't ready to be on my own after the horror I'd witnessed.

"I made some tea," Nessa tells me, and we all take a seat around the table.

I know they're waiting for me to spill. About Locklin. About why I wanted it to be a secret that I was staying here.

Everything.

I nod, thankful for the tea, and bite the bullet, choosing to get it out sooner rather than later. Paddy and Nessa are the closest people to parents I've ever had, and they deserve the truth. They helped me at one of my lowest, most terrifying moments in my life. I had only just met them, and they had brought me soup in bed and had provided me with shelter, all to protect me from the evil that is Yakov's crew of Russian traffickers.

"I was in a car accident over four months ago." Nessa gasps, placing her hand over mine. I squeeze her fingers. "I woke up in the hospital twenty-two days later with no idea who I was or where I had come from."

Swallowing, I continue, "I had amnesia, but the only thing I could remember was Locklin. Only, I didn't know who Locklin was or if my mind was playing tricks on me, considering that I couldn't remember Portia, or Cooper."

"Dear girl . . . ," Nessa whispers.

"One day, a detective came to see me." Making eye contact with Paddy, I tell him, "Detective Bryan O'Shaunessey." Shaking my head, I add, "I didn't know who he was then, or a month later when I ran into both him and a Detective Cavanaugh."

My breath hitches, and Paddy eye's squint. "Neither said they knew me. Neither told me who I was."

"No!" Nessa gasps while Paddy curses, "Sons of bastards."

"I was still having dreams of Locklin, and I had a dream about the attack at the shipping warehouse. So when Bryan told me the brake lines had been cut on my vehicle, I was scared, not knowing who I could trust."

"The fucks still dinnae tell ye?" Paddy asks.

I shake my head and vehemently whisper, "No."

He starts pacing. Wanting to get it all out, I power through. "I kept remembering this song I sang to him."

Nessa adds, "Ye were always singing to the boy, even when he wasnae around."

I swallow past the anguish and finish telling them about the YouTube video, Scarlet and her stalker, Locklin getting shot, and how I ended up here.

"We know he ain't dead since he called, Nessa," Paddy assures when Nessa's eyes go wide at the mention of Locklin getting a bullet.

"He'll be fine, Nessa. He was expecting to be released from the hospital two days after I left," I tell her.

"Who'll look after him?" she asks, worried, and Paddy adds, "He's a grown-ass boy who shoulda acted like a man!"

Placing my hand on both of theirs, I tell them, "I'm sorry."

Nessa shakes her head. "It is nae your fault, Jerrilyn. What ye went through? And fer *you* to be alone? And singing? In public? . . ." She starts to ramble.

I tell her, "The only reason I chose to sing was because I knew in my heart whoever I sang to in my memories was the father of my child, and I was desperate to find him."

Nessa gasps, and I don't bother hiding the tears that fall.

"Our boy?" she whispers.

I whisper back, "Your boy. But he never came for me, Nessa." Choking back a sob, I say again, "He never came."

She pulls me close and crushes me in her arms. I finally let the sobs go on her shoulder. I want to feel terrible that I've probably tainted their view of their beloved nephew, but the truth is I know Paddy and Nessa think of me as their own, too. And if I need any more answers—answers regarding the men who were after me, who were trying to hurt me—I know Paddy won't lie.

He'll tell me what I need to know because I'm his family, too.

I can't feel guilty about fiercely loving these two and wanting to be with them. My memory is back, but now I have questions that Locklin wouldn't answer. But clearly, he never told Paddy about the accident because he was just as shocked as Nessa.

I pretend I don't notice Paddy's inner turmoil, when his head tips toward the ceiling, when he blinks back emotion he doesn't wish to share. Softly, to be certain, I ask him, "He never told you about the accident, did he, Paddy?"

He shakes his head and turns around, looking devastated. "No, Lass. Three months ago we spoke; 'e said ye were fine."

Leaning back in my chair and taking a healthy sip of my tea—wishing it were something stronger—I ask, "Do you know who would have cut my brake lines?"

Shaking his head, he says, "Not certain. Lots changed in ten years, but Vasily is still out there."

Stilling my quivering chin, I nod. The man who attacked me, the man Locklin hit over the head with the crowbar used to open shipping crates, is still alive. I already knew that when I recovered my memory; even so, it's a harsh reminder that the nightmares from my past still walk the earth today.

Hating that Locklin is the only person who has the answers I need, I shudder and place my arms protectively around my stomach.

"How far along are ye?" Nessa softly asks.

"Four and a half months. I got pregnant around the time of the accident." She smiles and I add, "It wasn't planned, Ness. I spoke with the doctor once I got my memory back, and she said it was most likely the antibiotics that countered my birth control shot that was near due. But nothing is one hundred percent effective."

She nods, still smiling. "Any bairn is a blessing. Does he know?"

Paddy places a hand on my shoulder, and I nod.

"I won't keep him from *him*," I tell them.

"A boy," Paddy confirms.

I smile. "A boy. I told him in the hospital, after I told him I had my memory back. What he does, knowing about the pregnancy, is entirely up to him."

Paddy shakes his head. "He will nae abandon his boy."

He closes his eyes at the unspoken reality.

He won't abandon a child.

He'll just abandon me.

"I'm sorry, Jerrilyn."

I squeeze his hand in support. "There's nothing for you to be sorry for. I'm here. I'm staying for a while. And I'm going to focus on nothing but getting some rest and perspective on this whole thing." I sigh. "Even getting my memory back, I still just feel lost."

MIND LIES

Nessa takes our cups to the sink. "This is yer home too, Jerri. Ye stay here as long as ye need."

"Thank you. I don't exactly have a plan; I just wanted some quiet. And I knew the first place Locklin would go when he left the hospital would be my flat in Boston." Shaking my head and rubbing my temples, I add, "I didn't want to see him. I don't want to see him at all right now. He's not a bad person, and he's very good to you guys. But I'm sorry. I just don't know if I'm going to be able to forgive him for what he did to me. Did to us."

Moving from the chair, I stare out the window at the little lake behind the cabin. I know I can't stay here and do nothing forever. I know at some point it will come to an end. But I guess facing reality, facing Locklin, just hurts too much. I don't want to deal with it, and perhaps this is running away from my problems, which is nothing new. I ran from Ireland before. And even if this, running, is the coward's way, I feel like this is where I need to be right now. I feel like Paddy and Nessa's company will bring me peace.

And that's the only thing I need right now—peace.

The only thing I want.

The rest can wait.

I'll focus on my baby.

I'll get Paddy to prod Locklin for information about the accident. Lock doesn't need to know I'm here, but he'll know once I got my memory back that I would have contacted his aunt and uncle. I guess he never expected me to tell them the truth, seeing as he didn't when he called, but such is life.

Sometimes, life is full of liars.

And sometimes, those liars break your fragile heart.

CHAPTER TWENTY-FIVE

LOCKLIN

I bang on the door. Out of respect, I give her a few moments before pulling the key from my pocket, opening the door, and disabling the alarm as I go.

I never spent much time in Jerri's apartment. Not because I never wanted to, but because of her friends who always come and go. I punch the code into the alarm panel before sluggishly taking the stairs; my chest fucking hurts. I move as quick as my gunshot-wounded body will allow.

Fucking prick.

I'm half-grateful that the sorry bastard who shot at us at the theater wasn't after Jerri. It was a blessing and a curse knowing that the sick fucks from Yakov's crew hadn't caught up with her. It's also a kick in the fucking teeth not knowing exactly who messed with her car.

"Jerri?" I call out. I don't know why; I can already sense the emptiness.

She's not here.

When she brought me back here weeks ago, when someone had tried busting into her apartment, I couldn't help but get lost in the picture above her bed.

I knew she kept it. Sometimes I forget how much it meant to her. She hates that she can't put photos of us out for all to see. It hurts her that she's always the third wheel whenever she goes out with her friends, but like the bastard that I am, I still keep my distance.

I still make her do everything alone.

Because what was more important than getting justice for Siobhan?

What was more important than making sure Jerri stayed safe and as unconnected to me as possible?

Nothing.

It has been my mission, my goal, for the last seventeen years, and I vowed I'd stop at nothing until I fulfilled that goal.

My promise to a ghost.

There was one time I doubted my decision: when she finally left me to my mission and started dating that suit-wearing fuck with the shiny shoes. I followed the prick for a week, then I went out on business, came back, and followed the prick some more.

MIND LIES

I had Bryan run him for me, check him out to make sure he was good enough for Jerri.

No one is good enough for Jerri.

Mr. Suit was clean.

Didn't lie, didn't cheat, good savings account. He had a long line of women he'd been with, but when my Jerri walked into his life, he settled down.

He loved her.

But she didn't love him back. Not once did she look into the fucker's eyes the same way she looks into mine. And that, that right there, is the only reason I left her alone . . . because as much as she wanted to step away and play house, I knew she would come back.

I knew she would end up with me.

But she didn't.

After him, we did our usual on-and-off game over the years. But she always came back. Not once did I ever doubt that she *wouldn't* come back to me, because it has been Locklin and Jerri for twelve years.

Until it wasn't.

Looking away from the painting, I notice a folded piece of paper on her bed, with my name on it.

"What did you do, Lass?" I mumble before sitting down and picking it up, already dreading the words I'll read but unable to stop myself from opening it.

Locklin,

I knew you'd come here.

Just as I knew you'd always choose vengeance over us.

It's a tough pill to swallow, acknowledging that. But it's time to be honest with myself in knowing I will never mean as much to you as she did. I don't hate her, or you for that. In fact, I respect your dedication to commit so fiercely.

Dedication aside, I won't be second fiddle anymore, because this life is not just about me, or you. It's about someone much more important who deserves absolutely everything.

Our son.

I meant what I said in the hospital, so please don't mistake this letter as anything but what it is:

Me telling you once and for all that I'm done.

What you did to me is unforgiveable.
I truly thought when I woke up in the hospital that not knowing who I was was the most painful thing to ever happen to me. My heart hurt and my head

MIND LIES

was empty, and all I hoped for was to feel something other than the agony of being completely alone.

Consistently having memories of a man no one knew, a man who appeared to love me—to have him not show up, not comfort me—was a death in itself.

You cannot imagine what it feels like to go to sleep at night with memories of you and I entwined together with me singing to you and you in turn making the most passionate love to me that I've ever experienced.

But then I wake up.

I wake up and you're not there. You don't show up to comfort me. You don't show up to let me know who I am, that I'm not fucking crazy, and that my fond memories of us together are true.

You did absolutely nothing.

And you broke my fucking heart.

Excuse my language, but I'm bitter, angry, and so incredibly disappointed in you. I once believed you would do anything for me. I once believed that no matter what happened to me in this life, you would be there for me.

And once, even though you told me you cared for me deeply, I took it for something much more. I took it to mean you loved me.

But you don't love me, Locklin. You've clearly held onto those words since you last said them to Siobhan, and deep down I think you want them to stay with her.

Well you know what?

I deserve love, too.

I know that now.

I deserve so much more than what you have given me, Locklin.

I deserve everything.

Someone who will show up when I miscarry. Someone who will wait twenty-two days at my bedside as I struggle to wake up from a coma. Someone who will tell me who I am and how much I mean to them when I wake up.

Someone I mean the world to.

I deserve someone who will hold my hand when I give birth to our child.
I deserve a man who will kiss me good morning and good night. A man who will hold my hair

MIND LIES

during morning sickness and rub my back when I lie in bed at night.

A strong and kind man who will willingly meet my friends and suffer through dinner parties and weddings. A man who is never afraid but extremely proud to be my plus-one.

A man who, regardless of life's circumstances, is completely and utterly devoted to loving me.

I deserve a man who isn't afraid to love me.

You are not that man.

Please don't look for me, or try to get in contact with me. There's really nothing left to say to each other, and I need a clean break from this. If you're cursing right now because you have something to say, please know that I don't want to hear it.

I don't want to hear from you at all.

I do promise to contact you when our child is born, and should you wish to be a part of his life, we'll make that happen.

I wish you well, Locklin Cavanaugh. May your mission of vengeance not take you from those who love you.

Jerri

"Fuck."

I re-read the letter at least a half-dozen times, hoping it will hurt a little less. Instead, it just drives the knife deeper in my chest.

Our son.

"FUCK!"

Storming from the bedroom, I come to a halt before a figure leaning against the island.

"What the fuck are you doing here?" I growl at Cooper. Perfect fucking Cooper who dotes on his wife. She's a hot wife, and I'm a bastard because I know he's a good man. I want to think he doesn't know who I am, but his casual stance against the island says otherwise.

"You need to let her go," he tells me.

"Like fuck I do," I answer.

He shakes his pretty fucking head at me. "I've known Jerri for ten years."

"I've known her for twelve!" I reply, arguing like a five-year-old on the goddamn playground.

He rolls his eyes and continues. "Never in all of those years have I seen her hurt as badly as she did the day she left you at the hospital."

I open my mouth, but he shakes his head. "She was gutted, Locklin. She's one of the strongest women I know, and she could barely stand on her own two fucking feet. I thought it was bad the day Portia showed up here and found Jerri in her closet." He shakes his head. "Man, her damn eyes were nearly swollen shut because she'd been crying all night. Her closet was torn apart because she was trying to find a clue that you were real, that she wasn't fucking crazy."

I swallow past the razorblades in my throat.

I did that to her.

"Getting the picture I'm painting?" he says heatedly without slowing down. "I held her hair while her head was in the goddamn toilet from carrying your fuckin' kid. I drove her to every fuckin' town where we figured you two had been just so she could remember and try to find you. It was me, giving up my wife to come here and distract her from crying all damn day because of you!"

"I would never do anything to intentionally hurt her."

"Too fucking late! You broke her, you bastard. Now she's gone for the simple fucking reason that she didn't want to see your face!"

Another knife to the chest.

I'm a bastard.

Cooper scrubs his hands down his face before walking toward the door. "Leave her be, Locklin. You want her to heal? You want your baby healthy and the mother not stressed out all goddamn day? Leave her be. You may not want or care about her, but the rest of us sure fucking do."

I want to yell at him that I care about her more than anyone else, but I know it'll fall on deaf ears. I'm not an idiot; I know actions speak louder than words, and all these people, her friends, have to go on is whatever she has told them. After what has happened, I'm sure none of it is good, and I don't fucking blame her.

I used to pride myself on looking after her. I used to send her food when she worked late, and rub her back when it hurt. I used to set the coffeemaker for her and kiss her goodbye before I left in the morning. But all that was before Vasily got his hands on her, and since then, the only thing I do for her is make sure she's safe.

And sated.

A far cry from all the things I used to do.

Folding the letter and putting it in my coat pocket, I jog down the steps and out to my truck, eager to move, to find her.

To do something.

Punching the security code back in, I exit, only to be greeted by my cousin.

"My lucky day or what?" I bark at him. He shakes his head at me and says, "She left a week ago."

I spread my hands out. "You didn't think to fuckin' tell me that sooner, you cocksucker?"

As with most of my jabs, he ignores it and says, "I think it was for the best."

"What? Her leaving or you not telling me?"

"Both," the prick answers.

"I've looked out and cared for that woman for twelve goddamn years! And you don't think I deserve to know she took off? Where'd she go?"

Sighing, he puts his hands in his pockets. "You did look out for her, Lock. Nobody would say you didn't. But in all the years I've had your back in looking out for her when you weren't around, I've never seen her so broken, man."

"Why does everyone keep saying that? She's not broken; she's the strongest damn person I know!" I bark back.

"Everyone keeps saying it because it's the damn truth. And if you weren't such a stubborn fuck, you would have realized how much she meant to you before you broke her heart." He moves from the truck and jabs a finger in my chest. "I hate that I fuckin' listened to you when you asked me to lie. I fuckin' hate it, Lock, and I hate the way she looked at me when she found out. She hates me now, too. That's on me. I'll take it and I'll make amends with her when she comes back. But you?" He shakes his head. "Damn, Lock. You fucked up this time."

Slapping his hand out of the way, I yell. "You think I don't know that?" I instantly regret yelling when the burning in my chest forces me to lean against the truck to catch my breath.

I'm not bulletproof.

Strangely, the lingering burn in my chest isn't from the bullet—it's my goddamn heart.

"Take some time, Lock," Bryan mutters before getting in his truck.

Time.

Something I need more of.

With *her*.

CHAPTER TWENTY-SIX

"He's been here twice in the past week asking for you—wanting to know where you're staying," Portia solemnly tells me.

"I'd ask if you told him, but I know you better than that," I reply. I stare at her on the computer screen, watching as she bites her lip. "Portia?"

She sighs. "He also followed Cooper and me, and I'm assuming he was hoping that we'd lead him to you."

Frowning, I ask, "Followed you where?"

"We were headed to that market in the south end. Cooper spotted him and had a little chat."

"Jesus Christ," I mutter.

"He's desperate to find you, Jer. Cooper almost looked sorry for him after they finished talking."

"What'd Locklin tell him?"

Her face fills with a mixture of sorrow and hope when she says, "That you're the only thing worth hanging onto." She swallows. "And he won't let you go."

Clearing my thick throat, I lean back in the patio chair and push the words as far back into my brain as they will go. He has no right to step into my personal life now, no right to bombard my friends—my family—with his halfhearted attempts to get me back. I came here to be free of him, clear my mind, and focus on anything but him.

"Damn, it looks beautiful there, Jer."

Smiling back at my best friend and feeling grateful for the change in subject, I nod in acknowledgment as Portia compliments the stellar backdrop of rolling hills and the lake behind me.

"It's peaceful. I can't complain, although I do miss you guys. How's Cory handling the extra responsibility at the shop?"

Pursing her lips and swiping hair out of her eyes, she tells me, "If he'd stop acting like a goddamn queen all the time, we might actually get more shit done. That new shipment of handmade Afghans came in, and when I tried to pair them with the furniture, he threw a hissy fit because the teal-colored afghan apparently didn't match that particular tan-colored couch." Her hands flail as she imitates him. "God fucking forbid it looked too, and I quote, 'beach house casual' when it was supposed to look 'modern chic.' Forget strangling his highness with his bowtie; I'm gonna blindfold the fairy fucker with it instead."

My tea spurts past my lips and dribbles down my chin. I can't hold back the laugh. "Oh my god, you two. I honestly don't know how anything gets done when you work together."

Raising a brow, she agrees. "I know, right? He can't be getting it on the regular if he's this uptight. I'd ask him what's up his ass lately, but I'm afraid the answer would be nothing. Poor Marcus; they must be blue—Agh!" she screeches, jolting forward on her stool.

"Sorry, Pixie. Didn't see you there," Cory says, scowling at her after purposely knocking her off her seat.

"Violence, Cory? Really? That's what we're resorting to?" she throws back.

I see him cross his arms over his chest on the small screen, the top of his head cut off from the Skype conversation. "First of all, beach house casual did not suit the look we have going in here. Second, although your threats of blindfolds are mildly kinky, my sex life is far more interesting." She opens her mouth, but he cuts her off. "And last, they're *never* blue."

Leaning closer, she hisses, "How in the hell are you so uptight all the time then? I bet my tits you don't get it on the regular!"

"So it's a small bet, then?" he deadpans.

Her jaw drops. "You gay bastard!"

He nods. "Back to the insults, Pixie. Truth hurts, doesn't it, Ms. Tiny Tits?"

"Okay, okay," I try to reason, earning a scowl from both. "I'm gonna leave you guys to it, alright? Don't kill each other before I get back."

They carry on their argument, throwing out a few "I love yous" before I sign off.

* * *

"I've missed you, Lass."

His voice in my ear waking me from sleep doesn't startle me.

It warms me.

It's only been three weeks, but god how I've missed him. He doesn't show at my apartment above the shop often, but when he does it's always a short visit. He comes in when I'm asleep and leaves before the chance of someone walking in in the morning.

"Missed you too," I mumble, adding a moan when he takes my ear lobe into his mouth.

MIND LIES

"How much?" he rasps, licking and kissing his way down my throat, pulling the strap of my nightie down my shoulder as he continues his journey.

"Enough to wish you'd stay," I tell him, not expecting an answer.

"A few hours, Lass. Stay awake with me?" he asks as he pushes me onto my back, kissing his way down my chest, pushing the material up as he goes.

"Always," I whisper, sitting up a little so he can remove the offending garment that stands in the way. When his naked skin touches mine, I sigh, having missed the contact.

Having missed the presence of a man in my bed.

Not just any man, only him.

Locklin can be a slow lover and a fast one, but during these middle-of-the-night visits, he always starts slow, waking my body one delicious kiss at a time from the top of my head to the tips of my toes and back again.

"Are you ready for me, Jerri girl? he whispers against my lips, sucking the bottom one into his mouth as his hands move between my thighs.

"So ready," I let out on a moan, eager for him to fill me.

Eager for him to take me.

Make me his.

Only his.

My back arches off the bed when he works himself into me, painstakingly slow, but oh so beautifully. It's not just sex with Locklin, it's everything you've ever imagined when you think of two souls becoming one.

Wrapping his arms around my back, he holds onto my shoulders to keep me in place while he thrusts into my body, pushing harder each time in hopes he can get closer.

Deeper.

My fingernails dig into his back when he pushes me over the edge. Free falling into an abyss where only he can take me.

It's a place where I can't move, nor speak, as bright lights flash behind my eyelids, as my body begins to feel weightless.

Free.

But we're not free, because we're still hiding.

Our souls entwined, our bodies worlds apart.

MIND LIES

"I love you," I whisper, nodding off despite my promise to stay awake. I'm sure I hear him whisper back, "My water, Jerri girl," but my sated mind doesn't question it.

My body doesn't move to keep him close, and my lips don't open to ask him to stay.

I know he watches me, like he always does until I fall into slumber, and the only reason I know he's gone is when I hear his motorcycle rumble down the street in the wee hours of the morning.

CHAPTER TWENTY-SEVEN

"It's been two weeks, and I'm sure now's as good a time as any," I tell Paddy, convincing him to call Locklin. He's gone back and forth, and naturally we wanted to wait a bit to see if he showed up here. It isn't common, but it wouldn't exactly be uncommon either.

Locklin would normally call to make sure Paddy and Nessa were home before a visit, but given the circumstances, it wouldn't be unlikely for him to seek out his family when he's feeling lost.

"He has yet to tell you the truth about everything, Paddy. I highly doubt he'd show up here and lie to your face."

Thankfully, Paddy picks up the phone. I think he's hurt that Locklin has yet to call to tell him about the accident, about what happened to me. I also think it hurts him to have to confront him about it.

I assured him we needed answers, and Locklin was the only one who had them.

"Still a brick short of a full load," Paddy snarls down the line, his mood gone from thoughtful to pissed off in two seconds flat.
"What's up your ass?" Locklin shoot's back.

MIND LIES

"It ain't what's up me arse that you should be concerned about. You should be more concerned with me stickin' my foot up yours!" Paddy shouts back.

Silence.

"You speak with Jerri?" Locklin solemnly asks to which Paddy continues his tirade.

"You're goddamn right I spoke to 'er! Never pegged ya as a lyin' thief."

Locklin growls back, "I had a plan!"

"Plans to break the poor Lass's heart! Well fair fucks to ya too, Lad. And lyin' to me? Ye called three months ago and said my girl was fine!"

"I didn't lie; she was fine. And I wasn't ready to tell you what was going on. Listen, Paddy—"

"No. You listen to me! I want to know what ye been hidin'. I've supported ya yer whole life, Boy. But you be on my ships, usin' my resources, and it's me who has been hidin' yer trips back and forth. Now you tell me what in the hell is goin' on and why ye been keepin' it yourself?"

"Yakov found me," Locklin says so quietly you would think he whispered it.

"Come again?" Paddy asks, face nearly white as a sheet.

"I was at the shipping port in Hamburg. Four containers had been shipped from Russia and had entered ports as they travelled south, but nobody had found the women yet." He sighs. "It was like a shell game, trying to track the containers. Anyway, the next stop was Hamburg, so that's where Lee and I went. We waited almost two fucking days before we saw anything."

I wait on eggshells. Locklin has been after Yakov since before me.

After Siobhan.

His status as informant gives him a little pull in some places, and a lot more in others. When he met with G2, the intelligence service of Ireland, after what happened to Siobhan, he was originally met with a long line of red tape.

After years of pulling his weight, using Paddy's ships and his business as a foot in the door to make friends and contacts at different ports across the Eastern Seaboard, Locklin realized the Russians weren't just running women, but guns too. The tape began to shorten.

Locklin has not only helped pinpoint meeting locations and drop points but has also put his own ass on the line to rescue innocent women, regardless of his own fate. I'm sure it was admirable—heroic even—in the eyes of G2, and that allowed Locklin to spread his wings a little further, gaining more access at the ports and more backup when he needed it.

Irish intelligence didn't have the manpower to folly around from one port to the next chasing a ghost. Having Locklin offer to do the legwork while on Paddy's shipping runs was a blessing. And I was always able to sleep a little easier at night knowing that Lee, his contact at G2, was never far behind him.

"It was a setup." Locklin's voice cuts through my musing, and goosebumps break out on my skin. "Twelve years, Paddy. Twelve years of me doing business in shipping, and I made a mistake."

I sit across the table from Paddy with my hands over my mouth, waiting with baited breath.

"Tell me, Boy," Paddy grumbles.

"A truck came in late that night, dropped off a container, and loaded another. Lee followed the container on the truck while I stuck to the one that had been dropped off at the ship. Two fuckers stood guard near the thing. I figured they were waiting for the lift to hoist it on the ship, as usual. I took my chance and knocked one of them out while fighting the other, 'til the big Russian prick kicked me in the ribs, winding me."

"Jesus, Locklin. What happened to your ribs?"
"Nothing for you to worry about, Lass."

"Don't fucking 'Lass' me this time, Lock. They're broken, and black! You can hardly breathe!"

"I wasn't out long, maybe two minutes. But when I woke up, they were gone. They got a few more hits in while I was out and then left me there."

"They dinnae just leave ya there," Paddy says.

"I know. Thought it was fucked when it happened. Spoke to Lee about it, and we figured they didn't wanna attract more attention to themselves at the docks. It wasn't busy that night, but it wasn't quiet either. They're known for shooting people, or beating them to death. A shot would have been heard, and if they were on a timeline with a container full of women, they didn't have the spare minutes to beat me to death."

A shot would have been heard.

Didn't have time to beat me to death.

This is the severity of what Locklin does. He doesn't get paid for it; he didn't spend his youth dreaming to fight off murderers, pedophiles, and rapists. He wasn't trained to kill people.

But he still keeps going.

"That was a week before Jerri's accident," Locklin heatedly tells us, and I try my hardest to hold in the whimper wanting to escape.

MIND LIES

"What happened? How did they know you were 'ere?" Paddy's accent is thick, his emotions affecting his speech.

"I didn't get it. I really fuckin' didn't, Paddy. Thought I had a tail when I went to meet with Bryan one day, but he ended up getting called out so that meeting didn't happen. I got in touch with Jerri on the burner we use; it'd been a month since I'd seen her last. I shacked up at one of the motels in Brockton and met her at the coffee shop the next morning. We spent the day together. She then came back to the motel with me but didn't stay the night." He trails off—and I know why.

I remember the fight we had that night, the first night I had ever refused to spend the entirety of it with him.

"I need to bag off for a while, Jerri. Short visit again this time, Lass. Then I need you to promise not to contact me. You need anything, you call Bryan. He'll help you."

Between the broken ribs, bruise on his jaw, and his aloof behavior after we just made love, I know something is wrong. And for the hundredth time, I'm so sick and tired of being left in the fucking dark.

Why can't he trust me enough to tell me? He thinks I won't worry about him as much, but it makes it worse. Not knowing where he's going, or how to get in touch with him, makes it so much worse.

And it hurts.

Not just because it's insulting, because it's one more roadblock between us.

"The same fucking car I thought was tailing me the day before was parked outside. If I were smarter . . . fuck." He sighs heavily. "If I were smarter, I would have known, but I didn't fucking think. All I could think about was getting Jerri the fuck out of there before whoever was in that car came through the door. So I started a fight with her."

I gulp, half grateful he didn't mean the awful things he said that night.

"I started a fight because I knew she was stubborn enough, that she'd refuse to spend the night with me afterwards. And I was right—she left. She fuckin' left, Paddy, and I didn't follow her because the car stayed right where it was fucking supposed to. What I didn't think about was that the goddamn brake lines on her car were cut before she even pulled out of the parking lot."

I gasp. The sound was loud, unfortunately loud enough that the phone resting between Paddy and me on the table catches the sound.

"Jerri?" Locklin surprisingly asks, shocked. "I know it's you, Lass. Paddy doesn't talk with me about all this shit in front of Nessa. *Answer me*," he rasps.

Ignoring the tingling in my throat, I rasp, "Finish the story."

"Jerri, I don't—"

"Finish the damn story, Locklin."

A deep sigh is followed by, "I left my bike in the parking lot and left out the back door on foot. I hadn't made it a block before seeing the car pulling out. It kept distance but stayed on my tail. I hit a twenty-four-hour diner and made a call to Bryan. I ordered a coffee and watched the car park amongst the trucks in the side lot. When Bryan showed up, I met him in the bathroom and confirmed what I already fuckin' knew: They didn't find me 'cause they were smart. They found me because they put a tracker in my phone when that Russian prick broke my ribs."

"Jesus," Paddy mumbles.

"They didn't want to kill me. They wanted the bigger fish and to find out who has been intercepting their shipments. Good news was it didn't monitor calls, just location. No doubt they assumed I was part of the muscle tryin' to take down the trafficking ring. Track my phone, find the bigger fish. I got Bryan to check on Jerri, and when he told me she was in a coma," he pauses, as though he were speaking of my death. "When he told me, I got back on the ship and headed back there to have a meeting with Lee and some other members of G2.

"The fuck of it was when I got back, Patrick at the dock in Belfast says he got a call from Hans at the dock in Germany. Hans told him he was having a smoke with some of the dock workers, going on about how it's hard to find good dock hands anymore. Some prick named Ivan then starts talking about a guy named Locklin, says he ran into him a few times and talked to him about getting on a different boat. Couldn't remember Locklin's last name though. He wondered if anyone could help him out."

"Son of a bitch," I whisper, my stomach dropping and my danger-free bubble feeling as though it were about to burst.

"They won't find you, Lass," Locklin reassures me.

Shaking my head, I ask, "How can you say that? They found you, Locklin. They cut the fucking brake lines on my car. How can you think that they won't find us? And why do you think it was safer for you to not tell me all this? Huh?

"What do you think would have happened if one of them came to visit me while I had amnesia? I had no idea who was out to hurt me, or that they were Russian. Christ, Locklin, you could have gotten me killed by withholding that information!"

"Dammit, I had eyes on you, Jerri! I would never leave you unprotected. I put that app on Bryan's phone so he would know each and every time you left the apartment, and when you did, he was on your tail. If it weren't him, it was a private detective he has used in the past. I *never* left you unprotected."

I sniff. "No, you just left me altogether," I murmur.

"I didn't hear you, Lass?"

Paddy gives me a sympathetic look, having heard me, and asks, "What do we do now?"

"You two do nothing. Lee and his men have a few leads, and as far as we're concerned, the Russians left Boston. There has been no sign of them in months."

Paddy sighs. "I dinnae like this, Lad."

"Neither do I, old man. They don't know about you, so the only thing I'm asking is that you keep Jerri safe," Locklin replies.

I scoff. "You thought *you* were safe, Locklin. Look how well that turned out. I don't for one second think you'd put us in danger, but for Christ's sake, open your eyes! You want to keep chasing ghosts, that's fine. But when it hits this close to home . . ." I trail off, afraid to finish.

Paddy finished for me. "You need tae think 'bout what's more important, Boy. Chasin' a ghost, or livin' with a few shadows."

The chair legs scrape across the floor as I push away from the table.

"Jerri?"

Shaking my head, I ignore Paddy, heatedly staring at the phone, and answer, "There's nothing left to say."

I ignore his outburst and continue walking until I hit the lake.

CHAPTER TWENTY-EIGHT

LOCKLIN

"Don't be scared. We'll be in and out," Siobhan giggles as she leads me through the fence to the shipping yard, practically dragging me behind her.

Like a fool, I follow.

I always follow.

Since my horny, sixteen-year-old self got hold of her two years ago, I've been following her everywhere.

And once I got my dick wet, there was no turning back.

Her father would fuckin' kill me if he knew what happens when we're out at night. We may be eighteen, but that doesn't change the fact that he'd cut my balls off and feed them to me for dinner.

"Siobhan, slow down!" I hiss at her. I know the docks like the back of my hand, ever since my dad took off and I started staying with his cousin, Paddy. I've spent nearly every minute down here.
I love the docks.

The water, the hard work that Siobhan says makes my body lickable, and the men I get to meet from all over the world makes it interesting. My dad's a piece of shit. He never taught me anything other than how to lie your way out of a shitty situation . . . and the best places to gamble. He made his life on bets. However, I'm grateful that ever since I turned ten, I've been making mine out of honest work.

Paddy has been more of a father to me than my own.

"Well then hurry up!" Siobhan's voice cuts through my musing as we weave through containers on the way to the docks. Why she wanted to sneak in here, I have no clue. Her dad works for a trucking company that frequents the docks, and if it weren't for her tailing along with him one day, we never would have met.

Now we're inseparable, and even though she seems to get us into shit wherever we go, I can't help but follow. She's my first girlfriend, my first love, regardless of the fact she's fucking crazy.

Last week she wanted to try acid, just to see what all the hype was about. I didn't join her, but after that experience, I hope to hell she never wants to do it again.

The week before, she'd jumped off the Clover Street Bridge, just to say she'd done it.

I didn't join her then either.

MIND LIES

She has lived a sheltered life, but as soon as she hit eighteen, she became more brazen, sneaking out in the middle of the night so she could hang with some of the East Street Gang to score drugs. Just so she could say she tried them.

The list goes on.

I hoped that since it was just the two of us tonight she wouldn't be dragging us toward trouble. Paddy told me she's a spark waiting to hit a pile of gasoline.

I told him I didn't care because I loved her.

He told me to be careful. He would never stand in the way of me making my own mistakes.

I never saw Siobhan as a mistake. But lately, these past few months, I have been seeing her as a liability, as someone standing between me and a jail cell, or death. And instead of pushing me away from either, she's pulling me toward them.

"Here!" she tells me, and I look up to see some of the East Street crew along with a few girls she went to school with.

"What the fuck, Sio? I thought it was just us tonight?"

She gives me those big brown eyes, batting her eyelashes at me. "Lock, why aren't you any fun? You used to be fun, but now all you want to do is couple stuff. Why can't we hang out with them?" she pouts.

I cave for a moment, and remain silent. I like couple stuff because it keeps her out of trouble. I like taking one of Paddy's boats out, just the two of us, because I know it's safe and I won't have to worry about what trouble she wants to get into.

I also like fucking her, which I can't do in a group of people.

But I don't tell her any of that. She wouldn't care anyway. Lately, all she cares about is the East Street crew and those rail-thin twins she has been hanging around who snort coke all day long.

She likes coke too.

I'm not a pussy—I've tried it.

But I didn't need to keep doing it. Not because the shit's expensive, but because I'd rather be spending my time with her.

Shaking my head, I tell her, "Sio, you want us to hang out with other people. That's fine. But do we really have to do this every night? Get high, hang out with a bunch of people we don't give a shit about, and sleep all fucking day? I have to work tomorrow, Sio."

She scowls at me. "I thought you loved me, Locklin?"

MIND LIES

I sigh. She always does this.

"I do love you, Sio. More than anybody."

She melts a little in my arms before kissing me.

"One hour. Then we'll leave. Okay?" she promises.

Reluctantly, I nod, knowing it won't be an hour.

It will be four.

I swallow back the words I really want to say and follow her.

* * *

I wake with a start, scrubbing my hands over my face and shaking off the nightmares of my past.

Siobhan.

I remember that night, much like all the others. If I had known it would only take two more weeks for Siobhan to become hooked on more than just blow, I would have grabbed her hand and dragged her out of there.

In my mind, I think that would have helped. But deep down I know I'm wrong because Siobhan did what Siobhan wanted. And there wasn't a man on this earth who could have told her otherwise.

If she had the choice to run away with the carnival as a child, I'm sure she would have. She was a free spirit, but a dangerous one. She jumped in with both feet, regardless of the fire.

And that's what scared the fuck out of me.

That she wasn't scared at all.

She had no regard for her own life or those around her. She'd been sheltered for so long her only choice when the cage opened was to rebel, to run and fly and stretch her wings as far as they would take her, no matter how strong the wind.

At first I found it inspiring.

But then I learned it was ignorance.

I tried. Fuck, did I try. But she never listened.

It only took those two weeks before I never saw her again, before the drugs became more important, and the only people she wanted to hang out with were those who could supply her with more. I'd blame the gang, or even the twins who marched alongside her; but, the truth is, I know the only person responsible was herself.

And if she weren't so careless, so clueless, she wouldn't have been wandering around the docks, higher than a goddamn kite by herself late at night.

MIND LIES

When her father called Paddy to tell him she hadn't been home in two days, Paddy cursed me out. I would never do anything to disrespect Paddy; he'd done more for me than anyone else in my life. That being said, I told him everything.

Then we went to look for her.

And I haven't been the same since.

Finding her on the dock that night broke something in me. It broke the part of youth that remains innocent—it also broke my faith in love.

Was I not enough for her?

If I was, would she have sought the reckless path she took?

Paddy always assured me there was no saving something so wild. She was like a lion held in captivity being let loose in the wilderness. There was no taming her.

Like a spark, only she wanted to be bigger. She didn't stop until she found a flame.

The flame was the drugs.

She burned so fucking bright you would think she would take down everything in her path. Ultimately, she just took down herself, to the lowest pit of hell, when she got strung out, when she stumbled upon

Yakov's crew while wandering the docks late one night.

That's when flying free got her killed.

I don't know if Siobhan tried to free the women she found in a container that was ready to be shipped off to god knows where. All I know is she'd been beaten so badly when Paddy and I found her that she was waiting for death.

She plead for me to save the girls. And then all she kept mumbling as she began to die was that name. Yakov. I promised her I would save the girls, even though I wasn't entirely sure what that promise was at the time. Who knew women were being trafficked into the very port I practically grew up in?

I sure as hell didn't, and neither did Paddy.

So I made the promise, and I've been nearly killing myself every day since.

I couldn't save Siobhan. But maybe, just maybe, I could save someone else.

But I'm getting tired.

I've spent the better part of my adult life chasing a ghost.
I know that now.

From the day Siobhan was killed to today, I've done

nothing but try to bring Yakov's crew to justice.

But it didn't end there. No, it never fucking does.

Yakov is just one man, with one crew of sick and twisted motherfuckers who get off on trafficking women. Yakov is also just one fish in a big pond. I've worked hard trying to get information—to interfere—on the skin trade while keeping up an appearance by working for Paddy.

Long story short, I've helped put a lot of people in jail.

I've even seen a few killed.

Most importantly, I've saved a lot of innocent women from Siobhan's fate.

But not them all.

And that's part of what keeps me doing what I do.

But not all of it. No. The last of it is that I'm a fucking coward. Jerri was the first woman who I enjoyed fucking for more than one night, and when I found her in the hands of Vasily all those years ago, my worst fucking fear came back to haunt me:

Losing someone else.
So, gone was the attentive Locklin she'd come to know. If I kept my distance, kept doing what I do, I told myself it wouldn't hurt so badly if I did, in fact, lose

her.

I'm a fucking idiot.

I know I'm lying to myself, but I've refused to believe it. Jerri is strong, resilient even. No matter what shit I put her through, she always bounces back.

And I've taken advantage of that.

For twelve fucking years.

I know what I've been doing is wrong, how I've treated her. I know I need to change, but that's an easier thing to say than do. How do I quit what I've been doing and break a promise to Siobhan?

Better yet, how do I get the woman who means the most to me—the woman who carries my child—to believe I'm worth it?

I wasn't worth enough to Siobhan, and as much as I feel like a damn pussy for saying it, I wonder if I won't be enough for Jerri either.

If I give her everything . . . what if it's still not enough?

What if, after all the sacrifices I'd have to make to be with her, she would decide it isn't worth it?
Would decide I'm not worth it?

I'm a proud man, and that's the hardest fucking pill

MIND LIES

to swallow.

Mostly, because I fear it's the truth.

CHAPTER TWENTY-NINE

"God I love your cooking," I mumble around my spoon as I take the last bite of stew from my bowl. Nessa's practically preening, not only because of the compliment but also because she's grateful she has more than two mouths to feed.

Nessa and Paddy were never fortunate enough to have their own children, which is probably why they did so well with Locklin when he came to live with them at ten years old. They truly wanted kids, so when they were given the chance, they spared no love or expense in giving him everything they could.

It breaks Nessa's heart now to know what Locklin does day in, day out; not because she isn't proud of him, but because she worries that one day the phone calls will stop.

Because she worries that one day he might not come home anymore.

Along with that worry comes a woman eager to resume her motherly role. In my case, it's the small things, such as the stew she just fed me for dinner; and the large things, such as how often she spends on the internet searching for healthy meals to help the baby grow, or how she's bought a crib and change table, and all the clothes currently occupying the closet in the nursery she's made.

I never had a plan, really, when I came here three weeks ago, but staying until the baby was born was only a thought at the time. Nessa would have me here forever if it were her choice, and I love her even more for that. But the bottom line is I still haven't figured out exactly what I want, or need, to do. When I do think about it, my head spins.

I miss Portia like crazy, but our near-daily Skype conversations help curb that. When I was in Boston, I didn't get that luxury with Paddy and Nessa. I didn't get to stay in touch as often because I never wanted anyone to know about them.

When I look back now, I think it probably would have been okay to make more contact with them. But as the years wore on, it became the norm to stay somewhat out of touch.

Besides, how do you suddenly explain your family in Ireland to your friends in Boston without telling them the whole story?

On top of that, Locklin has been paranoid about my safety since we first got together. Hiding and lying about my past has become as normal as making a cup of coffee. After one year turned into two, and two into three, I knew nothing else.

All I knew was I couldn't go back to Ireland. I

couldn't let myself be that much closer to Yakov's crew, again, and worry about leading them to Paddy and Nessa.

After that awful night in the warehouse, it was a given. It isn't as if they couldn't figure out who I was. They'd seen me before, knew where I worked.

And later, as Locklin's friend Lee informed him, they knew where I lived.

My flat had been ransacked.

I had left my purse behind at work one day. Identification inside.

No brainer, really. I had to hide.

When Locklin called Lee to tell him what had happened to me, he basically said I had no other choice but to hide. G2 wasn't going to stick me in some sort of witness protection program to testify about what I saw that night in order to help hang Vasily, because *he* would never rat on Yakov.

If he did, he signed his own death certificate.

As Locklin once said, "Any smart man knows that jail is a little girl's tea party compared to being in the hands of Yakov."

So we were on our own.
And six months later, I was settled back in the States

under the protection of Bryan O'Shaunessey with a new last name a social security number.

That was over ten years ago.

Thankfully, I never had to call Bryan for help, but when I look back, it makes me miss all the time I could have shared with Paddy and Nessa. It didn't take long, but they wormed their way into my heart in the six months I stayed with them.

We visited a handful of times. Once when Portia went on vacation with Cooper, Locklin and I came back to Ireland for two weeks to spend time with the lovely couple. It was never enough though; it always hurt to leave.

Now that I'm back, I feel a mixture of peace and a mild fear.

I fear that I'm that much closer to the Russians, but I'm at peace because I feel home.

And that's tough. It's hard being torn between two places.

I have no desire to return to the docks unless I'm getting on a boat to go somewhere, and I'm certain that I'm safe hidden at the little cabin. But I suppose my feelings might change when the cabin fever sets in, when I realise I have nobody in this country other than Paddy and Nessa.

I also don't have a purpose, such as I had with the

shop.

I've spent days online purchasing and finding new treasures to ship to the shop. I've also been doing payroll and other clerical work from here since I have the time. It helps, gives me something to do in the day since Nessa insists on feeding me. And aside from tidying up after myself, there really isn't a whole lot to do.

There's a small barn with a few horses on the side of the hill. I venture there every morning to visit them, give them a good brushing. But that too only takes up a little of my time.

"Ye won't be havin' time when the babe gets here, Jerrilyn. Enjoy it!" Nessa had told me.

I take her word for it and help out where she lets me. She's a pushy older woman who works from sunup to sundown looking after those under her roof, but she wouldn't have it any other way.

"Thanks, Ness," I tell her as I place my bowl in the dishwasher. "I'm going to head back for the night. I'll see you in the morning."

Grabbing my shoulders, she places a kiss on my cheek. "Get some rest, dear girl."

Swinging by the lounge, I give Paddy a tap on the back as I pass by and say, "Until the morning, Ol' Man."

He sighs and nods his head.

"Paddy?" I ask, confused since he's normally more vocal. Normally, he has some smart-ass comment to fling back at me.

"Aye, Lass. 'Til the mornin'," he grumbles.

"Everything alright? Did Locklin call?"

He shakes his head. "Nothin' for ye to worry about."

I don't believe that at all, but he seems contemplative so I leave him be and begin the mile-long trek to the cottage.

There are pathways all over the landscape, and I follow the one heading toward the water as I begin the walk home. Paddy often offers to drive me; he even left one of his old trucks at the cabin for me to use to get back and forth. But this bucolic walk is not a burden.

It's a blessing.

After my fifth refusal, he stopped bugging me. But he made me promise to call or text Nessa when I arrive.

* * *

LOCKLIN
I watch her from the covered porch as she makes her

way along the lake.

Jerri girl.

It has been almost a month since I called her last, since I heard her soulful voice.

God, she's beautiful.

It has been almost six months since I've held her, made love to her.

Tasted her.

I've been a stupid son of a bitch for letting something so perfect slip through my fingers, but I vowed that day in the hospital bed that I would never fuck this up again.

I would never hurt her again as I have in the past.

I would never, not for the rest of my life, take for granted how important she is.

One could argue that she's been weak in the past for choosing to stay with me, a man who has nothing to offer but incredible fucking and the occasional meal. The fucking part has always taken precedence over food, so I can't even say that I eat with her often.

Unless I'm eating her.

Our trips to the coffee shop were as close as we'd

gotten to sharing a meal because it was the busiest time of the year for me: fall through spring. Human trafficking slows down in the summer months because nobody wants to worry about their merchandise cooking in a container on its way to the port.

It's the end of November now, a busy time for business. But for once I don't feel the guilt setting in. I don't feel that weight I normally have on my shoulders of not working twenty hours a day, hell bent on saving every defenseless woman I cross paths with.

Jerri continues her walk toward the cabin at a slow pace.

She always loved it here, and you can tell by the way she takes her time, by the way she stops occasionally to take in her surroundings, to absorb the beauty of the landscape. I simply absorb *her*.

The way her hands rest protectively on her stomach, which has grown with our child. She'd be five or six months pregnant now, and my God, how it suits her. The emerald-green tunic she has on is molded tightly to her perfectly round stomach. Her hair has grown a few inches, and her skin is paler from the lack of sunshine.

But she *glows*.
Not wanting to scare her from where I stand in the shadows, I walk out toward the light and wait until her hand is firmly gripped on the railing before speaking to her. There's an odd sensation in my throat, as though there were a golf ball lodged in an awkward place.

Swallowing past the offending lump, I manage to rasp, "You look beautiful, Lass."

Her head whips toward me, face whitening like a ghost. Her fingers dig so hard into the railing I'm surprised I haven't heard it splinter.

She heaves in a breath, and like the true bastard I am, I watch her tits. They are much larger than they used to be, having moved up her chest. Her neck flushes pink, and when I follow her flawless skin, I see the color matches her cheeks.

She's fucking stunning.

There's a fire in her eyes, a fire that I missed when she tore me a new asshole and gutted me at the hospital. The fire I've admired and envied, and I'm glad she has it back. It's better news for me because if my Lass has some fight left in her, it means I still have a chance.

It means I haven't completely fucked everything up.

"Why did you come here, Locklin?" she whispers, eyes still blazing, face contorted in agony as though it physically hurts her to speak to me.

My fingers twitch with the urge to touch her, so I ball them into fists at my side before I do something stupid like grab her and kiss her fucking senseless.

"For you, Lass. I came here for you."

She sighs in frustration, closing her eyes to gather herself before opening them with new resolve. Gripping the railing tighter, she ascends the steps and says, "Then you've wasted your time. If and when you come here, it should be for your family, not for me. Go and see them. Ness misses you."

Shaking my head, I follow her up the steps and tell her, "I did come to see my family, Lass."

She huffs. "Then why aren't you with them?"

"I am, Jerri girl. My family's right in front of me."

Pausing with her hand on the door, she looks over her shoulder with the same expression on her face I probably had when she left me with nothing but an ultrasound picture.

"You can't come here and expect to win me back with words, Locklin." Shaking her head sadly, she adds, "You can't win me back at all."

Ignoring the burn in my chest, I grab on to my fiery Irish temper. "You're wrong, Lass. I'm here to prove it to you."

She laughs humorlessly. "What are you going to do, Lock? Beat down my defenses, make me love you again? And then when you have me right where you want me, hop on your motorcycle in the middle of the night and take off?" She scoffs. "I'm not signing up for that life agai—"

I cut her off, choosing not to acknowledge the "make me love you again" comment that implies she doesn't love me anymore, and tell her, "I quit, Jerrilyn." When she stops her tirade and turns to face me, I continue. "I met with Lee when I got off the phone with you last and told him I was done."

Walking into the pub, I spot Lee at our regular table. It's not an inconspicuous place to meet, but two men sharing a pint in a pub is as common as it gets around here.

Taking a seat across from him, I rub my hands over my tired face. I've been awake for nearly thirty-six hours. Ever since I told Jerri and Paddy what happened, I haven't been able to sleep.

I wish I were haunted by what Yakov would do to me if he found me again, or haunted by the memories of the shit I've seen over the years—the women and children. But that's not what keeps me awake at night.

For once, it's something entirely different.

I can't sleep because I'm haunted by the fact that my Lass may not want me anymore. I'm haunted because she may look for the man who will rub her back, make her breakfast in bed, and be her plus-one at a fucking dinner party.

And thinking of her with another man while she's carrying my child eats at me. It pains and angers me enough to keep me awake at night.

MIND LIES

"I know what yer here to say," Lee says, pulling me from my thoughts to the man in front of me.

Lee's become a friend. Well, as much of a friend as someone can be when in this line of work. If we meet for a drink, the talking is limited, but the comfortable silence is supportive. Lee's a good man. A hard worker. If he says something, he means it, and if he doesn't speak, it's because there isn't anything important to say.

I don't know all the details to Lee's demons, as he knows mine. Of course, I had to share my story about Siobhan when I was asking around for help, but Lee is not so forthcoming.

Not that I blame him. If I never had to talk about Siobhan's death again, it would be too soon. All I know is there's a void in his eyes that speaks to me. Or maybe it speaks to the eighteen-year-old me who found his girlfriend beaten to death.

Either way, I've been a lucky bastard to have him as my contact with G2. Even luckier is the fact that he's boots to the ground when I need him. When I started this, I was strictly a gatherer. With my contacts at many of the ports, I could get insider info that G2 didn't have. But that information grew to be too big for just one person. Once Lee and I rescued Jerri, it lit a new fire in me—a fire that wanted to do more than just sit around and get information.

A fire that led me to the shooting range more often.

And when I wasn't at the range, I was at the gym sparring with Lee, or some other unlucky bastard at the receiving end of my wrath.

That fire turned into anger and bitterness, but I held onto it because that kept me focused.

Focused not on the woman who was nearly taken from me. Focused on the mission.

My promise to Siobhan.

"What do ya think I'm here to say?" I ask.

The linebacker-sized agent runs a hand over his buzz cut before settling his vacant eyes on my own. "That it's over for ya, and I need to find a new partner."

Partner.

That's the thing about Lee. He respects me. Never saw me or simply used me as a means to an end, a middle man to gather puzzle pieces while he put them together.

No.
He treated me as an equal.

I can't say it's been the same for some of the other agents I've met. Some are so uptight that you would want to pry the stick out of their asses and beat some fucking sense into them with it.
Nodding, I ask, "How'd you know?"

He smirks, but there's no mirth or humor in his eyes. "I've seen her, Lock. I ain't fuckin' blind."

I smirk back. "Aye. Carryin' a babe looks good on her."

Lee goes to have a drink of his beer but pauses and then sets it back down. "She's pregnant?"

I nod, half-confused because I thought his comment was regarding the pregnancy. But obviously the prick was just commenting on her looks. I don't blame him; Jerri's stunning. But that doesn't mean I want every other bastard to think so.

"How far along?" he asks.

"About five months with my son." Fuck it feels good and scary to say that.

My son.

"Why the fuck ya still sittin' here, Locklin?" He shakes his head in frustration. "Thought you were a dumb shit when ya kept workin' with me after that night we rescued Jerri. Kept askin' myself, 'What man in his right fuckin' mind has a good woman to go home to and chooses to do this?'"

Shaking his head, he looks out around the bar and gathers his next words before settling his eyes back on me. "Now you got a son on the way, but for the past five months you been runnin' in the shadows at night with me instead of bein' with yer fuckin' family?"

Slamming my beer down on the table, I say, "I finish what I start, Lee. We had a job to do, and that job isn't finished because Yakov is still out there. I don't care if we've taken down at least a dozen of his men over the years. It won't stop for me until we get him."

"You're a fuckin' idiot, Lock." He spits at me in frustration. "This ain't about Yakov anymore. This is about your promise to a fuckin' ghost." Leaning closer, he adds, "Ghosts can't warm your bed at night, Lock. And they sure as fuck can't give you family. You got both of those waitin' for you. You had one waitin' on you for a decade, and yet you sit here with my sorry ass?"

I feel like a fuck, and he looks as if I kicked his dog. No longer held back by boundaries, I ask, "What the fuck put you here, Lee? Why's it not okay for me to chase a ghost, but you can?"

Chugging a healthy portion of his beer, he looks off, lost in thought, and says, "Had a family once, Lock. I'd drop this job in a heartbeat for more time with them. But they aren't here, and I've got nothin' left to lose. But you? You got somethin' worth waking up for every day, and she's a hell of a lot warmer than that ghost you're chasin'."

Lee was right.

"I hooked Lee up with Patrick at the dock in Belfast.

He's going to bring in another agent to work on bringing down Yakov. It's too risky for me anyway since I was followed. But I'm done, Jerri."

I can practically see the wheels turning in her head. I've said the words she's waited so long to hear, for a decade. I thought it would be harder, but Lee was right. I belonged here all along. It only took me twelve years, a bullet, and a good tongue-lashing from my fiery Lass.

When she starts nodding her head, I know I've got her. I know I've done something to make her happy. Licking her lips, she starts to speak, and I do all I can to focus on her eyes and not her mouth. "That's good, Locklin. I'm sure it was a tough decision to make—"

"Easiest decision of my life, Lass."

Giving me a small smile, she tells me. "You deserve freedom, Locklin. You deserve your own life. I'm happy for you, truly I am." She shakes her head. "But don't mistake my happiness for forgiveness."

She's fucking killing me.
Rubbing my chest, I watch as she walks into the house. "Go see Paddy and Ness before they go to bed."

I grumble, "Already seen Paddy."

CHAPTER THIRTY

Of course he's been to see Paddy. And that's why Paddy was somber after dinner, the slippery old bastard. He knew how I would react. He also knew I wouldn't want to see him.

So why did Paddy let him come here?

Any other day, Paddy would have told him to take his lyin' arse elsewhere, so long as elsewhere wasn't anywhere near me.

I watch as Lock rubs his chest, either feeling pain from the bullet or something else. I don't know.

"Go home, Locklin."

He looks to the house and then to me. "Paddy won't let me in the house."

I raise a brow at him. He adds, "Told me not to ask Nessa either. Said I'm not allowed to sleep there until I pull my head out of my arse."

"Why didn't you tell him you quit?"

Crossing his arms over his chest, he says, "I did. That's not why he thinks my head's up my arse."

I frown, "So go stay at your flat in town."

He shakes his head. "Got rid of the flat ten years ago, Lass."

"I thought you kept it. I know you didn't stay *here* all those times you came back."

"I stayed on the boat. If I had any free time, I wasn't gonna waste it in an empty flat when on the other side of the pond was a flat with my woman in it."

God help me.

"I'm not your woman anymore, and I don't want you to stay here, Locklin. If that's the case, I may as well head back to Boston."

Reaching around me, he opens the door and gestures into the cabin. "I thought you might say that, so I'll remind you that going into early labor on a ship with no real medical team could be a disaster. What if something went wrong and you were still days from reaching land?"

He has a point, but I don't tell him that.

"And you haven't used your original passport since you arrived in Ireland twelve years ago. It's possible Yakov is no longer looking for you, but he wouldn't forget you either. I also know nobody has crossed him or witnessed his crimes and lived to tell about it. If we're smart, we'll assume using your passport will raise a red flag and alert him to where you are."

"If I stay, it doesn't change the fact that I don't want you here," I tell him, rubbing my lower back. Between the walk and standing here having a conversation I never wanted to start in the first place, it's aching.

His eyes soften, ever the astute one when it comes to the needs of a woman's body.

Just not her heart.

"You need to rest, Lass."

Pointing to the door, I tell him, "And you need to leave."

He shakes his head. "Never. I'm never leaving again, Jerri."

Too tired to argue, too tired to continue a conversation that won't quit unless he wants it to, I wave over my shoulder as I head to the bedroom. "You want to stay where you're not wanted, Locklin, that's fine." Pausing when I reach the doorway, I look over my shoulder at his solid frame, which dwarfs this little abode. "But I haven't forgiven you. Go see Ness; she'll be more charitable."

I don't wait for his reply. I simply shut the door to what was once my haven, my place of peace.
Peace went out the window the minute I found him on my porch.

Leaning my head against the door, I mumble, "What are you doing, Locklin? Why couldn't you have just stayed away?"

It would have been easier.

After washing my face, I change into my nightshirt and get into bed. Only when the house is quiet and the stars are brightest do I give into my tears.

* * *

I've been lying awake in bed, listening to the sound of pots and pans in the kitchen. Sometimes Nessa comes to cook me breakfast, but I have a feeling it's not her.

If Ness was here, she'd be talking to herself, or humming.

There's no humming.

Sleep didn't come easy last night, and I'm tired, more tired than usual. But apparently that's the norm when carrying a child.

They suck the life out of you.

There's no warning when the door to my bedroom opens, which lets me know it's definitely not Ness.

Locklin's body takes up the better part of the doorway. In one hand, he has a glass of orange juice. In the other, he has a small tray.

"Morning, Lass," he says, face brighter than yesterday, dressed for the day in a pair of jeans and a grey long-sleeved shirt.

Sitting up in the bed, I lean against the headboard. "What are you doing, Lock?"

He sets the orange juice down on the nightstand and places the tray on my lap. Swallowing thickly, I take in the plate of food.

Egg's Benny.

"I haven't quite mastered the poached egg part of this," he says, waving his hand toward the messy pile of eggs. "In fact, I watched a YouTube video on poached eggs three times, and I think it's a fucking joke because I did exactly what it said, and they look, well, like *that*."

Working hard to keep a straight face, I try not to laugh. "I'm sure they taste the same as pretty eggs."

He nods, thinking seriously about it. "You're probably right."

Clearing my throat, I ask, "Why aren't you with Nessa? I told you she wanted to see you."
He sighs and takes a seat in the chair by my window,

angling toward the bed. "I went to see her this morning." Running his hands through his thick hair, he adds, "She's not my biggest fan at the moment either, Lass."

I swallow past my bite of eggs. "I didn't tell them the truth because I wanted them to be angry with you, Locklin. That wasn't my intention at all."

Waving a hand, he cuts me off. "The only person people should be angry with is *me*. That's not your fault, Jerri. That's all on me."

Locklin has always been straight to the point, but this is more candid. He's open in a way I haven't seen before.

He lied to you.

My phone starts ringing, and I grab it from the night stand. "Could you . . ." I don't finish speaking because he's already getting out of his chair.

"Morning chat with Portia, I know." He pauses at the doorway and adds, "When you're finished, I'd like to talk. I'll be on the back porch."
Before he closes the door, I add, "I told you I didn't want you to stay here, Locklin."

He throws back, "And I told you I wasn't leaving."

Then he shuts the door.
"Shit," I mumble when I pick up the phone.

"What the hel—*lo* woman! How you doing today?" Portia asks.

"Cooper's around, and you almost cursed, didn't you?"

She whines, "I've been trying for over six months, Jer. It's impossible. If there's someone who can go a month without swearing, I wanna meet them and ask how they do it. I was on a good swear-free streak until last night in bed when I asked Cooper to F-word me, so I had to start all over again! And the kicker here: Coop loves dirty talk in bed, but he still told me that was a fail! So what am I supposed to say? Sex me harder, Coop? It doesn't sound near as good or as dirty. If we keep this up, I'm going to be talking the way Christine talks around her kids when she's all, *'He put the P in her V.'* I can't live like this, Jerri. Honestly, who doesn't swear?"

Finally, she pauses to take a breath. I answer, "Holy people? The clergy? Nuns?"

She scoffs. "They do so, my friend. You don't go around talking about *Hell* all day and not swear."

I form a reply, but she cuts me off. "Anyway, what had you cursing the S-word, you lucky B?"

I sigh. "Locklin's here."

She lets out a low whistle. "That didn't take long. I thought he had arrived there two days ago?"

Frowning, I ask, "How do you know when he was supposed to get here?"

"Because he told me," she simply replies.

"Did you not think it'd be a good idea to pass that information along? We talk nearly every day. How did you leave that shit unsaid? What the hell, P?"

She sighs in contentment. "First, tell me how good it felt to drop the S- and the H-bomb, and then I'll answer your question."

"It felt fucking fantastic. Now spill."

I swear she's having an orgasm when she mutters, "Gosh, I miss my F-bombs." Clearing her throat, she then dives in. "He showed up at the apartment a little over a week ago. After a few good curses with Cooper, he let him in."

I swallow. "Cooper let Locklin into your apartment?"

"I know. I was shocked to sh-shoshana, too. Quick save with shoshana, right? There's more where that came from. So yeah, he let him in, and get this . . ." She pauses for dramatic effect. "They shared a beer together, Jer. A *beer*!"

"You're kidding?"

"I'm not. You can't make this shellac up."

"I feel oddly betrayed by Cooper. But my pregnancy

hormones want to weep, P, because that's all I have wanted for the longest time. Only now, after I told him I was done, does he finally insert himself into my life, and my friend's lives. How messed up is that?"

"It is messed up, Babe. But I think he had good intentions."

"What's that supposed to mean?" I ask.

She sighs. "You know I'm a pretty neutral person, Jer."

I snort. "Neutral my ass. You can hold a grudge unlike anyone I know. The question is why is the grudge fading in this case?"

"I think he's really sorry, Jer. And I know you don't want to believe it—no wait—you want to pretend you don't, but I know you still love him. I know that because even if Cooper betrays me in the most awful of ways, I would still love him. You can't just turn that shiatzu off. That being said, I think maybe you might want to give him another chance."

"P, are you alright?"

"Ugh. F-fund it, I'm pregnant."

I nearly drop the phone. "What? When?"

"You better not ask how because I f-fundraising hate when people ask that."

"Good save again, P. And I knew there was something wrong. There was way too much sentimentality in that last spiel."

"I know. I feel like a weepy, old woman. I found out the night before Locklin came to the apartment. That might have been why I was so accommodating, considering I just found out I got my spawn-carrying card. When I think about it, it's probably why Cooper was so accommodating, too. I mean, he just found out he was gonna be a dad, Jer. Maybe they connected on some dad-to-be level, you know? I went to bed, and they were still talking."

Walking into the bathroom, I place the phone on the vanity as I go through my morning routine.

"I just don't understand why? Locklin doesn't ask for anyone's permission in anything. And ultimately he wouldn't give a shit what Cooper thought. So why talk to him?"

"Are you peeing right now?" Portia asks, to which I respond, "When your spawn sits on your bladder, you won't care whose listening or watching, so long as you get your ass to the toilet in time. That's my first pregnancy tip for you. Congrats by the way. You guys deserve a big family."

You can hear the smile in her voice when she says, "Thanks, Jer, and sorry for not telling you sooner. That scare with you at Marcus's shop made me want to wait twelve weeks before telling anyone."

"How far?"

"Eight weeks along. And I don't think Lock was looking for permission; Cooper said he was earning his respect."

"Are you telling me you didn't eavesdrop?" I ask her.

"Of course I did, for at least half an hour. But when my ass started to go numb from sitting in the hallway for so long, I went to bed."

"Hmmm. So did you garner any useful info from your thirty-minute stakeout, or should I go ask Locklin myself? You know what, don't answer that. I don't want to know."

She's quiet for a moment and then says, "I'm going to say one thing, Jer, and that's hear him out. I know you said you don't want to talk to him, but holy shishkabob, the man has a way with words. And if he says even half to you of what he said to Cooper, then I think you might have a change of heart."
I sigh. "That's just it, P. They're words. They've always been just words, and I don't for even a minute think that I can get over how I felt that day when he was in the hospital. I don't think I can get over not being wanted."

"Babe, listen to him. It sounds like you guys haven't done a lot of actual talking, and I think that if you do, you might gain a whole new perspective."
Placing my hair into a knot, I mutter, "I'm letting you go now. Not because I don't love you, but because

your practicality is starting to scare me."

"Cheese and rice, just talk to him. Love you."

"Love you too, Lady."

CHAPTER THIRTY-ONE

LOCKLIN

I feel as if I've sat here for fucking ever waiting for Jerri to come out of the house. I don't mind waiting for her, but I'm anxious.

I need her to talk to me.

I need her to hear me out.

If she doesn't, it's just going to take that much longer to get her to see that I'm dead fucking serious about wanting her in my life.

I've always wanted her in my life.

But my actions spoke louder than words: I had been absent too often for too long.

Never again.

When she finally comes out showered and dressed almost an hour later, I'm nearly lost for words. I used to sit and watch her sleep before leaving in the middle of the night. I know how beautiful she is. In the daylight, she's as beautiful as ever.

MIND LIES

The day is cloudy, as are most in Ireland. I wait for her to take a seat next to me, but she continues down the steps toward the path leading to Paddy and Nessa's house.

"I'd really like to talk with you, Lass," I tell her as I stand. She barely slows and responds, "Then you'll have to talk on the way to the house. If you haven't noticed, I barely fit in the shirt I have on and my pants won't button up. Ness called and said the clothes I ordered online are here, and I'd rather not walk around with my pants undone."

I look down Sure enough, her small, round belly is poking out the bottom of her shirt, and the button on the pants she's wearing is being held together by what looks like a hair tie.

"I can drive us," I tell her as I jog down the steps.

She doesn't stop. "I walk there every day. I like it."

Clearly ending the discussion, I follow in step behind her. It isn't lost on me that I'm following another woman, but the difference this time is that it's not toward danger, or death.

It's toward the very person who can give me life.

We walk in silence for the near-mile to the main house, where Paddy and Nessa greet Jerri with welcoming arms. I'm not near as fortunate with the two people I consider parents.

"Ye pull yer head outta yer arse?" Paddy asks from where he stands in the doorway, arms crossed, blocking my entrance.

"I'm workin' on it, ol' man."

Nessa slaps him on the arm. "I would never keep ye from yer home, Locklin. But mark my words, me boy: ye upset Jerrilyn while she's carryin' that bairn, ye'll be seein' what's on the other side of my wooden spoon. And I ain't talkin' about the handle; I'm talkin' 'bout the cast iron pan that sits under it."

Raising her eyebrows to drive her point home, I nod and say, "I won't upset her, Ness."

I'm going to upset her. That's a given. But if I told Ness I'd try, that wouldn't be good enough. She nods and puts her arm around my shoulders. "Come on in. I just made some tea."

Paddy watches me, as though I were about to steal something, until we settle at the kitchen table. Nessa begins piling a dinner-sized amount of food on our plates, and it's not even lunch.

"So much better," Jerri says when she comes out of the bathroom dressed in a loose paisley-print shirt and those tight, black, stretchy pants all women seem to fucking wear these days.
She turns around to grab a cup, and my eyes zero in on her ass, which has grown at least two sizes. I love every extra inch of it.

MIND LIES

"Fuck!" I curse when Paddy slaps me on the back of the head.

Hard.

"Ye don't look at 'er like that," Paddy grumbles.

"Watched you look at Ness like that for the past twenty-seven years, you horny, old bastard," I shoot back.

He smirks. "Nessa's mine to look at. Jerrilyn quit belongin' to ya the day ye broke her heart."

I grumble, making sure the women aren't listening. But they're too preoccupied going through Jerri's new clothes. "Fuck's sake, Paddy. I'm tryin' to fix it. Until she actually lets me talk to her, there's fuck all I can do other than what I'm doing now."

Paddy pops a tart in his mouth and mutters, "So ye just keep playin' with yer 'gina then?"

"Haven't got a 'gina to play with, you grumpy prick."

He nods. "Could've fooled me, Lad. Ye called Ness to ask fer cookin' lessons this mornin'. Think she's got some extra hair rollers in her dressin' table if yas are doin' makeover's next."

I sigh and resist the urge to run my hands through my hair, which has grown past my ears. "Jealous,

Paddy? You're gettin' a little thin on the top. That why you always keep your hat on?"

He scowls and barks, "Mind yer elders, smart arse."

"You mind yer mouths. I won't have yas talkin' like that when my grandbaby gets here," Nessa chirps before she and Jerri take a seat at the table. Since Nessa's word is law around here, we talk about mundane things like the boats and the weather as we eat and drink tea. When we finish, I gather Jerri's things, two boxes full of new clothes, and follow her home.

* * *

"Why did you go see Cooper?" I ask Locklin later that afternoon. After I put all my new clothes in the wash, I settle in with my feet up on the large sofa as Locklin tidies up his mess from cooking breakfast this morning.

He wipes his hands on the towel and comes into the living room with a beer for himself and a water for me. Taking a seat on the other end of the sofa, he answers, "It's like that saying, 'You don't know where you're going until you know where you've been.' That's the best way for me to describe it. I've lost a lot of time with you, Jerri. And that's on me. I know it is. I'll work hard to get that time back, Lass. But I need to know where you've been first."

I tilt my head, mildly confused. He carries on. "I know you better than I know anyone, Jerri. But those people were a part of you, and I never made the time to care about that. I never made time to dig deeper, to get to know that part of you better—who it is you are with them. I can't take back what I've done and how I've acted for the past ten years, but if I learned anything from getting shot and waking up in that hospital, it's that I need to try harder."

They're just words, Jerri.

Placing my water on the table, I clasp my hands together and tell him, "Locklin, I appreciate the effort. I really do. I'm grateful you want to be here, to be a part of our child's life. But that doesn't include a romantic relationship with me."

He closes his eyes, pained. "I was fighting for the wrong thing, Lass." Then, he opens them again and turns to face me. "The wrong person. I think I knew that before, but the guilt—fuck, Jerri—the guilt eats at me."

"What are you saying, Locklin?"

Leaning his head back against the couch, he looks to the ceiling then closes his eyes. "She called me that day," he whispers.

I swallow. "Siobhan?"
He nods. "I hadn't talked to her and had been avoiding her calls because she was always with the

twins, or the gang, stoned out of her fuckin' tree." Shaking his head, he adds, "I hated that, Jer. I absolutely hated those drugs because I felt like I wasn't enough, like I couldn't give her enough. So she needed to find what she was missing elsewhere."

Reaching out, I put my hand on his shoulder. "I think addiction effects everyone differently, Lock. If she got that hooked that fast, I don't think there's anything you could have done about it. That's not on you—that's on her."

I give him a squeeze and place my hand back in my lap, but he reaches out and places his on my foot, needing the contact to finish his story.

"I answered the call because I always did. I may have turned down hanging out with her near the end, but I always answer when she called. As usual, she sounded fucked up, hadn't gone to bed in who knows how long. So when she asked me to meet her at the docks, I told her no. I had no desire to hang out with her and those useless fucks she spent time with."

"You think that if you had gone, you could have saved her," I softly say.

Nodding, he tilts his head my way, eyes pained. "Yes, Lass. I do. So when I finally did find her later that night, it made it that much worse."

"Her death is not on your shoulders, Locklin. Did she call you to help her? To get her out of there?"

"No."

"Had you have gone down there, do you think she would have left with you?"

"No," he whispers.

"Then it doesn't sound like there's a whole lot you could have done. She made her choices, and though they were shitty ones—and no woman deserves what happened to her—she still chose the path she walked."

Rubbing his hands over his face, he sighs and lifts his head from the couch. "What I'm trying to tell you is that something broke in me that day, Jerri. I felt inferior, scared, and fucking useless as an eighteen-year-old. What happened played a great role in shaping me into who I am. But, Jerrilyn . . ." He pauses. My eyes meet his. "Never had I known true fear until you left my hotel room that night . . . and ended up in the hospital. It fucking gutted me, Lass. What I thought was fear as eighteen-year-old boy holds no weight next to what I felt when I got that call from Bryan. It hurt me to argue with you to get you to leave that night. But damn it, Jerri, I nearly died from fucking heart failure when Bryan called me."

He gets up and starts pacing. "And worse, I couldn't fucking see you because I was on a goddamn ship in the middle of the ocean. Bryan didn't call any of your friends because we were worried that *they*, Yakov's cronies, could still be watching you. So we hired the PI and his team to look out for you while we tried to figure out what the fuck was going on, if Yakov's crew had left Boston. It was one big clusterfuck, and the whole time I was drowning, Jerri. Fucking drowning."

He spins to look at me. "Do you have any idea how hard it is to look at you and not touch you? Do you have any idea how bloody hard it is to watch the light go out in your eyes, to not be able to put it back there? It's painful, Lass! But while it was killing me inside, all I could think about was you. And if you knew what I was doing, and that I'd been followed, you'd try to run with me, again."

I wipe the tears from underneath my eyes and ask, "And you didn't want me with you. I get it, Locklin."

"No, Lass." He vehemently shakes his head. "You would have followed me to the pits of hell, and I didn't want that for you. You made a family with your friends at the shop. That's more than I ever gave you, and if I tore you away from that, I knew you'd hate me. It may not have happened immediately, but it would fucking happen. How could I do that to you? How could I ask you to give up everything for me, again?"

He sits on the couch and brackets my legs with his arms. "I couldn't, Jerri, because it's fucking selfish of me. And I didn't want to be responsible for someone else's death. I didn't want to be responsible if you weren't fuckin' happy, if you were to wake up one day realizing I wasn't enough for you."

I let out a humorless laugh through my tears. "You

stupid, stupid man."

Pushing his hands away, I get up from the couch and look down at the man in front of me, a man who has said all the right things but remains completely fucking clueless.

My pretty and reckless.

Or at least he used to be.

"I didn't stay with you out of obligation or lack of direction. I didn't follow you, stick by you, and be there for you just because I loved you. Even I'm aware that love isn't always enough. I did it because *you* were my family, Locklin. You were the first person to make me feel." Wiping my cheeks, I finish. "You don't get to pick and choose who you have that feeling with, Locklin. It chooses you."

He moves to stand, and I shake my head. "I don't want to talk anymore. I'm going to lie down."

He nods. "Fair enough. My goal wasn't to upset you. Fuck, I'm doing this all wrong."

It's my turn to nod my head. "I need time. Just . . . give me some time, please."

CHAPTER THIRTY-TWO

Three weeks.

That's how long it's been since the talk I had with Locklin.

It's also how long he's been hovering.

Paddy tried to get him to go to work on the fishing boat, but Locklin wouldn't budge. Whether he's staying because he's worried about Yakov or my pregnancy, I'm not sure. But he's rarely far from me.

When I go to brush the horses, he works on the barn or cleans out the stalls.

When I walk down to the bench by the lake to read, he parks his motorcycle on the nearest path to clean it. That bike's been with him for a decade. An easy mode of transportation that he can get on and off the ship easily.

Now I sit beside him at the doctor's office while I wait to get in for a check-up.

"Ms. Sloane?"
I smile at the nurse. Locklin grabs my arm to help me from the chair. We've barely spoken since we left

the house, but that's been the norm. He's just *there* all the time. From the time I go to bed to when I wake up in the morning, he's *there*.

"You don't need to come in, Locklin," I softly tell him so as not to disturb the quiet waiting room.

He sighs. "I told you I'm not leaving, and I'll keep saying it until you believe me. I'm not leaving, and if there's a chance they do a sonogram today, I'd like to see our son."

"Okay," I tell him, letting him lead me to the exam room. I wore a long dress today, so when the nurse tells me to get on the table, I take off my panties and get under the paper sheet, pulling my dress up over my abdomen.

"Fucking hell, Jerri. You could warn a man," Locklin grumbles before snatching my panties off the chair so he can take a seat. He then puts them in his pocket.

"You do know where babies come from, right?" I smartly say.

He groans. "I remember putting him in there. Vividly."

Ignoring the urge to press my thighs together, I let out a whoosh of breath. Thankfully, the doctor comes in, saving me.

"Afternoon, Ms. Sloane. I'm Dr. O'Leary," the man announces. He exchanges a few pleasantries with Locklin and I before running through the regular questions.

"If you think I'm letting that man touch your pussy, Lass, you might want to know I'll break his fingers before they get anywhere near it," Locklin whispers in my ear.

I swing my head to face him, bringing us nose to nose. "He's a doctor, Locklin. Calm down."

He shakes his head, still looking at me, and says loud enough for the doctor to hear, "We would be more comfortable with a female doctor."

"Locklin!" I scold before Dr. O'Leary turns around and lets out a small laugh. "It's not the first time that request has been made, but I assumed you knew I would be your doctor before you made the appointment. But, it's no problem. If you're comfortable with it, I'll perform the sonogram and then ask Dr. Banks to come over to perform the exam when she's finished with her next patient."

Locklin answers, "That sounds fine."

I clear my throat. "Thank you, Doctor, and I'm sorry for the inconvenience."

He nods as he lubes the wand for the ultrasound, clearly getting a kick out of Locklin's antic; he's still fighting a smile. Locklin opens his mouth when he sees the doctor squirt gel on my lower abdomen. "Not one word, Locklin. Not one word."

Wisely, he closes his mouth, but the scowl on his face remains until he hears the telltale whoosh from the baby's heartbeat. I watch his face more than I watch the monitor, memorizing his expression as he sees his son for the first time.

"Strong heartbeat, Ms. Sloane. Your due date is mid-January. But I'd say first week of the month and he'll be fighting to get out. He's a big lad."

I nod, still looking at Locklin, watching a mixture of happiness and awe cross his beautiful face. Watching him watch our son is a moment I plant into my brain to savor as a happy memory.

We created a life together. And in that is something beautiful, regardless of how little we've been communicating.

Powerful.

He's seeing that power for the first time, and for the first time in weeks, I can truly say my heart feels warm.

Full.

"He's a tumbly little one, but as you can see he's a healthy boy. All ten fingers and toes, and fixin' to be the next Connor McGregor." The doctor laughs before removing the wand. "Dr. Banks will be with you shortly."

I nod. "Thank you, Doctor."

Moving to grab the paper towel, Locklin puts his hand on my wrist. "Not yet, Lass."

I follow his eyes to my bare stomach. "Look, Jerri." He's focused on the lump moving across my abdomen.

"It's his foot." I stop and hiss in a breath.

Only then does Lock move his eyes. "What's wrong?"

I shake my head and give him a small smile. "He likes to kick my ribs. It doesn't hurt, but it catches me off guard."

He swallows before moving his hand to my stomach. I don't stop him. I just continue to smile as his warm hand settles on my bare skin for the first time in what feels like forever.

"You need not kick your ma, Lad," Locklin says to our son. I grab his hand and move it to the left. "Feel that?" I watch his face light up as he nods. "That's his foot. And over here . . ." I move his hand and push. "That's his head."

Locklin sighs. "Incredible, Lass." Leaning in, he places a kiss on my stomach and then moves and places another on my forehead, where he whispers, "My water."

It's been a long time since I've heard those words. I think the last time he said them was when we got back together after I left Tom. When asked what he meant, all he said was *someday*. I don't get the chance to ask now because Dr. Banks enters the room.

Someday.

* * *

After retrieving my panties from Locklin, which he grudgingly handed over, I ask a nurse to point me in the direction of the bathroom.

"First door through there on the right, Ms. Sloane. I'll meet you at the desk with your paperwork."

"I'll get it," Locklin tells me, to which I argue, "Locklin, I can pay for my health care."

He shakes his head. "Did you pay for all the other appointments?" At my nod, he continues, "Then I owe you for those as well as this one."

I open my mouth, but he just turns his back to me and walks the ten feet to the desk.
"Whatever," I mutter as I turn the corner to the bathroom. Once I'm finished, I straighten my green, long-sleeve maxi dress and exit the bathroom.

"Oomph!" The wind is knocked from my lungs when I run into the man in front of me. "I'm sor—"

Gun in front of my face.

Prepared to scream, I open my mouth to yell for help—but he points the gun at my stomach.

"Walk."

Nodding furiously, I put one foot in front of the other. The strange man clamps one hand on top of my shoulder and pushes the gun into my abdomen to drive his point home.

Only six feet from the bathroom door is an exit, and once we reach it, my brain catches up.

He has a Russian accent.

I'm probably going to die—or worse; I'll be handed a fate much like the women in those containers.

I don't think anymore, just act quickly before the door to the office closes.

"Locklin!" I yell at the top of my lungs. The big Russian grabs hold of me around the waist and hits me across the head with his gun.
I fight the dizziness and the pain as he tosses me into a van parked far too closely to the door.

I should have screamed sooner.

MIND LIES

I watch as he tosses a heavy envelope on the ground in front of the door. Then the van bolts off toward the street, taking corners too fast, slamming hard on the brakes.

"His tires are flat, Vasily. He not follow us," says the man who threw me in the van. The hair on my neck stands up. Biting the bullet, I lift my head from the floor and look directly into the eyes of my nightmares.

"Da, you remember. I see it in your eyes. Fear and memory," he says, laughing in sick satisfaction while maneuvering the van through traffic and down side streets. I edge closer to the door, slowly, hoping I can jump out if they slow down for a turn.

"Nah, ah, Raven," he says while waving his gun toward the back seat. I ignore the raven comment and ask, "You're going to kill me anyway, are you not? Should it not be my own decision whether I die jumping from a moving vehicle or being tortured and shot in the head?"

Vasily laughs, a full-out, humorless laugh, and points his finger at me in the mirror. "I knew I like you, Raven. You Americans have fire."

I shake my head. "No, we just have common sense. And if I'm going to die, I would rather it be on my terms, not after you torture me."

Still laughing, he says, "Why you think we torture you?"

"Because if you wanted me dead, you would have shot me already. You need me for something, and I'd rather not find out what that something is."

Smiling, he rolls down the window and lights a smoke. "This common sense is entertaining. So much fire, Raven. And fight?" He nods. "I did not know it was you at first in Boston motel. I think this Locklin guy we after hire hooker. But then I see you and bam! It comes back to me. I never forget faces. You woman from shipping company, and he the man who hit me over the fucking head."

Fucking hell, he knows who I am.

"Yuri cut brake lines already on car." He pursues his lips. "But I come for you, Raven." Taking a drag, he carries on. "Stick through the neck, blood everywhere. All I see is tattoo." He points to his shoulder. "I come to take you, Raven, but you already dead."

He blows smoke across the cab at Yuri and says, "Boo!" before they begin laughing their asses off.

"You fighter, Raven. Come back from dead."

I swallow past the bile rising in my throat and hold my hands over my stomach, rubbing in small circles. I'm not sure whether I'm soothing my baby boy or myself, but I keep doing it until my breathing returns to normal, as I watch the unfamiliar signs pass by outside.

"He come for you, Raven."

Whipping my head toward the front, I ask, "Excuse me?"

He shrugs his shoulders. "Locklin. He come for you when it is time."

The pit of dread in my stomach grows larger, but I ignore it when we pull up to a warehouse. It's a dilapidated, old building next to the treeline at the end of an abandoned street. Windows are knocked out, and trash litters the parking lot. Clearly, it still has hydro, though, because when Vasily presses a button on the dash, one of the three large garage doors opens.

My eyes take a minute to adjust to the light. But when they do, I nearly faint.

Cages.

There are four large cages. Concrete separates them, and a chain link closes the front of two, bars close the others.

"Oh my god," I whisper.

Vasily laughs. "How you Americans say it? New digs?" He nods, proud of himself for remembering the slang. "Yes. New digs for Raven."

The garage door closes behind us before Vasily opens the van door. He stands in front of me so that I may be reminded of his size. The sheer power behind the monster is overwhelming as he barbarously grabs my arm, pulling me from the vehicle.

"Come, Raven, I show you," he says as he drags me toward the cell. "I put you here, fighter. The other girls," he says, waving a hand to the ones with the chain link, "they not fighter like you."

I look to the chain-link cells and shudder, resisting the urge to cry when I see four women huddled in the first.

Eyes cast downward.

Bruises and red welts on their wrists.

The same sight I saw twelve years ago.

Once he crosses the threshold to my cell, he lets go of my arm and waves his hands around as if to show me how wonderful my new home is going to be.

"This old wildlife doctors. He work on things like bears and wolves. These bars," he says while banging his hand against them, "they for the bears."

I shiver and say, "I guess that would explain the smell."

He laughs. "Ah, Raven, you silly girl. No bear live here in decade. The smell is death." Pointing to the next cell over, he says, "Last girl have disease. She need sugar to live, but she do this"—he jolts his body back and forth, imitating a seizure—"and she not breathe anymore."

Shaking my head in disgust, I hiss, "It's called being diabetic, you sick fuck. You might wanna try feeding your captives. Maybe they'll live longer next time."

"Ha! Fire!" He spins around to see the other women. "My Raven a fighter. What we do with fighters?"

The women don't answer but simply keep their eyes cast downward where they sit huddled together on a dirty blanket. Their clothes are torn, and dried blood caked their once-tear-soaked cheeks.

"We discipline!" Vasily shouts before backhanding me across the face. Caught off guard, I stumble, slamming my elbow into the wall before reaching a hand out to balance myself.

"Raven, Raven, Raven. I like fire, but you do not tell Vasily how to run his business."

A door slams shut in the distance, and he smiles, "Ah, boss is here."

Taking shallow breaths to beat the dizziness back, I lean against the wall and listen to the sound of footsteps getting closer while wondering if the boss is Yakov. My eyes follow shiny shoes up to a suit-covered body. I come face-to-face with a much older man, mid-sixties I would guess. He has thinning hair and a scar under his eye. He has crow's feet around those eyes, but they're not from smiling, more like from squinting in the sun or being an asshole all the time.

"She's pregnant?" the man asks Vasily.

"Surprise, Yakov!" he replies.

"Good. It the mans?"

He nods.

"Extra security. Man fight hard for child. We be prepared," Yakov says, adding, "No harm to child. It worth more than the girls."

My unborn child is worth more than the women?

Clearing my throat, feeling certain they aren't going to kill me because my child is somehow worth something to them, I speak up. "Locklin's one man, and you could have killed him at the doctor's office. Me too, for the matter." They both settle their eyes on me, Yakov's with brows raised as if I've spoken out of turn, and Vasily's displaying a sick satisfaction I don't want to understand. "If we're not dead yet, clearly you want something that can't be gained from killing, and the only thing that could be is information. I have no desire to die today, or to watch someone be hurt. It's possible I could answer your questions."

Vasily claps. "This called common sense, Yakov. She full of wisdom, my Raven."

Yakov shrugs. "I do not care how we get information, so long as it is obtained. Yuri?" The man comes when called and speaks with Yakov for a moment before leaving. When he returns, he has two chairs. Yakov places one outside the cell, and Yuri carries the other one inside before returning to his post.

"Sit," the Russian orders. I do as I'm told because my head is pounding.

"Vasily tells me you clever girl. So you going to tell me how you evade my men and hide for . . ." He looks over his shoulder at Vasily, who answers: "Twelve years."

"Twelve years."

CHAPTER THIRTY-THREE

LOCKLIN

"Are you all ready for the wee one to arrive?" the nurse asks as I sign forms and pay the bill in cash. "We will be," I tell her, not because I want to carry on a conversation, but because I lose myself in the memory of feeling my son kick for the first time.

I've watched Jerri like a hawk this past month, and that includes noticing every time she smiles, when she places her hand on her belly, or when she sings to him without even noticing. I've been envious of her touching her belly, which I can't freely do, and jealous of the unborn lad when he gets her soulful voice—the same one that used to calm me when I was making love to her, afraid I might never hear it again.

Afraid I might never see her again.

Always worrying I might never feel her touch again.

Touching her today was like coming home, only this time, I wasn't afraid to leave. I wanted to stay right where I was with my skin touching hers, my boy eagerly kicking against me.

I need her in my life. I've known it for a long time,

but now it physically aches when she's not near. I don't have the adrenaline driving me forward to chase ghosts anymore. Now all I have is a driving need to be with her every second of every day.

It's not healthy. It's nearly obsessive.

But I don't fucking care.

"Locklin!" Jerri's shrill scream echoes through the office, and I tear off toward the sound.

The bark of a man.

The slamming of a door.

"Jerri!" I shout when I round the corner, pushing open the heavy exit door that had just slammed shut and watching a dark van peel out of the parking lot. I don't stop running until I get to our car. But I see slashed tires—so I keep running.

"Jerrilyn!" I shout, distance gaining between the van and myself. It swerves around a corner and heads west, out of town.

"Fuck! No!" Slowing down, I dig through my pocket until I find my cell phone and dial 9-1-1.

"She's gone!" I bark down the line. Ignoring the operator, I continue, "Black van heading west on Harris Street." I rattle off the first four digits of the license plate, then add, "A pregnant woman abducted from

O'Leary's Clinic. Find her."

I hang up the phone and dial Lee. "They got her," I tell him before he has the chance to say hello. "They fucking took her from the clinic!"

"Where are you?" he asks.

"O'Leary's Clinic, south of Harris."

Then he says, "Five minutes," and hangs up.

Walking back to the car, I rip open the door and grab my gun from the console, sticking it in the back of my jeans. There's a crowd gathered outside the door, and one of the nurses runs toward me, white as a sheet.

"Sir?"

I'm sure I look far from friendly. Her hand shakes as she holds out an envelope with my name on it. "I think this is for you, but I wasn't sure if I should touch it."

I shake my head. "The police are on their way. I'll pass it along. Thank you."

She nods and scurries off. I open the flap to the envelope, but before I can pull out the contents, Lee comes barreling into the lot. He doesn't park, only slows the car as I open the door and get it.

"Police are looking, and two of my guys at G2 are lookin' through traffic cams to get a location. The rest won't help until they know it was the Russians. Until it can be confirmed it's them, it's just a regular abduction."

I ignore him and reach inside the envelope.

Pictures.

"Fucking hell," Lee curses beside me, his eyes switching from pictures to the road.

There are quite a few of me in Boston. Pictures of Jerri coming and leaving my motel room that night. At the bottom of the stack is a photo of girls huddled together in a cell.

Dirty.

Bloody.

Raped and waiting to be sold.

"Flip them over," Lee tells me.

Unless you want Raven to have the same fate, you will call, is written on the back of the last photo.

There's a number underneath the message, and I pull my phone out of my pocket, prepared to dial.

"Wait," Lee says. "That might be enough to get G2 in on this."

I whip my head toward him. "You're fucking here,

aren't you?"

He shakes his head. "I'm here as myself, not part of G2. Five minutes, partner. Just let me make a call."

"She could be anywhere by now! It's been ten minutes, and I know you know what happens in ten fucking minutes!" I shout, pointing in the direction the van was headed as we blindly try to find it.

"Colin," Lee barks through his hands-free. He regales him about everything that had just happened and the pictures in my lap. "Run it through the boss, and put a trace on this number."

"Done," Colin chirps back before the line goes dead.

"Now you call."

I dial the number twice, my fingers failing to work. It rings nine fucking times before someone answers.

"I see you got my package?" the Russian prick answers.

"I did. Care to tell me how I can fix this problem?"

"You've been fucking with my shipments. I do not like when people fucks with what is mine."

I bite my tongue but throw back, "You can't own a person. They're not for sale."
He laughs. "Everything for sale! For a price."

I shake my head. "That what you want? Money in exchange for a life?"

"Silly Irishman." He continues laughing. "You and I need to have a little talk."

"So talk. I'm listening."

"In time," he says. "First you need to ditch your getaway driver."

Lee and I share a look before the Russian adds, "I have eyes everywhere when I sense a threat. I make it my business to know people before I take them down. I do not like messes. And you, Irishman, are making a fucking mess."

"Alright, I'll ditch the driver. What next?"

"You go to Jarvis Industrial Park."

I frown. "There's nothing there but concrete."

"Exactly. I see you coming from a mile away. Alone. I will have you picked up. See you then."

"Proof of life. I'm not coming unless I speak to her."

"Ahh, the fiery Raven," the smug fuck says before throwing in, "Vasily is quite fond of her," adding fuel to my fire.
Then, "Lock?"

I breathe a sigh of relief and tell her the only thing I can think of in case this doesn't turn out as I hope.

"My water, Jerri girl."

* * *

"They won't kill you yet. They need something from you," Lee tells me. I nod my head. My hands are clenched into fist on my thighs, craving to drive into something.

Someone.

"Not trying to talk me out of it?" I smartly say, not because I care what his answer is, but because the past sixteen minutes in this fucking car have been the longest of my life. And talking makes the time go by quicker.

Gripping the steering wheel harder, he replies, "No."

I know there's a fuck of a lot more than what meets the eye with Lee, but even now, in a situation like this, he doesn't bother to enlighten me.

His business, not mine.

I don't pry because what's the point?
Men are simple; if we want you to know something, we'll fucking tell you. If we don't, there's a reason

why.

"End of the road, Lock."

I take one last look at Lee. We've become more than just partners, despite the fact that we rarely made small talk over the past twelve years. It's bigger than that. He doesn't have to be here right now; he didn't have to act without G2 and risk a suspension to fucking help me.

But he is.

Not because he owes me anything, but because he's a good fucking man.

I take a look around the desolate landscape. The buildings in the industrial park are long gone. The result of a fire that broke out six years ago, leaving nothing but concrete behind. Opening the car door, I give one last nod to Lee. "Don't do anything I wouldn't do," he smartly says, and I nod back.

"Wide open, then?"

He gives me a sober look. "Wide open. Go get your girl."

I shut the door and bang on the roof twice. I don't watch the car disappear, but instead turn and walk with speed toward my meeting point, well aware that I'm wide open without a weapon and could be taken out at any time.

They don't want me dead.

Yet.

The Russian's want me alive. For what I have no fucking clue. Could be information, but then why not ask the driver, Lee, to come too?

Maybe they just want to beat and torture my sorry ass for all the headaches I've caused them over the years, but it feels as if they've gone to too much trouble for that to be the case.

At the moment, I really don't give a shit. I need to get Jerri out of this mess, and if I can make that happen, I don't give a flying fuck what they do to me.

When I reach the top of a small hill, a car comes into view. I can see the outline of two men, and when I get near, a third man exits the back seat with a gun trained on me. I don't raise by hands but instead walk slower. Standing five feet in front of him, I stop.

He's about my size. Not as fit but matched for weight.

"Lift your shirt and turn around."
I do as he asks, showing him I have no weapons, then proceed to do the same with my pant legs. Once he's satisfied, he points to the car. "Inside."

His accent is thick. Either he fucking sucks at speaking English or he's a man of few words. Not that I want to speak to the prick, anyway. No. What I really want to do is reach out, grab his arm, and snap it in the middle.

The gun would fall, and I'd catch it before it hit the ground while elbowing him right under his nose.

Hopefully, I could get shots off faster than the two in the front seat could draw, but the truth is I've never shot someone.

Never killed anyone.

The only time I've had to fire my weapon is for sport.

For practice.

The car weaves out of the concrete desert, and I continue thinking of all the way I could kill these sorry bastards. It's not long before we arrive at a warehouse. I know this place; it used to be a wildlife rehabilitation centre but closed down over a decade ago for some reason or another.

We're about seven miles out from the docks. Through the bush line, it would only be about a mile before you hit the water.

Perfect location for trafficking. There'd be no security to worry about at the shoreline. No dock hands or undercover G2 agents would get in your way. It's a prime location, one they wouldn't show me if they planned to keep me alive.

I'll get you out, Jerri girl.

Even if I die trying.

I try not to think about how much I fucked up over the years. Evading these fucks for twelve years is a pretty goddamn good stretch. But the mess I made with Jerri . . .

I could have been out.

I could have quit this shit. I could have left it all behind, made a life with her.

Paddy told me many times over the years to pull my head out of my arse, and this is exactly what he meant. It wasn't just leaving Lee, G2, and the abducted women behind—it was having something worth living for when you did.

I'd live and die a thousand deaths for that woman, and don't I feel like a stupid son of a bitch for wasting all the time I could have had with her. The Christmases and the dinner parties. I've never been to a fucking dinner party, but I'd do it for her. I've never been somebody's plus-one on a wedding invitation, but I'd gladly fill the damn role.

I'd do anything.

And now it might be too late.

MIND LIES

I might not get to hold her hand, wipe the hair out of her eyes, and breathe with her through the labor of our boy.

I might not get anything.

The large garage door opens on the front of the building. We pull into the hollow space. It's nearly empty, save for the few tables and chairs scattered around. My eyes scan past the cages. They're too far away to see anyone inside, but all too familiar, sadly.

Lee and I came across a setup like this one outside of Hamburg a few years back. Nothing prepares you for it, but after the shit we've seen inside shipping containers, nothing surprises you anymore either.

Getting out of the car, I walk forward when a gun is pushed into my back. "Ah, the shit disturber listen well. I give instruction to shoot you in the arms if you not come alone."

"Why not the legs?" I ask.

The well-dressed man in front of me, Yakov, answers, "Then we have to carry you. No fun."
This is the first time I've ever seen Yakov in the flesh. As far as I'm concerned, it's the first time he's left Russia. According to Lee, the man flies so far under the radar they lose track of him.

Often.

Clearly he leaves the country when that happens, considering he's standing in mine.

"Where is she?" I bark, impatient, needing to see my girl. The asshole smirks and motions behind where a laughing man exists the cell with bars on.

Vasily.

Should have killed him. I should have fired my weapon for the first time all those years ago.

"Raven needs rest. How you call it?" He tilts his head to the side and wipes his bloody hands on a rag. "Ah, yes! Beauty sleep."

I charge forward, all the building rage surfacing. All the hate, pain, and suffering I've witnessed rises to the top as I take in the lifeless body of my Lass, sprawled out on the hard concrete floor, blood covering her face.

Bruises on her flawless cheeks.

Eye swollen shut.

"Don't do anything I wouldn't do," Lee had said.

Kill them.

Kill them all.

CHAPTER THIRTY-FOUR

Yuri pulls the phone from his pocket and nods, handing it to Yakov.

"I see you got my package?" is Yakov's greeting when he answers the phone. I can't hear the other side of the conversation, but I know it's Lock when he adds, "Silly Irishman." He continues laughing, leaning back in his chair as though he were having a chat with an old friend. Completely at ease, not a worry on his mind. "You and I need to have a little talk." I watch him nod. "In time," he says. "First you need to ditch your getaway driver."

Getaway driver? God, I hope it's not Paddy. He was in town today. The docks are only twenty minutes from the doctor's office.

"Ahh, the fiery Raven. Vasily is quite fond of her," he carries on, and I shiver, praying to god Vasily doesn't like a goddamn thing about me as he passes me the phone.

"Lock?" I speak just above a whisper, not wanting the men in the room to intrude on our conversation. Vasily rips the phone from my hand right before I hear, "My water, Jerri girl."

I hug my arms protectively over my stomach, and

Yakov waves a hand in a gesture that says, "Carry on," in regards to the talk he wanted to have.

"It's not that impressive, really," I tell him, stalling for time.

He crosses his legs and leans back in his seat. "I think otherwise. Twelve years." He nods toward Visily. "I nearly kill Vasily for not finding you. After six months no word from you or police, I let it rest."

I swallow. "So you didn't look for me all this time?"

He lets out a small laugh. "Penance for Vasily. I do not chase people. He look for you"—he waves his hand back and forth—"off and on. If someone come forward and say, 'I see this man,'"—he points to Vasily—"then Vasily goes down. I do not go with him."

I get the picture he's painting, clearly. It's exactly the same as what G2 had told us. If Vasily had been caught for any crime, and if I were asked if he had been involved that night, he'd be the only one doing time.

He would not rat on, roll over, or fuck with Yakov.

"You either change name, live under rock, or work for government to hide this long. Vasily get your name, even social security number from apartment, and he still not find you. I want to know how?" Straightening in his chair, he looks over his shoulder and loudly says, "Yuri? Empty girl's shit bucket and open window. Fucking stinks in here."

The girls cower farther into the wall, if that's possible, as Yuri collects the degrading bucket and takes it outside.

"Better. Now talk."

Fidgeting with the sleeve of my dress, I tell him half-truths: "I guess you could say I took a page out of your play book. If you could hide women and traffic them god knows where, why couldn't I escape the same way?" He nods for me to continue. "I knew shipping schedules like the back of my hand, so I had lain low for a few days before getting onto one of the ships that was heading to the States."

Pursing his lips in thought, he asks, "You hide on ship for week or more?"

Thinking fast, I tell him, "I bribed one of the deck hands. He brought me food and snuck me inside at night for bathroom breaks."

I don't want him to know about Paddy and Nessa, so I hope my story is believable enough that he won't ask for more detail. They always say less is more, so I stick to key points to keep it straight and hopefully satisfying.

"Then you hide in US? How?"

I shrug. "Odd jobs, fake IDs, and eventually a new social security number. I'm sure you know that money can be powerful. Once you save enough, you can buy just about anything."

He shakes his head. "You do not work for government?"

I shake mine back. "I don't work for the government."

Letting out a low chuckle, he says, "Vasily, she regular girl and you not find her?"

Vasily doesn't like the jab. The daggers he throws my way solidify that. "I good at finding people, she lie."

I swallow. "I'm not lying."

Vasily's lip curls. "You hide, but I find you with the dock worker, Locklin, in Boston. Same man who fuck with our shipments here."

I nod, thinking fast. "He's the dock worker I bribed to help me escape."

Vasily shakes his head. "He's not dock worker. Men at the docks say he negotiate shipping cost for companies."

I roll my eyes, grateful he has yet to mention any of Paddy's ships, the connection between Paddy and Locklin. "Everyone starts somewhere. When I met him, he was a dock worker."

"When he—" Vasily starts, cutting himself short when he gets a text message. "Ten minutes."

Yakov nods. "Desperate man do desperate thing. I need him desperate. Fix it, Vasily."

Yakov stands and straightens his already-pristine appearance before walking out of my view. The man from my nightmares smirks and sing-songs, "Raven, Raven, Raven. Now we have some fun."

I stay seated in the chair with my arms over my stomach. I'm helpless against him, but if I'm sitting, I can't be raped. Surely he won't punch me in the stomach if their goal is to sell my child.

"How long until baby come, Raven?" he asks as he stands in front of me, fist clenched at his sides. Swallowing, I answer, "A few months."

Smiling, he says, "Pretty Raven. Face long way from stomach." Then his fist hits the side of my face with such force it knocks the chair sideways. I cry out, expecting my body to hit the concrete, but two large hands grasp my shoulders. He rights the chair.

I open my mouth, to plea with him to stop, but a blow comes to the other side of my head before I've even opened my eyes. The pain from his backhand earlier intensifies as black spots cloud my vision.

"S-s-stop, please," I cry, not once putting my hands in front of my face; they're still wrapped firmly around my stomach. His hands are still pressed firmly on my shoulders to keep me seated.

Laughing, he asks, "Why stop? Why you not fight, pretty Raven?"

Blood flies from my mouth when I wail, "If stressed, I could go into labour, you stupid bastard! Then where will your black market baby money be?"

I get no warning when he backhands me again before placing his fingers around my throat. "Sleep, Raven."

I choke against his hold, finally removing the hands from my stomach to claw at them and his wrists. I feel the blood on my fingers as he lifts me up by the neck and lowers me to the floor. Blackness clouds my vision, and I pray to all things holy that we make it out of this alive.

* * *

LOCKLIN

"What the fuck have you done?" I growl, hands clenched at my sides, murderous gaze aimed at Vasily. "I wanted proof of life!" I shout, pointing into the cell. "What the fuck is that?"

He laughs, but I don't let him get any words out. I don't care about the men, the guns, or the piece of shit in front of me. Taking two steps forward, I pull back and swing as hard as I can, hitting him right in the temple. I almost smile at the sight of the big fucker falling flat on the ground.

Weapons are drawn, clicks telling me safeties are released. Since I'm not an idiot, I don't bother fighting them. With Vasily down, it's five against one.

"Guns down," Yakov calmly says, as if he had just asked us to have a seat at his table for motherfucking tea.

Kill them all.

"I finally meet the man who has been fucking with my shipments." Clasping his hands behind his back, he asks, "I want to know who you work for."

I scoff. "I don't work for anyone but myself, you piece of shit."

He raises a brow. "A vigilante? How noble of you, Irishman. And why would a man become vigilante? Why not stay at home and"—he waves a hand toward Jerri—"raise babies?"

Clenching my hand into a fist, I decide there's nothing left to lose. "Her name was Siobhan. She was beaten and left for dead on the docks almost twenty years ago."

The fucker shrugs. "So now you run around saving women?"

I shake my head in disgust. "You killed her, you son of a bitch. The last name that came out of her mouth was Yakov."

He tilts his head, trying to remember, then shakes it. "It does not ring any bells."

I scoff and glance down at my watch. "I'm sure you don't remember half the people you kill."

Waltzing around without a care in the world, he says, "I know I did not kill the one you speak of because I kill fast. Not dirty." Waving his arms around, he adds, "My men do dirty work, and this suit"—he fixes his lapels—"cost three thousand dollars. I have no interest in blood. Yuri?"

The man in question steps forward, walking around Vasily's still yet alive body, "Who is the woman the Irishman speak of?"

Yuri shrugs. "Long time ago, boss."

Yakov sighs. "It was not Vasily. He enjoys watching the light drain out of eyes."

Yuri nods, as if that were common fucking knowledge, and says, "Wait, wait. Girl come across container when we move women from container to truck. She attack Sven. Red hair?"

I swallow and nod, so Yuri keeps going. "Red hair, big money. But when we grab her, she crazy. Puke all over and eyes go." He motions to the back of his head.

"So we throw her off the truck."

All in a day's work, you sick sons of bitches.

"Needle marks, all up her arms. Even if she not die, no one believe her," he continues.

She's dead, you fuckin' bastards.

"Enough," Yakov says, issuing the silence, staring at me for a long moment. "You don't work alone."

Shaking my head, I answer, "No, I don't."

He scowls, and I take a minute to sweep my eyes over Jerri's cell. She's breathing but hasn't moved. Vasily starts moving and lifts himself to a seated position. His eyebrow is nearly torn off, blood oozing down his face.

It pleases me.

"Who was the driver?" Yakov asks. When I stall, he nods to Yuri, who then points his gun in Jerri's cell. "Legs or arms only, Yuri."

Stalling for time, I joke, "It's not as though she's in a position to hurt you. You really need a bullet to slow her down?"

Sighing, he says, "I need a bullet to speed you up, Irishman. And I can't kill her because I can get up to thirty thousand dollars for the child."

"You sick fucking—"

"Hey!" Yuri shouts, pointing the gun back at me, so I slow down.

"Babies? You sell fucking babies? The women trade not enough? Fuck me, why not just knock them all up before you sell them?"

He nods. "Oh, we do. But babies not as pretty when they come from junkies, whores, and street people. She"—he nods toward my Lass—"a healthy girl. Now, who was the driver?"

Two minutes.

"His name is Lenny," I fib. Yakov nods to the men behind me who then grab my arms. Vasily stands up and delivers a swift blow to my ribs, right below where I was shot. Two more follow right in the face.

"Who does Lenny work for?" Yakov asks, allowing Vasily to land another punch to my chest before I kick him in the stomach. I spit blood at his feet. Some lands on his pristine shoes. Satisfying.

"G2, motherfucker," I reply.

I watch the smirk fall off his face for a moment before he straightens his shoulders in a manner that suggests he doesn't give a shit who tries to take him down.

MIND LIES

You'll think differently soon.

Grabbing the gun from Yuri, he points it directly at my head. "Nobody fucks with my business. Not you, not her, and definitely not G-fucking-2."

"Get low!" is roared from behind me, and I dive down, taking one of the Russian fucks holding my arms with me. Shots ring out as I fight with him, wrestling for the gun. He elbows by aching ribs, and I lose my breath, which gives him the upper hand as he reaches for the gun. He then swings back, gun in hand, hitting me across the head with it. When he sits up with the gun raised, I think this is it. I'm a dead fucker. But the blood raining down on me isn't my own.

Women scream as three men dressed in black garb and bullet-proof vests rush in. I grab the gun from the dead Russian's hand and push him off me, desperate to find my way to Jerri. The bullet hole in the center of Yakov's head lets me breathe a little easier as I pass him and enter Jerri's cell. Vasily is five feet in front of me, soaked in blood from shoulder to ankle.

"Don't fucking touch her," I growl, aiming the gun at his head. Turning in my direction, I see the pleasure on his face. I don't understand why until I take notice of the gun aimed straight at my unborn son.

That lump I'm familiar with rises in my throat once again, and I tell him, "You shoot, you're fucking dead."

He chuckles, a wet sound as the blood runs out of his

mouth. "Irishman, I'm already fucking dead."

And then he pulls the fucking trigger.

CHAPTER THIRTY-FIVE

"Agghh!"

"No!" Locklin shouts. "Jerri, stay with me, Lass. Hang on."

I try to open my eyes, but it hurts. I push through the pain. I need to see him. I need to know I'm not dreaming.

"Lock?" I whimper when I feel my body being moved.

"I'm so sorry, Jerri girl. So fucking sorry," he cries as he holds me in his arms, rocking me back and forth.

"Lee!" he shouts, causing me to stir. "We need an ambulance, now!"

I hear them talking, but they seem muted. The blood rushes in and out of my ears as I press my face into his chest, breathing in his scent.

"Open your eyes, Lass. You can't go back to sleep yet. Open your eyes," he keeps saying, and I keep trying. Reaching up, I touch my eyes with my hand and feel the dried blood coating my lashes. Placing his hand on top of mine, he shushes me, and a woman says,

"Here."

I hear the sound of fabric ripping before a cool, wet cloth is rubbed gently over my eyes. The blood softens. The stickiness washes away, and thankfully my eyes start to open. The muted lighting in the cell is a blessing, and the first thing I see is Lock's face, which is inches from mine.

Tears run down his cheeks, and he presses his lips gently to mine. "Stay with me, Jerri girl."

I try to nod, but my head falls back on my shoulders, dizziness making me blink my eyes repeatedly. I try to clear it, the dizziness. Locklin keeps whispering in my ear as he lifts me from the floor, and a woman with a torn shirt stands there, a piece of her tattered shirt in one hand, a bottle of water in the other. She nods at me, our camaraderie among the cells now over, and hell forever behind us.

I fight the darkness as my head bobs on Locklin's shoulder. Dead bodies litter the floor on our way out of the building, and men dressed like commandos are huddled around the small group of terrified women. Blankets and water are handed out, and the women reach for them with a liveliness you wouldn't expect from someone who had just cowered in a cell a moment ago, petrified.

I try to wave, but it hurts.

Everything hurts.

"Lock?" I whisper.

The lights of an ambulance are visible in the distance. I focus on the flashing. "I'm tired."

He presses his face into my neck and weeps. "Stay with me, Jerri girl, and I'll tell you a story, okay?"

I think I nod into his chest. I'm not sure because I can barely feel anything. His arms loosen from my body, and I call his name. "Right here, Lass," he whispers against my forehead as I'm lowered onto a stretcher and loaded into the ambulance.

His hands grip my own, his thumb moving in soothing circles as he rests his forehead against mine. I feel a prick in my arm, hear medical jargon being spouted off about my condition and the baby.

A gunshot wound.

"The baby?" I cry, eyes barely open.

"Shh, Lass. Our boy is fine right now. I was going to tell you a story, remember?" I tilt my head toward his voice and open my eyes.

"Kay."

He smiles. God, it's beautiful. There's blood covering half of his face. Tears stream down his cheeks, and two days' worth of stubble covers his square jaw.

But he's beautiful.

I tell him so.

He laughs. "The drugs are kicking in. I guess I better hurry before you fall asleep on me again." I give him a dopey smile. He carries on. "I once told a woman that I loved her, but I don't think I really knew what it meant at the time. Those words are thrown out so freely, Lass. They're overused and underworked. You can love someone, but not like them. You can love them, but not care for them." He sighs. "I've cared for you, deeply, Lass, more than I have ever cared for another. And I don't just *like* you . . . I'm practically *obsessed* with you."

Reaching up, I place my fingers on his full lips. He kisses each finger before holding them to the side of his face. His cheeks wet from tears. "In the past twelve years, I've helped rescue one hundred and eighty-three women."

His throat works. He clenches his jaw. "One hundred and eighty-three, Jerrilyn. Black, white, Asian, Russian, Irish." He barks out a harsh, painful laugh. "Twenty-three, seventeen, thirty, ten. It didn't matter the age. It didn't matter their ethnicity, where they came from. It didn't matter if one were a prostitute and the other a child entering high school.

"When that cage, container, or warehouse door opens, none of that stuff matters, Lass. And it doesn't matter if they've been in that cage for five hours, five days, or five weeks—they all want the same thing. They all *beg* for the same thing. That thing is not their parents, children, or friends. It's not even healthcare."

Leaning close, he places his free hand on the side of my face and harshly whispers, "its water, Jerri girl. They beg for fucking water."

You're my water, Jerri girl.

EPILOGUE

Jerrilyn

"Oh my God."

"I like it much better when you moan my name, Lass," he says with his mouth firmly attached at the base of my neck.

"Stop teasing me," I groan, digging my nails into his back as he continues to thrust gently and steadily into my body.

"Patience, Jerri girl," he says as he pushes deeper, grinding his hips before placing his mouth on my own. I push my fingers into his hair and pull none too gently. "Locklin, please!"

He sighs but doesn't push harder. "I don't want to hurt you."

I growl, "You're hurting me by denying me my orgasm."

He clasps his hands around my shoulders, and I wrap my legs around his firm arse, pulling him deeper into me. "Christ, woman. You're killing me."

I nip his bottom lip and pull, forcing a groan to erupt

from his chest but spurring him on enough to fuck me harder. "Yes," I moan, falling back onto the mattress, taking all that he gives me.

Locklin, my unselfish lover who loved me all along, even though I was deaf to his words.

You can survive without love.

You can survive weeks without food.

You *cannot* survive without water.

"Eyes, Lass," he whispers against my lips.

When my eyes connect with his, we're joined in every sense of the word, from toes to mouths.

From skin to soul.

There's no doubt, worry, or indecision.

There's no fear or insecurity that he may leave.

We're one, Locklin and I. And although it may have taken a long time for us to get here, I know, as does he, that never would either of us been in this place with someone else.

If we did, it would be settling for less.

And regardless of what has happened over the years, I get it now.

I fucking get it.

Whether it was when he rescued me in that warehouse or when he told me the reasoning behind me being his water, I'm not sure. What I do know is there's not a soul on this planet who has loved me, and will continue to love me, like Locklin.

I used to think him selfish, and perhaps he was for a time. But until he learned, on his own terms, how to get rid of the ghosts from his past, there was no way I ever would have had one hundred percent of him.

And while there was a time in my life when I had settled for a part of him, I now know the abundance of having all of him.

Given our turbulent history, I can only call it tragically beautiful.

Much like the man—my pretty and reckless.

"Sing to me, Jerri Girl."

I sigh. "Only if you make me come."

His eyes crinkle around the edges as a smile takes over his handsome face. "Done."

"There are a million of you,
But only one for me,
They may be new,
But can't you see?

There's only one for me.
And that one is you,
No matter what you do,
Know that I need you.

No matter what you see,
Know it's only you for me.
No matter what you see,

Know it's only you for eternity."

"Beautiful, Jerri Girl. Now come." His hands hold tight—one on my shoulder, the other on my neck—as I go to blissful heights and let out the first moan of pleasure in months.

"Locklin!" I half-moan and wail as he follows me over, squeezing my body so tightly to his that it's hard to tell where he ends and I begin.

"Whaaa . . ."

Locklin grasps my hips and gently removes himself from my body before leaping off the bed and pulling his lounge pants on.

I sigh. "You know, its okay for her to cry a little, right?"

He turns and scowls at me. "It was your idea to put her in her own room."

I fight the smile and the laugh wanting to escape my mouth. "She's two months old, Lock. How long do you suggest we let our children sleep in the same room as us?"

He flings the bedroom door open and speaks as he walks across the hall. His voice tapers off but comes through on the monitor beside our bed.

"She doesn't like to be by herself," he grumbles. "Do you, Lara? Come to Da."

Her crying wanes, as it does every time he holds her. It's getting to the point where I think she does it on purpose just so he can come to the rescue and rock her until she falls asleep. "You don't like being on your own in here, do you little Lass?"

I hear her gurgle sounds and the motion of the rocking chair in her bedroom. She was just fed an hour ago, so I know she's not hungry. "I'll stay until you fall asleep. How about a story?"

I put my nightshirt back on so that I don't give our son an eyeful in the morning when he comes to wake me up. I snuggle down into bed and listen to my husband's deep, soothing voice serenading our girl.

"There was once a beautiful Lass, more beautiful than any other in the land." Lara coos as he continues. "She had the voice of an angel and the body of a goddess, but that wasn't what caught the attention of the most stubborn man in the Kingdom. No, it was her eyes. They told a story all on their own. So much so that even after the awful villain tried to steal the light from them, they still shone bright every time the most stubborn man in the Kingdom made contact with them.

"You see, it didn't matter how many men from the kingdom looked at her. It didn't matter how powerful or handsome they were, because the light in the beautiful Lass's eyes only shone for one stubborn man. You know why, Lara girl?" She doesn't answer; she's probably fast asleep, but he continues. "Because the stubborn man was sent to protect her, care for her, and treat her as though she were the last drop of water in the middle of a desert. He vowed once he escaped the darkness and shadows he lived in that he would treat her as best he could for the rest of his days and all eternity. And any man who had been in the desert knew that this was the highest form of assurance. Bigger than fate, bigger than love. Bigger than anything.

"So, together at last, the stubborn man gives her enough water to never know thirst. And in return, the beautiful Lass gives him enough light so that he will never be lost in the shadows of darkness again."

I wipe a tear from my cheek, a smile engraved on my face.

"Sleep, little lass," he whispers before returning to our bed moments later. I relax into his embrace with my head on his chest, listening to his heartbeat as I do every night before I fall asleep. Taking a deep breath, I place my lips over his heart. "I love you madly, Locklin Cavanaugh."

I keep my lips there for a moment, thankful for him, our healthy boy, and our growing little girl in the other room. I'm grateful for this cabin and our children's pseudo-grandparents on the other side of the property.

We made it.

It took over a decade. It took nearly dying and Locklin fighting for something I didn't completely understand.

But we did.

EPILOGUE

LOCKLIN

"Oh, he's so handsome!" Jerri gushes over the foul-mouthed little bastard.

Portia always did call her child her spawn, and I never bothered to correct her because he is.

The spawn of fucking Satan.

I watch the little prick eyeball Lara from across the room. Even at six months, she knows he's a bad seed. She's a watcher, my little lass, and she can spot the evil from where she sits in her jumper. I may have had a talk with her and her brother before I got here, without Jerri present, of course, because she would have kicked my ass.

Or she would have deprived me of sex for a week.

Witch.

My boy is almost three now, and after a man-to-man chat, he understands he needs to protect his little sister from shit disturbers like Portia and Cooper's son. Josh has no manners, swears like his mother, and has taught my boy that if you throw your vegetables far enough at dinner—you don't need to eat them.

As I said, little prick.

MIND LIES

I motion toward Lonán. He comes and stands between his sister and I. "Smart move, Lad." He looks up to me and nods, his serious little face a mirror image of my own. I take a moment to remember how lucky I am as I place my hand on his shoulder.

To have this family isn't something I have ever dreamed about. It's not even something I had hoped for. It took me a long time to pull my head out of my arse, as Paddy would say. A long time to realize that living in the shadows and chasing ghosts wasn't going to warm my bed or my stubborn heart.

It took Jerri nearly dying.

Twice.

I'll never forget the day my life nearly ended, right along with hers. I'll never forget any of the days I spent with Jerri, but it tears me to shreds and makes me all the more grateful to know what we've overcome to get where we are today.

Tears stream down her face when I explain why she's my water.

Why she's everything to me.

"I'm your water," She whispers back, as if she gets it and wishes she'd have understood the meaning sooner. A smile touches her beautiful mouth, and I press my lips to hers. "My water, Jerri girl."

The air slowly whooshes out of her lungs, eyes losing light and color draining from her face. The medic shouts, "She's crashing! Sir, I need you to move back."

I grip her hand more fiercely as the ambulance slams to a halt, the rear doors ripped open.

"Sir!" she shouts again. I jump into action, hanging onto my Lass's hand and helping them lift the bed from the ambulance to the ground.

"Multiple contusions. Gunshot wound to the hip."

I talk to her as I run beside the stretcher, a medic trying desperately to pump air into her lungs along the way. "Stay with me, Jerri. Don't you fucking die! Stay with me, Lass."

The doors are pushed open, and the medics wheel her into the emergency room, tearing my hand from hers as hospital staff surround the table.

"Jerri!" I shout. An older nurse puts her hand to my chest.

"You can't help her in there, Lad."

She shuts the doors as I watch through the window. They begin cutting the dress from her lifeless body. It makes a slapping sound when it hits the floor—it's soaked in blood.

"Jerri! I'm right here, Lass!" I shout, banging on the window, not listening to a goddamn thing the medical team says because I need her to hear me. I need her to know I'm here.

That I'm not leaving.

MIND LIES

Ever

They wheel surgical trays toward the bed and hoist her legs up in stirrups.

"No. Fuck no, let my boy be okay," I weep, not giving a shit who watches me, a grown man, cry.

A strong hand lands on my shoulder and squeezes. I don't need to turn to know its Lee. He stands, giving me silent support while we watch them administer blood, stick a breathing tube down her throat, stitch her side, and poke around her belly at the same time.

"Sir?"

I don't bother looking. I refuse to take my eyes off her.

"Sir, I brought you some clean clothes. If you change, I'll take you in there. The doctor would like to speak with you."

Finally peeling my eyes off my Lass, I nod in thanks at the older woman before tearing my clothes off in the middle of the hallway. Lee says, "Thank you, Elaine." And I make a note to thank him *and his connections later. I ignore the looks from nurses as I strip. Whether they are ogling my body or the bruising all over my chest, I don't care. Within seconds I'm pushing through the door. Jerri's hand rests back in mine.*

I can't kiss her as they work on her face, but I watch as the doctor moves his hand around her belly. "The baby's in distress, Mr.?—"

"Cavanaugh. The father," I choke out.

"Mr. Cavanaugh, the babe's not due to come out but he needs to. He's a good size, so I'm certain he'll be fine. But there's too much stress on both after the trauma. I'd like to perform a caesarean. I recommend it."

I nod. "I don't care what you do, Doc, so long as you try your fuckin' hardest to keep both of them breathing."

He motions to a nurse, who then begins prepping Jerri, before placing the scalpel to her stomach. I turn my head and press my lips to the palm of her hand, praying for them to be okay.

I won't take either of them for granted ever again. I won't let Jerri feel as though she's not wanted, as though she's not the most important person in my whole goddamn life. I'll finally tell her that even when she was with that prick, Tom, even when I was away from her for months at a time, I never, not once, slept with another woman.

I didn't even think about it.

Because it's always been Jerri.

It's only been Jerri.

A wail pierces the air. I open my eyes and take sight of my boy.

So little.

A nurse furiously scrubs his filthy little body, which only angers him further, before hustling him over to a different table. Then another doctor rushes into the room.

"Is he okay?" I rasp, feeling torn between hanging onto Jerri's hand or letting go to see my child.

The doctor nods. "A little fighter, this one. Strong heartbeat, good lungs. Gonna need to spend some weeks in the NICU until he's grown, though. Better to be safe."

I let out a breath, and since they're finished cleaning Jerri's face, I press my lips to her cheek.

"A healthy boy, Lass."

"Would you like to hold him for a moment before we take him?" I wipe my cheeks on the scrub shirt and nod. I'm a sore fuckin' sight for my boy to see, but I don't care. The nurse sets him in the crook of my arm, and I hold his little head in the palm of my hand.

"Hey, little Lad." He looks up at me with bright, curious eyes, and I vow in that moment to never leave my family again. Never again will I let any harm come to them, and if that means moving to some shanty in the middle of nowhere, then that's what we'll do.

Jerri later died on that table.

She died and my fucking heart broke when they tossed me to the other side of the room so they could work on her.

It took sixteen seconds for her heart to start beating again, but it might as well have been an hour because it was the longest sixteen seconds of my life.

I eat, breath, and live Jerri.

I hover around her like a bee to a flower, now, never letting her out of my sight for too long. She may let on that it drives her crazy, but I know better.

I'm obsessed with her, and she's infatuated with me. And after so many years apart from each other—after everything we've been through, everything I put her through—*this* is our time.

This is our time to love and live and be a family.

It's our time for a new normal that doesn't include us being separated for weeks or months at a time. Once Lee shot Yakov his cronies disbanded. Some were caught, some were killed, but it's safe to say the threat to her safety is over. The bottom feeders of Yakov's clan don't have the resources or the want to harm Jerri.

I still see Lee from time to time, a pint here and there. If it weren't for the tactical watch he put on my wrist he wouldn't have saved us that god awful day. So, it's safe to assume all rounds at the pub are on me from here on out.

"Would you stop scowling? You're scaring the poor kid."

Jerri leans into my side, and I put my arm around her shoulders and kiss her forehead. "You can't scare the devil, Lass." She opens her mouth to speak, but I press my lips to hers. "We're not leaving our children with that boy. Lonán already asked if he could stay with Cory and Marcus."

"Locklin!" she whisper-shouts. "He barely has any friends, and he's not going to make any if you keep sabotaging his sleepovers."

I shake my head. "I've sabotaged nothing, Lass. Lonán knows he's a bad seed."

"Tell me you are not talking about my baby?" Portia scolds from behind us. I raise my eyebrows, challenging her. Thankfully, Cory comes to my aid.

"Pixie, that hell-raiser you call a child scares even me. I don't blame the guy for not wanting him around his kid. Last time Marcus and I watched him, I woke up to him sitting on the end of the bed with a pile of my bow ties. He'd already tied one around Marcus's wrist, and he looked like he was thinking of strangling me with the one in his hand."

Portia smirks. "Can you blame him? Which one was it? Purple with stripes?"

"Not the point, Tiny Tits. If I wanted to sleep with a Chucky doll, I'd buy one."

"He does resemble Chucky," I muse. Jerri punches my arm.

"He's a free spirit!" Portia argues.

"Anyway," Jerri continues as Portia and Cory carry on their argument. "Cory and Marcus just got back from their honeymoon. I doubt they want to look after the kids; they're probably tired."

I give her a look because she knows all too well they will take the children whenever they can have them.

There's no *doubt* about it, especially since they haven't seen them in so long.

We've been spending most of our winters in Ireland, travelling back to Boston for the spring and some summer months. Our schedule isn't a regular one, but we've made it work. Of course that will change when the kids start school, but until that time, Jerri has been happy to have two homes.

Whatever makes Jerri happy is what Jerri gets.

I'm just happy I have a family to call home. These three are my life—I'll take them any way I can get them. Jerri's shop here is still thriving, and she's looked into opening up another in Ireland once Lara is bigger.

"Look! I told you she'd love it." Marcus's glee gathers our attention as he holds my daughter like a prized pony at the fair. I'll hand it to him; he does treat my girl as exactly that.

As he should, because she is.

I take note of the tiny, Lara-sized cardigan, which has been covered in tiny shining jewels. "Are they stick-on? She could choke, Marcus," I say.

The saucy man points a finger at my face, and the conversation dims. "Do *not* underestimate my bedazzling skills. Did any of my BeDazzle's come off Lonán's jean jacket? Hmm?"

I frown. "Those silver things?"

He rolls his eyes at me. "Those *silver things* were original BeDazzler Flathead size 20 studs, and I know for a fact that none of them came off because I know how to run my machine."

Cory rolls his eyes, and Jerri gives me wide ones. "Honey, do not talk ill of that man's BeDazzler."

I raise my hands. "My apologies, Marcus."

He gives me a quick nod of his head. "I'll accept. But only because Jerri promised to show me pictures of your trip to the Outer Banks."

I frown and Portia adds, "He gets to see your hot man-body without a shirt on."

Jerri laughs and I curse. The man has no shame, but so long as he continues to treat my children like gold and my woman like a queen, I'll put up with his antics.

When everyone leaves our apartment above the shop, I practically pounce on my wife after she turns the deadbolt. She gasps when she feels me press my body to the length of hers.

"Turn around, Lass."

She does, slowly.

I don't want slow.

"Do you know how long it's been since I've been inside you without the worry of interruption?" I ask against her neck, devouring her skin as I pull the strap of her dress from her shoulder.

She shakes her head. "A couple days?"

"Seventy-eight hours," I deadpan before grabbing her dress, ripping it right down the middle.

Her eyes glaze over, heat overtaking them, as I remove every last stitch of fabric covering her beautiful skin. I don't bother with my own but simply release my aching cock from the confines of my jeans and grab two handfuls of her fine arse. She obliges by wrapping her legs around my waist, and I waste no time in sinking into her in one hard thrust.

I take her hard and fast, her cries feeding the beast within that wants to be buried inside her twenty-four hours a day. The beast that wants to put a tribe of children in her to mark her as my own.

Our teeth clash and our tongues duel before I tear my mouth from hers and return to the spot on her neck that makes her whimper, cry, and beg.

I run my tongue along the raven taking flight up her neck, tattooed on her shoulder. It used to stand for a horrible time, a time when the word "raven" made her shudder so much that she considered having it removed.

So I pay special attention to the newer part of the tattoo.

"You've risen from the ashes, Jerri girl. I believe that's some of the myth behind the bird, is it not?"

The next day, Jerri came home with *my* tattoo clutched

firmly in the bird's grasp: a Celtic triquetra, talons holding onto it for dear life, ash's trailing behind knot.

The same knot that's been tattooed on my chest for decades.

"If I've risen from the ashes, I'm bringing you with me. No more ghosts, Locklin."

I didn't think I could care for her more. I didn't think it was possible. But fuck, that day she did me in.

Took the breath right from my lungs.

No more ghosts, Locklin.

As I sink deeper into her body, there isn't a thought of the ghosts from my past. They may have shaped me into the man I am today, but it's this woman, this beautiful fucking person in my arms with the voice of an angel and eyes that bring me to my knees, that overpowers anything and everything that was once dark in my life.

She's the air I didn't know I needed to breathe.

She's the light that chased away my shadows.

She was, and always will be, my water.

THANK YOU

Thank you so much for reading! Let's keep #LOVELOCKLIN alive @Harlow_Stone

Mind Lies was a hard one to write. Not because I didn't love the idea, but because originally I wanted to base the book completely around Jerri singing and the YouTube video. While it was a great theory in my head, I couldn't keep it interesting without adding my usual flair for dramatics like the Russian's, the mystery behind her past and why she was hiding, etc.

I love suspense in novels and I hope I kept you guessing and turning the pages in this one. I'm not as proud of this book as I am The Ugly Roses Trilogy, but I sincerely hope you enjoyed it all the same.

I'd like to thank Christine Stanley at The Hype PR for helping me deliver every single one of my books. I came into this business with my head in the fog not knowing a damn thing about getting a book out and this woman has answered every single one of my questions on the way. Not only does she work hard, but she enjoys what she does and that in my opinion is a great person to work with.

Give her some love here:
https://www.facebook.com/thehypePR

My favorite beta reader, Rachel Green. You help make my books shine flawlessly with those priceless peepers of yours! Thank you for being such a speedy reader and coming through so quickly for me.

My editor Greg, thanks for putting up with my endless questions and embarking on this wonderful journey with me!
To my readers: You truly make this worthwhile. If it weren't for your reviews and support I wouldn't be where I am today. Thank you so much!

Want to chat about current and upcoming books?
Hit me here:

@Harlow_Stone
www.facebook.com/harlow.stone.author
www.harlowStone.com

And PLEASE take time to review. It only takes a minute or two and means THE WORLD to us authors.
We love your feedback.
The good, the bad and the ugly.

Goodreads Link:
http://bit.ly/24xV8Rb

Amazon Page Link:
http://www.amazon.com/-/e/B00WYF1QXE

Stay up to date with new releases by signing up to my newsletter! I only mail about once a month, and it's a great

HARLOW STONE

way to get first dibs on excerpts, giveaways and new releases!

http://eepurl.com/bJSDYj

© 2016 HARLOW STONE / KATE KEARNS

Made in the USA
Charleston, SC
21 July 2016